# WHORES ON WHEELS//
# CLONES ON STEROIDS

# WHORES ON WHEELS//
# CLONES ON STEROIDS

Ted Knuckey

**To order additional copies of this book, contact:**
Xlibris Corporation
1-888-795-4274
www.Xlibris.com
Orders@Xlibris.com
51993

# CHAPTER ONE

Two shots, Yeah, it was two gun shots. Too loud for most pistols and even some rifles.

Now I was wondering if I was awake or just dreaming. To add to my confusion, everything was quiet. Suddenly my doubts disappeared as a pack of coyotes started yapping. It sounded like the exuberance of a fresh kill. The howling and barking was missing, but the yapping announced the excitement of the moment.

Low, angry growls joined the unmelodious yappers. Now fully awake, I switched on the light and glanced at the clock, two twenty. A hell of a time for such a rude awakening. Sport was facing the door on a defensive mode. His teeth were bared, ears laid back and a ridge of hair on his back stood upright. His low growls completed the picture. My adrenaline pump went into overdrive as I rolled from the bed.

I grabbed the 30-30 carbine from the rack above the door. I eased out onto the porch while levering in a shell. Disciple was snorting, raring and pawing the ground. Damn strange behavior, even for a stud horse. I cursed the blackness and moved cautiously into the night. I was between the house and the corral when a half laughing female voice startled me.

I stopped in my tracks as she spoke from the darkness behind me. "Dutch, you're going to freeze your balls off, running around like that."

I suddenly realized I was standing there wearing only cowboy booths, a pair of shorts and my Stetson hat. Not surprisingly, I felt naked and ridiculous. The rifle, I clutched at port arms, did nothing to comfort me. I started to turn toward the speaker, when the voice, now giggling, said, "I see my warning was too late."

I said, "Damn it Mary, it's cold out here. Didn't your husband ever explain to you what happens when it's cold. Besides what are you doing out here?"

"I'm looking for my husband. I'll ask him when I find him. I don't know if he knows, since I never let him get that cold. Now tell me, what are you doing out here half naked?"

"There isn't any moon, how come you can see me and I can't see you?"

"I eat more carrots than you do. Besides you're between me and the house. With the front door open you're a perfect silhouette. If you're gong to sneak around in the dark, you should turn off the front room light. Now stop avoiding the question. What you doing out here?"

"I thought I heard shots. Then those damn coyotes yapping finished waking me up. The studs snorting and raising hell sounded urgent so I came out. I thought it might be important, but if I'd known you were out here I would have gone back to sleep. Now will you go downwind about 50 yards and quit teasing my stud. Hell my dog is even excited."

"You can't blame me for this. It's not my time of month, Your dog will have to come up with some other excuse. As for the stud, hell, he's never needed a reason. I came out to see what all the commotion was about and found Ralph had saddled up and rode out."

"I'm freezing," I said, as I turned to go into the house.

Three shots in rapid succession stopped me and I backed quickly to the corral. I squatted against a post while telling Mary to get down.

"I am down," she replied as the stud behind me started to run in circles and then whinnied. Sport pushed against me as he uttered a low guttural growl. I put my hand on his neck and in a calm voice tried to comfort him. Then Mary yelled.

"Horse coming and coming fast!"

"Damn it, Mary, you not only see better, but you can hear better." I listened and then continued, "Stay out of his way, if he heads for the barn."

The hoof beats echoed out of the darkness and only stopped as they slid into a stall. There was an agonizing prolonged silence which ended suddenly with Mary's scream, "It's Ralph's horse!"

I ran to the barn, switched on the light, and spoke softly to the horse. I cautiously grabbed the reins and observed his heaving chest. His mouth was open, as he slobbered and struggled for air. I unstrapped the cinch and removed the empty saddle. His hooves were in constant motion as he continued trying to pull away. His ears were laid back and his eyes were bulging and rimmed in white. I followed his movements and used the saddle blanket to wipe the lather from his back. I shook my head and said, "Something really spooked him," I turned to look out into the darkness and asked, "Can you hear anything?" there wasn't any answer, Mary was gone.

# CHAPTER TWO

It was warmer with my cloths on, but it was still cold. The open air of my early military jeep offered no protection. The headlights were barely adequate and I strained to see. At best, the drive was rough while zigzagging across the uneven terrain. A glimpse of movement in the darkness caused my to rapidly turn the steering wheel and accelerate toward the area.

Mary did not even look up as the headlights illuminated her backside. She continued to trudge across the pasture as I drove up beside her. She was half carrying and half dragging a 12 gauge double barreled shotgun. She said something, but the pounding of the ancient 4 cylinder motor drowned her out. I raised my voice in order to be heard, and said, "Get in."

She kept walking, until I cut the motor. Then barely looked up as she replied. "I'd rather walk. Bouncing around in that damn thing hurts my butt."

Mary was small, and was dwarfed by the huge shotgun. I reached over, grabbed the barrel and pulled it from her grasp. She stopped walking, shrugged her shoulders, mumbled something, I couldn't hear, then climbed into the passenger seat.

"Have you ever shot that thing?" I asked, as I handed the gun back.

She shook her head from side to side and said, "No." She set the butt plate on the steel floor between her feet. Her left hand grasped the stock, just below the trigger guard. Her right hand clutched the barrels. She used both hands to firmly hold the gun steady against her left shoulder. I did notice the barrels extended above her head over 2 feet. I felt uneasy, but maybe she and the gun were secure enough for a short trip.

We drove to the top of a small knoll, where we could watch the pasture area. I shut off the motor and killed the lights. We sat silently listening for any sounds before I spoke. "If Ralph loaded your gun, like he usually does, you have a rifle slug in the left barrel and a double aught in the right. Don't ever make the mistake of pulling both triggers at the same time."

"Would it really be that bad?"

I shook my head, smiled, then replied, "Ralph bought that damn gun at some auction when he was a kid. Hell, it was an antique then. They haven't made a gun like that, in maybe a hundred years. Both barrels have big pits and with the deep steel butt plate either barrel would kick hard enough to tear off your shoulder. Both barrels fired at the same time could lay you up for a month. I'm surprised Ralph lets you carry it."

"He doesn't know I have it. In fact he told me to leave it alone. He gave me a little pistol to protect myself. I think it's a 22 or something like that."

"Why didn't you bring it instead of the cannon?"

She remained quiet for a moment and then said. "Well, Ralph took his 44 magnum and I thought I might need something big."

Five rapid gun shots broke the silence of the night.

I instinctively stiffened, as Mary gasped. Seconds passed, before I started the motor. The shots did sound like they came from the same gun. The mag makes a hell of a lot of noise. On a clear still night like this, it would sound closer than it was. Yeah Ralph probably did the shooting.

I slowly moved the jeep forward while trying to see beyond the lights. Suddenly Mary cried out. "Over there, I saw a light. It looked like maybe a match."

I slammed on the brakes, killing the motor as I asked, "Over where?"

"Over there, over there."

I knew she must be pointing and I leaned toward her until I could see her outstretched arm. I fired up the motor and turned the wheels in the direction she was indicating. The jeep lurched forward with the release of the clutch. There was a teeth jarring jolt as we bounced into a dry, rock tilled ditch. Then the head lights erratically jumped, as the left front wheel struck a protruding boulder. I grabbed the back of the passenger seat and pulled myself upright just as the shotgun fired both barrels. Mary screamed and I instinctually grabbed the gun and pushed it away from her.

"I burned my hand," she complained.

"Damn it Mary, did you have those hammers back?" I asked.

"Yes, I guess. They're so hard to push back I did it before I left the house. You know, in case I had to shoot in a hurry."

In spite of the coolness of the night I had to wipe the sweat from my forehead. I took a deep breath and said. "And, you felt the gun slipping, so you stuck a finger inside the trigger guard."

"Yeah, maybe, I just grabbed that curved thing to keep the gun from falling. Don't you care I burned my hand?"

It was probably a good thing before I could answer another light flickered in the trees. Mary saw it at the same time and didn't question our bouncing toward it.

We wound up through the trees, trying to avoid the bigger rocks. Suddenly Ralph appeared from behind a clump of brush. I cut the motor as he walked up. He asked,

"What were you shooting?"

"Nothing, just your wife fired both barrels to protest my driving. Now what were you shooting."

"Also nothing. I fired up in the air to scare whatever was out here."

"Something was out here?" I asked.

"Yeah, it was really weird. Tonight was one of he darkest nights I've ever seen. There wasn't even a star out. I was perched on a rock listening for any noise. I was looking over toward the ridge, when I swear, I saw the blackness move. Hell it didn't even have any shape. It was movement without configuration and without noise. I thought maybe I was just imagining the whole thing. My horse was ground tied in the draw. You know, he would stay, but he took off even before I fired.. No, for damn sure something was out there,"

Ralph, an ex marine, ex cop and all cowboy leaned on the jeep for support. He looked down, took a couple of deep breaths, and spoke again. "It will be sun up soon and we can walk the ridge out. Maybe cut some sign."

I stared at the ridge and then asked, "What brought you out here in the first place?"

Ralph looked up and gestured toward the pasture, and said. "About 10 last night I heard coyotes barking and howling. They seemed to be in several locations and were talking to each other. They kept moving and it sounded like they were gathering. I could tell there were about 5 or 6 of them. I became concerned they were becoming a pack. You know, I have 20 head of sheep in the upper pasture and some of them are ready to lamb."

He turned his head away from me, as I asked, "Why didn't you yell. I would have rode out with you?"

"I thought you were asleep. Your lights were out." He hesitated, then continued in a lower voice. "Besides they're my sheep and I know you're not happy about my having them here."

I thought over my answer, before saying. "Ralph, our agreement is you take care of the place, and my stock. You can run what ever you want on the land. It's no secret that I'm not fond of sheep, but I like coyotes less."

He turned back toward me and seemed upset to see his wife. "Mary! Why are you here'" He asked.

# CHAPTER THREE

"Get up. Damn it, wake up." The loud demands startled me. At first I didn't recognize the voice. It was only after I organized my thoughts and focused my eyes was I able to shake myself awake. I looked up at Ralph, who was now mounted, on his run-a-way horse. I rose to my feet with difficulty and readjusted my hat.

I struggled for something intelligent to say and ended up with, "What took you so damn long? I must have fallen asleep. Remember it was your nocturnal shooting that woke me up in the middle of the night."

"Well, I had to take Mary and the jeep home, catch and saddle two horses, then ride back. Besides I haven't even been to bed and I'm still awake."

"Good for you." I said as I stepped across my saddle. "Now lead on and show me where you saw the night move."

We rode silently for over an hour crisscrossing the ridge. Several times we both got down and closely walked over dirt and sand. We checked every inch that might show tracks. We found none. Finally I moved over to the shade of tree and sat down on an uncomfortable rock. When Ralph dismounted, I asked, "Are you sure we're in the right area?" He took off his hat, wiped the sweat from his brow and nodded. He was quiet, as his eyes surveyed the plateau.

"Are you sure it wasn't the coyotes you saw?" I offered.

He shook his head then replied, "No the coyotes were over in the South pasture. If they spooked they would have come by me. They didn't and besides the last time I checked, coyotes leave tracks. In addition they were still yipping when I saw the movement on the ridge. What I saw, was a hell of a lot bigger than any pack of coyotes."

I scratched the back of my head before asking. "Was it as big as a man or maybe several men?"

"Hell, it was as big as a platoon of men, but wouldn't they have to fly to keep from leaving tracks."

"I just noticed there are a lot of crows and several magpies arguing about something. It sounds like it's down where you indicated you heard the coyotes. Lets ride over there."

"Good idea. At least we might find what the kill was."

We rode silently with each of us preoccupied with our own thoughts. We were half way to the lower pasture, when Ralph reined his horse over beside me. I glanced at him, as he said.

"You know, I wonder, if I'm going crazy. Lets look at the facts. No lights, No noise and no tracks. Then, I see a very large nothing moving through the night. It all adds up to my mind's gone. Hell I might even be dangerous. You're lucky you have Sport for protection."

"Protection from what? I hate to tell you this. Last night, Sport was scared by something and he tried to snuggle up with me."

Ralph shook his head before replying. "We both better start sleeping with night lights. You have Sport and I have Mary. You know I gave her a Saturday night special for protection and she thinks it's too small. She feels better with the shotgun and she doesn't know which end is which. The bright side would be, Sport and Mary might wake us up in time to find out we're being murdered. That, my friend would be a questionable blessing."

I opened my mouth to reply, but before I could speak I saw the crows, then the bodies. I reined my horse to a sudden stop, just as Ralph exclaimed,

"My God! Those damn coyotes. Oh God! I see two head down. Damn, Damn, Damn!"

We stepped down 75 feet away from the two dead calves. Dropped our reins, ground tying the horses. We started walking slowly in ever diminishing circles looking for clues.

"Is this how you investigated murders when you were a homicide detective?" Ralph asked as I took his arm and slowed his pace.

"Yeah, pretty much. You have to be careful because the scene is fragile. It can be changed every time someone enters. A clumsy examination can lose evidence. Once lost, it can't be replaced. Actually you have to assume you are changing the scene with every move you make. Caution is the rule. If you see a track, or any sign, stop and let me know. We will need to mark it until we can carefully make sure of it's preservation."

"It's a good thing you told me. I wanted to get to the bodies."

"That comes last. We know they're dead and we need to follow a system. In homicide investigations, nothing gets moved until it is measured and photographed. We're not going that far. We do need to see, if there's anything we can learn from whatever we find here. Just keep in mind this probably is our only chance."

He laughed as he said. "If you say so, but I think it is a waste of time. Hell we know they're dead. You said so yourself and we know the coyotes killed them."

"I don't think so. I don't believe the coyotes were responsible. I do believe they were ready for a free meal, but they didn't make the kill. First those two calves are about a year old and easily weigh 300 pounds each. Second, they are nose to nose. Coyotes don't like to work that hard. The way this is laid out, both animals had to be killed at the same time or placed nose to nose after their death. Now lets keep walking the area and wait until we get the whole picture before coming to any conclusion."

Fifteen minutes later we arrived at the bodies. The only thing we found on our walk was coyote tracks, fresh bird droppings and some indistinct squashed areas of the pasture grass.

Ralph stopped and watched. I slowly circled the bodies twice and then knelt down beside the largest of the two. I looked up and expressed my observations.

"We both have seen many coyote kills. Usually they start their meal from the rear end. They only tear into the rest of the body after they've finish the entrails. We don't have that here. In fact these animals have been dressed out." I stood up grabbed a hind leg and pushed it until we could see the empty body cavity.

Ralph stepped over and did the same to the other animal as he remarked. "They've been field dressed. Do you think I interrupted a bunch of rustlers?"

"I don't know, but I don't think so. I just noticed their eye balls are missing and their tongues have been cut out. Whoa, and look at this, their skulls have been cut open and the brains are missing. The cuts look professional, probably a stryker saw. Somebody did a complete autopsy on them."

"What do you think they were going to do next." Ralph asked as I looked around the area, without releasing the head I had been examining.

I pointed to the ground as I said. "No blood. No drag marks. No tire marks and no hoof prints. Not even from these animals. So what happened to them and how did they get here? Those pushed down areas could be footprints. Some are round and others elongated. None of them look like the prints we left." I walked twice around the bodies, frequently stopping and examining their hides. I stopped and waved my hand in a circular motion and exclaimed. "Damn, it just occurred to me. Those coyote tracks never came close to here. In addition there are no bite marks on the carcass's. They were just circling fifty yards out. Then we have those damn birds. Their sign is clear over by the rocks. They didn't come near here either."

"So what do you think we have?"

"One hell of a problem." I replied, I'm going to get a canvas tarp and state it down. We'll pull it tight over the bodies to protect them. Then it's time to call the Sheriff.

# CHAPTER FOUR

It was just as dark as the night before. I was settled at the base of a tree where I could maintain surveillance of both the ridge and the kill site. I had chosen to bring a horse rather than the jeep. Willfully conceding his senses were better than mine. I did refuse to admit that Mary or Ralph could see in the dark. In spite of Mary's claim of a generous consumption of carrots.

About an hour before daylight I decided to end my vigil. I was deep in thought as I rode back toward the ranch. I had remained in the area since darkness for two reasons. One to keep the coyotes away. The other, I was hoping to catch a glimpse of whatever Ralph had seen in the darkness. Unlike Ralph I came prepared and had a hand held spot light hanging on my saddle horn. I laughed when I thought of him out here with only matches. When I mentioned I thought it was dumb, he replied they were still brighter than my jeep lights.

I was 200 hundred yards from the ranch when the sky lit up from a oscillating red light. My horse spooked, throwing up his head and jumping sideways just as a loud voice, bellowed from a bullhorn.

"Dutch, Dutch Evans, we have the place surrounded. Throw down your weapons and come out with your hands up."

A bright set of headlights flashed from under the red light, just as a spot light blinded me. I felt my horse spin away from the light and then started bucking. He stopped only when we reached the corral. I stepped off, opened the gate, pulled off the saddle and bridle. I carefully shut the gate as the horse trotted over to the watering trough. I heard loud laughter coming from the bull horn and then a booming voice.

"By God, Dutch you still got it. Let me tell you that was one hell of a ride."

I caught my breath, before I answered. "I'm glad you enjoyed it Sam, but four o'clock in the morning is a hell of a time for a rodeo."

"Aw hell, Dutch it's pretty near 5 and you looked like you needed a wake up call."

"Yeah, well we have to take horses out to see those dead calves. You can ride the one I just brought in or I can saddle the stud for you." I said, as I headed toward the red lights..

Deputy Sheriff, Sam Brown was leaning back against the drivers door of his squad car and talking to a man standing to his left. I stopped as Sam turned toward me and introduced his companion.

"Dutch, this is Doctor Shaman Healum, a veterinarian from the Cattleman's Association. I met him a few years back at a seminar. Doctor this is Dutch Evans, the old friend, I told you about.

"Glad to meet you Doctor," I said as I extended my hand. Sam spoke again before the Doctor could respond.

"Doctor Healum flew down here on a red eye. I called him last night to get his advice. He's very interested in the scene you described."

I nodded my head and started to speak just as Ralph appeared out of the darkness.

He said, with a note of annoyance in his voice. "What the hell is going on out here? Sam is that you making all that noise? Damn it, you not only woke up all the chickens, but Mary jumped up and headed for the door with the shotgun. I caught her just in time. She promised not to shoot and said she would put on a pot of coffee, if you'd quiet down."

"Doctor this is Ralph Rangeler." I said as I introduced them and then continued. "Ralph and his wife Mary live on the place and take care of things around here. Ralph, runs their own stock so he has a personal interest in what happened. Mary makes a great cup of coffee and I think we should accept her hospitality."

Sam chimed in, "Yeah and if I know Mary, she's whipping up biscuits and gravy with a side of sausage and eggs. I vote we have breakfast before going out. It'll be sun up by then and we need to talk things over anyway."

Ralph, shook his head and sniffed the air. "Sam's right, even as we speak, I can smell the sausage cooking. Mary did say, before I left, we should consider Sam a suspect in this case. She believes he would butcher a couple of calves just to have an excuse to come out for her biscuits and gravy."

Sam was walking toward the house as he replied. "By damn, she's right. I can smell the coffee and sausage and my mouth is watering. Hell, I'll be dehydrated by the time we get there."

Ralph laughed and remarked. "I wish he was as good at sniffing out cow killers, as he is coffee and sausage."

# CHAPTER FIVE

It was close to eight, before we drove out to the pasture. I took Doctor Healum with me and had Sport tethered in the bed of my pickup. I wanted the dog to roam the area in hopes he could detect some sign that had been overlooked. I parked a hundred yards away and pointed out the bodies. Doctor Healum remained seated and then spoke. "They look like Red Angus from here."

"Yes, I just started raising them. I only have a small herd, so far."

"I didn't know anyone around here was into Red Angus. It's a great breed. Damn shame to lose a couple like this."

I nodded, without speaking, as he exited the truck. He picked up his bags and said. "You stay here and head off Ralph and Sam. I need to check out the scene by myself. When I finish, we can use the dog and talk."

"I will do my best. I don't know why they aren't here yet. They only had to jump in the jeep and move out."

"Yeah, but Sam was still eating. Damn, I never have seen anyone eat like that. Hell, he ate as much as the rest of us put together. I don't know why Mrs. Rangeler didn't hit him over the head with a frying pan. I would of, instead of whipping up a new batch of biscuits."

"He does have an appetite, but Mary knows how to handle him. She frequently shuts him off, when she gets tired of cooking. I suspect she would have closed the kitchen, if you had not been there. She wouldn't want you to think she was rude. You know what I mean?"

"Yes, I know, but still, he pushes his welcome. One thing before I go. Is this the pasture those calves were using?"

"No, they were grazing in the forest about three miles from here. Another thing, Ralph heard the coyotes gathering about ten and he rode out and spent the night. It was after two, when they seemed to find the calves. They ran off when he tired his gun into the air. Then I spent the rest of the night out here and they didn't come back. I didn't believe coyotes would be scared off of a free meal just by noise."

"You're right. Something else must have them spooked. Well, this isn't getting it done," he said, as he picked up a bag from the bed of the truck and walked off.

Sam and Ralph arrived and took Sport to walk out the ridge area. I waited in the truck and tried to come up with a rational thought of what had happened. My mind wandered, as I watched the progress of the investigation. Doctor Healum methodically examined each animal from the nose to the tail.

It was afternoon when he waved for me to join him. I looked up and tried unsuccessfully to signal Sam and Ralph They were under a tree at the top of the ridge dining on sandwiches. Sport stood at an alert stance between them. They were taking turns tossing him large chunks of their meal. Mary had provided an abundant lunch, but it was doubtful the Doctor or I would ever see any of it.

"Do you think the others would want to join us?" Healum asked as I walked up.

I laughed as I answered. "I don't think so. They're under a tree at the top of the ridge stuffing their faces with sandwiches. Sport has joined them and they're all pigging out."

"Really, I don't know how they do it. I'm still full from breakfast. Sam told me you're a private investigator, with an extensive background in law enforcement. He added, you were a highly respected homicide detective and you even went to medical school."

"Sam has a big mouth." I said, as I knelt down between the heads of the young calves.

Healum laughed and shook his head before he said, "Yeah, I guess when he's not eating, he's talking. Anyway, I have taken smears from the throat, ears and hooves. One thing about these cloven hooves, they're better than horses hooves for evidence. It is kind of like our toes, sometimes things get stuck in there. We won't know until I get it to the lab."

"Did you get anything else?" I asked.

"I kept the unusual for last. See these incisions on the neck." he said as he pointed to both animals necks.

I nodded as he spread open the incisions with his fingers.

"Both the jugular veins and the carotid arteries are missing."

"My God," I exclaimed.

There is more he said as he lifted the back leg and pointed to the hock, "All four legs on each animal have rope burns. I have taken samples of the fiber. It is either hemp of sisal. I won't know until I get them under a microscope, but they both come from plants in Mexico."

He hesitated and I asked, "What else?"

"Well, the incisions don't show any sign of hesitation. The pelvic was split with a saw as well as the cut removing the skull."

"A stryker saw."

"Maybe, a stryker. It could be some kind of a battery powered saw or they were butchered near an electrical outlet. One thing is for damn sure, these animals were not field dressed by a hunter or anyone with a hunting knife. Some cuts make me believe, it may have even been a scalpel."

"Wow, you're good and I think you're right."

"Thanks, but there is one more thing."

"What?"

"No blood. I have cut down and found the veins and arteries contain a clear fluid. I think it may be water, there isn't any odor."

"Water? Are you saying they went through an embalming procedure, but with water instead of formaldehyde?"

"Maybe, I don't know. I have taken samples and we'll find out. Then we have the next puzzle. How did they get here? There aren't any tire or wagon tracks. There isn't any drag marks and no evidence of a horse being anywhere near. It looks like they were dropped from the sky. But no one heard a plane or a helicopter and something had to arrange the nose to nose configuration."

I thought for a minute, then remarked. "Perhaps the nose to nose was a message or for shock value."

"Maybe, but there is one more thing, that may really shock you."

"What?"

"I believe these animals were alive while they were being mutilated."

# CHAPTER SIX

I was on the porch, enjoying my second cup of coffee, when Sport's barking alerted me. I watched, as a car pulled up by the corral and Doctor Healum stepped out.

I got up and said, "Good Morning."

He walked quickly across the yard and up the stairs before speaking. "Can we go inside?"

I nodded, and held the door open as he entered. We moved directly into the kitchen, where I motioned for him to be seated. I placed cups on the table while offering coffee.

He accepted before saying, "I'm sorry it took me so long to get back to you, but I've been very busy."

"That's all right. How about some breakfast? I'm not as good a cook as Mary, but I can whip up some bacon and eggs with a side of toast."

"Sounds good and it'll give us a chance to talk alone, By the way, I noticed the big corral when I drove up. I believe it is the first time I ever saw a corral eight feet high and made entirely of twelve by twelve lumber. What do you have in there, A mean bull?"

I flipped the eggs and bacon on the plates, put two pieces of toast next to them, before replying. "No, l have an ornery stud horse. He was the boss of a wild herd and he can't seem to forget it. I don't understand his problem. He gets all he wants to eat. They bring in mares from all over, for his services, and still he wants to escape. Believe me, if he ever does he will steal every mare from Mexico to Oregon. They were planning to kill him when we managed to shoot enough tranquilizer into his butt to save his life. You would think he would be grateful, but he's not."

Doctor Healum wiped his mouth with a paper napkin then asked. "Maybe he doesn't get enough exercise? Do you ever ride him?"

I nodded, and said. "I let him run in a pasture to the rear of the barn. It's double wired six feet across, eight feet high with the heaviest gauge wire I could find. In addition I have three strands of electric fence three feet before the heavy wire. So far it keeps him in. I have just recently been able to ride him, but it's a nervous ride. I never know when we are in for a fight. He has tried to kill me a couple of times by kicking, striking and biting. I don't dare buck off and I admit to pulling leather. In fact, if you check my saddle horn you might find teeth marks."

"Really, yours or his?"

I laughed and replied. "Mine."

"I understand. Sam said you were pretty good at saddle bronc riding and you use to win the event at various rodeos. I wasn't surprised to hear it. I was impressed by the ride I saw you put up the other morning."

"Sam's big mouth again, huh?"

"Yes, I guess. Now, I want to tell you why I'm here and some of it has to be just between you and me. Okay?"

"Of course."

"Well first, The results are back on the fluid we found in the veins. It was as we suspected, salt water."

"Salt water? What, normal saline?"

"Yes, probably 9% about the normal amount in the body"

"The next question is why?"

Doctor Healum shrugged his shoulders before answering. "I don't know except it certainly removes the blood, without contamination.."

"God, what do you think they are going to use that blood for, maybe transfusions?"

"Maybe, and it would be compatible for cattle. There is a possibility for a blood bank. I know them all and I will check them out. By the way the rope was sisal."

"So we know the water was normal saline and the rope was sisal. Those are facts. Do we know anything else?" I asked, as I rose from the table for more coffee.

He extended his cup for a refill before continuing. "Well we have history. Animals have been found in similar conditions in almost every Western state for the past fifty years. It hasn't been limited to only cattle and there have been pigs, horses and sheep. It maybe just a coincidence. Maybe we're dealing with copycats. None are like we have here. The nose to nose bit is something new and yours is only the first case. I think there's some significance, to the fact, one was a heifer and the other a bull. It probably means something, but I'm damned if I know what. There is one other case where two heifers were laid out side by side with their hooves outstretched and touching. I don't understand the meaning of that either. Both cases within the last month."

"Where was the other one?"

He took a quick swallow of the hot coffee, wiped his mouth and looked around to make sure we were alone. Apparently satisfied, he continued. "Okay, it was at the Haystack ranch. Four hundred miles from here. I tried to look into it and there's something damn strange about it. To begin with it's an area away from everything. The Sheriffs office is the only law for miles around. I called them for information and got transferred around for several minutes. Finally I ended up with a homicide detective."

I interrupted, "Homicide for a dead cow?"

He nodded and continued. "Yeah and that's not all. He kept telling me it was an open case and he couldn't talk about it. I asked him where the bodies were and he got real evasive. Then he refused to answer and asked me why I wanted to know. When I told him I wanted to examine them. He asked if I was some kind of weirdo and hung up."

"Didn't they even try to determine if you had anything that might help them?"

He shook his head as he continued. "Wait until I finish. They really made me curious and I called a few veterinarians in the area. I found one who knew Haystack. By the way the Haystack ranch is owned by a guy named Haystack. Anyway I was told Haystacks an original and was born and raised on the ranch. He still lives like it was a hundred years ago. I mean, no electricity, no phone and keeps pretty much to himself. He is married to his second wife and is extremely jealous. The local gossip mill believes he murdered his first wife and the Sheriff is covering it up."

I said, "I would have great doubts there. Murder is pretty hard to cover up."

I poured him another cup of coffee and he nodded as he continued. "Well now I will get to the point. You're a private investigator with a personal interest and no client. Am I right?"

"Yes."

"Well Sam was only half right when he said I worked for the Cattleman's Association. I do work close to them, but actually I work for a federally funded organization and they have authorized me to hire you."

I opened my mouth to speak, but Healum raised his hand to stop me. Then asked, "Please hear me out, before you make up your mind. First I don't want Sam to know about this. You and I know he would blow up and call that Sheriff and raise hell. We don't need anyone to burn our bridges before we get to them. Second you being an ex cop and homicide detective you may be able to open some doors I can't. Third, you are a cattle rancher and Haystack may talk to you. I have some limitations when I contact a cattle rancher and introduce myself as a veterinarian. They all get scared and won't talk. I guess they either remember or heard about the hoof and mouth disease. Remember, when we had to destroy whole herds. Now we have the mad cow disease and they are all scared. You see what I mean?"

I nodded and replied, "Yes, but you don't know how cold policeman get when they are contacted by a P.I. They're always afraid a P.I. will open their mouth and blow a case. Hell I don't blame them. I was the same way when I was on the force. Sam could probably open more doors than I, but you are right he would raise hell right now. I guess it would be better to wait. Then we could ask for his help at the proper time. Maybe, it could put it to him so he wouldn't take it personal."

Healum placed an envelope on the table. "There's a thousand dollars in there with the directions to Haystacks ranch. Try to get started as soon as you can."

"I haven't said, I would go."

"You will, because you're an investigator with a stake in this case."

I picked up the envelope with the comment, "You're right. I will have to make the arrangements with Ralph. He'll take care of things while I'm gone."

He shook his head and said. "Be careful what you tell Ralph. He and Sam are good friends."

"I will, but I don't have to tell him anything, other than I'll be gone."

"Good. Sam tells me you are not too happy about Ralph putting a bunch of sheep on the upper pasture. Then he was out there all night when the calves were dropped."

"Whoa, hold on. I would trust Ralph with my life. Now I know Ralph is strong, but even he couldn't carry a 300 pound calf, let alone two of them. Damn that Sam's big mouth."

"I hope you're right, but he did have a horse and right now everyone is a suspect."

# CHAPTER SEVEN

I would never admit to being lost, but I silently cursed the fact, I had no idea where I was. The road seemed endless, with relics of gas stations, motels, ram shackled barns and other remnants of a bygone era separated by miles of overgrown weeds. My concern raised its ugly head as the gas gauge continued the inevitable decent toward the E. The rolling hills on each side of the road with infrequent stands of trees offered little comfort. I wondered how far I would have to walk. I said, "If you run out of gas, the engine will quit. If the engine quits, the truck will stop. If the truck stops you'll have to walk. There isn't any alternative. That's the law. Now quit talking to yourself and slow down. Try to save gas. Coast down hills. When all else fails, get out and push. Damn it, quit talking to yourself. Save your breath for your walk. Then you'll need to talk to yourself."

Hell, I hadn't seen a car or truck or any other sign of life in over an hour. I had to keep going. The one thing I did know, I was too far out to go back. I slowed down and took my eyes off of the road to study the gas gauge. The needle seemed intent on dropping to the E as fast as my hopes of finding help. I noted, it was a nice day for a walk and tried to will my truck to make just a few more miles. I crested a small hill and noticed a dark spot a few miles ahead. I prayed it was not a mirage. The distance slowly diminished and I could make out the welcome silhouettes of a couple of gas pumps. My hopes soared as several buildings and at least four big rig trucks appeared. The engine coughed once and then went silent. I pushed with both hands on the steering wheel and tried to coast a few feet closer.

It was a long mile, in a hot sun. I cursed the heat and wondered, how it could be so cold at night and so hot in the day time? Anyway it was something to think about, as I hoofed it toward the possible oasis of inhabitation.

There didn't seem to be anyone around. The gas station door was secured by a large hasp and ominous padlock. The pumps were turned off and inoperable. The damn switch was inside and probably locked. I walked around the building shouting. "Hello, hello, any one here?" The only noise and sound of life came from my boots crunching on the gravel. I walked toward the big rig trucks, that were parked 50 yards away. I had very little hope, they could help. They all burned diesel and I needed gas. One bright hope, was they probably have CB's. I would be able to call for help.

I started to pass an antiquated restaurant. I anticipated broken window panes encrusted with dirt and cobwebs. Instead there was a neon sign barely visible through the dusty window announcing the establishment was open. I entered with the thought, this place would have to be upgraded to even be classified as a greasy spoon. But, what the hell it was the only game in town and I needed help. I hesitated as my eyes adjusted to the indoors and then slid into the nearest booth. A gravelly voice came from the other side of the room.

"If you want to be waited on, you can come over here and sit at the counter. I'm damned, if I am going to walk over there."

I looked toward the speaker and saw a large middle aged woman standing behind the counter. A cigarette was dangling from her lips allowing smoke to float upwards. It magnified her air of indifference as it passed over the nostrils and across a pair of squinting eyes. Her facial features were as rough as her voice. She had the look of a person who had given up on life years ago. I still hadn't moved when she again spoke.

"Well stud, what will it be? Do you want to move or stay there until you rot? It's up to you, I don't give a damn one way or another."

"I'll move." I said, as I went to a counter seat and added, "I just wanted to rest a minute. I ran out of gas and had to walk."

She took a deep drag on the cigarette and exhaled a cloud of smoke in my direction and asked, "What will you have?"

I held my breath until some of the smoke dissipated and then replied, "I would like a beer."

She took another long puff and stepped closer, before coughing and exhaling. She looked directly at me while replying, "So would I, but the nearest one is one hundred miles away. That's in either direction and you're out of gas. Now what do you want to eat? This is a restaurant you know."

There was a sign, in big block letters, above the kitchen service opening stating, "OUR FOOD IS DELIGHTFULLY DETECTABLE AND DELICIOUSLY UNHEALTHY." I read it without comment. I pushed my hat back as I turned and glanced at the trucks, then at the empty restaurant. I smiled and asked, "Where is everybody?" She crushed her cigarette out in the ash tray directly in front of me. Then, with an air of defiance she folded her arms across her breasts and leaned back against the wall. There was a tone of sarcasm in her voice as she said,

"I know, they say, go where the truckers eat for good food. Those truckers are all in the back showering and getting a little sleep. They may or may not want to eat when they get up. Now do you want to eat or not?"

"Do you have a menu,'?" I asked

"Yeah, but we probably are out of everything. Why don't you tell me what you want. Then I'll I see if we have it in stock."

"You said we. Is there someone here, who can pump gas?"

"Yeah, my husband. He's the cook and also runs the gas station, but he's sleeping. So if you want to complain about my attitude you may need to know one thing, I own the joint."

"Well, I wouldn't want to wake him, but do you belong to a strong union or can you cook something, when he's not here."

"She smiled as she replied, "Don't be a smart ass, cowboy or I will forget how to pump gas as well as cook."

I had the feeling unless I had something to eat I wouldn't get any gas. "Good, I will have a hamburger and a cup of coffee."

She started for the kitchen then stopped and asked. "Do you want that with or without chips?"

"Do you mean fries?"

"No, I mean chips. They come out of those little bags over there."

I looked at where she was pointing and saw a display rack of various chips. "Yeah, with one bag of chips."

"Get it yourself and don't try to stick an extra bag in your pocket. I know how many there are on the rack. Oh yeah, l forgot to ask, would you like a bowl of soup to start? It's home made."

"I might, what is the soup du jour?"

"Let me see, today is Tuesday so it's minestrone. Yesterday it was tomato. Today we drop in a couple of beans and a noodle and voila it's minestrone."

I laughed, "And what is it tomorrow?"

"Tomorrow, we start over with potato soup and on Friday we add a can of clams and it's chowder. That's what we have, when we have supplies and customers. Today we have a couple of cans in the cupboard, I don't know what kind, but I will find out if you want one."

"I thought you said home made."

"It is," she replied. "This is my home and I will open the can and unless you want vichyssoise, I will heat it. Do you want a bowl or not?"

I shook my head no, as I replied, "No, it sounds great, but I'll pass."

She came back and put a sandwich in front of me while explaining, "We are out of burger so you are getting horse cock and cheese on rye. Eat it and make believe it's beef, Hell for all I know it might be. "We need to get supplies and we will, if that the little bastard I'm married to goes to town like I told him to a week ago."

I took a bite of my sandwich and quietly remarked, "I take it you are the boss."

She stood directly in front of me and exclaimed. "You had better believe it. That sign out front says, Maude's Place and I'm Maude. How's the sandwich?"

The bread was dry, the cheese rubbery and the meat so old it was trying to curl. I remembered I still needed gas as I swallowed a large bite and washed it down with a gulp of coffee before saying, "It's fine, but maybe, I could use a little more mustard."

"Damn, you are a terrible liar. The baloney is so old I had to fight it to keep it from crawling off the plate. It was still younger than the cheese. I wouldn't eat the damn thing and I don't think you should. Unless your starving. I'm not going to charge you for it anyway."

I dropped the sandwich back on the plate and took another gulp of hot coffee. Maude promptly refilled my cup as she apologetically said, "I would offer you a piece of pie, but it isn't in any better shape than the sandwich."

I nodded my head in understanding as she continued. "We have a regular weekly delivery, but he hasn't been here for two weeks. He might be in jail or maybe he was in a wreck. We don't know and no one answers the only phone number we have for him. He would have come in from the West so he shouldn't have been caught in the flood just East of here."

She lit another cigarette, inhaled deeply then exhaled with a sigh of resignation. She wiped the counter and left the towel near my cup. I took a drink as she said. "I guess having the road closed is a blessing, because if people were coming, we couldn't service them. Those truckers have been here a week now and they may have to go back and start over. It would mean taking the longer southern route. One of them, I know wants to go North. He says, "If he has to go back, it will add three hundred miles to his trip, not counting the miles here and back."

I sat quietly listening to her tirade and as fast as I drank my coffee, she would refill the cup. Then she turned her back to me and busied herself wiping a spill on the back counter before she turned back with the remark. "I guess, I have been in a real bad mood lately."

I couldn't resist and I replied, "I never would have guessed."

She raised the wet dish towel and I thought she was going to throw it at me. She hesitated, then laughed as she replied, "Damn, you are one hell of a liar, but I'm beginning to like you. Where're you headed? That is if we ever get around to getting you some gas."

I glanced out the window before answering, "Well, l may not be going anywhere if the road is out. Then again I may be lost. I'm looking for the Haystack ranch, but I haven't seen a haystack in fifty miles."

"Yeah, you're lost." She laughed and then continued, "You missed the turn off about ten miles back. You should have turned at the cattle guard and taken the road North up into the foothills. It's about thirty miles from the main road and Haystack is the owners name. I don't know if you would see any hay or not, but the name is on the mail box."

"Ah, I remember seeing that cattle guard. Thirty miles you say. Well it's lucky I didn't take it. I ran out of gas getting here, only ten miles. Hell, I wouldn't have made half way and then I would have been lost for real."

She shook her head, laughed and dropped the wet towel back on the counter, before speaking. "Yeah, you sure would. Believe me there is one hell of lot of nothing up there."

I glanced out the window as one of the trucks drove out, headed West. His pulling out allowed me to see a motel, circa 1940, that I'd missed, when I walked in.

Maude watched him drive off and then remarked. "Well there goes one back. The truckers like this route since no smokeys are around to bother them. Damn, if they don't fix this road we won't have any business at all." She looked back toward me, grabbed the towel and resumed wiping oft the counter. She stopped and said, "If you're looking for work, you're wasting your time. I know for a fact, Haystack is not hiring."

I took a small zip of the freshly poured coffee and replied, "I'm not looking for work."

She remained motionless, for a few seconds, before lowering her voice and in a confidential tone asked, "Are you from the Government?"

I put my cup down, wiped my mouth and said, "No, why would you ask?"

She glanced over each shoulder with a furtive gesture. When she satisfied herself no one was listening, she placed both hands on the counter, leaned forward until her nose was almost touching mine and whispered, "Be very careful up there. Strange things have been going on and nobody knows what. I think it may be from outer space, but people say I'm crazy. Do you think I'm crazy'?"

I kept my face close to hers and whispered back, "No, but I have no answers. I appreciate the warning. I'll be careful. I'm just going up there on a business deal involving cattle."

"Well, I personally have seen bright lights up on the mountain and even sometimes I have seen what looks like fire."

"Can you see the ranch lights from here?"

Maude shook her head and whispered, "No." Then stepped back, laughed and said, "Haystack only has kerosene lanterns. Hell, you can't see his lights from his front gate. No, the lights I have seen come from way up on the hills behind his place,"

I heard someone walking and a door slammed. Maude smiled as she spoke. "Gus, my husband is up. The little twerp will be in here in a minute and we can get you some gas"

"Good, 1 would like to get going," I said as I threw a five dollar bill on the counter and motioned to keep the change.

A bald man in his fifties waddled into the room from the kitchen. He was half as tall as Maude, but three times as wide. He poured himself a cup of coffee and looked quizzically at me.

"I need some gas," answering his unasked question.

He nodded and asked, "That your pickup down the road?"

"Yeah, I almost made it."

He took a swig of coffee before speaking. "I noticed it when I got up and figured that's what happened. I don't suppose you have a can?"

I swallowed the last drink from my cup and signaled Maude that I didn't want a refill. "No, I hoped you would have one I could use."

"I do, It's only a two galloner, so it's easy to carry. I do have to ask for a five dollar deposit on it, so I know you'll bring it back."

Maude's mouth fell open as she turned to face her husband. Her rough voice rose to an angry roar. "What in the hell is the matter with you? He's here because he ran out of gas. Do you think your two gallon can will get him to the next station. You are really some kind of an idiot. If you had a brain you would know he has to gas up here. He wouldn't have a chance to steal your damn precious two gallon can. In fact it isn't even a can. It's a worn out piece of plastic. It probably leaks and should have been thrown away years ago."

He put down his cup and motioned for me to follow. Once we reached the pumps, he asked, "Where you headed?" I answered, "Haystack's ranch."

I stood quietly as he put the nozzle into the container. He looked up without turning it on. He pulled up his pants looked cautiously around and said, "I want to talk to you for a minute. Do you mind?"

"No, go ahead."

"I guess Maude told you about the flying saucers. I don't believe in such things. I have to say though, strange things do happen up there. Haystacks young wife is a real nice woman. Last time she was here she told me she was scared out of her mind. Damn shame, she is a real beauty. You know, the kind, when she smiles, it just kinda knocks the wind out of you. No one that pretty should have to live scared. Maude gets madder than hell if she as much as catches me looking at her. If you ask me Haystack himself is behind what ever it is that's happening up there. I always thought he was a little teched in the head. I probably shouldn't say this, but I think you should know, his wife is the second Mrs. Haystack. He was only married to the first one a couple of years. Then one day she was gone. No one or nobody seems to know where or why. There was talk, but it was just gossip and you know how that is."

"Yeah I know. Were there any kids?"

"Nope, and in less than a year old Haystack brought home this mail order bride. He told me he got her from a catalog."

"A catalog?"

"Yeah and a real looker like her, it's hard to believe. She is some 10 years younger than him. Hell, I think she was a child bride. I have always thought she was only about 16 when he brought her home. Then, another thing, she didn't speak much English when she got here."

"What language did she speak?"

"Damn if I know. Some said it was Russian. Haystack kept her up at the ranch. He didn't bring her around for more than a year. He's jealous as hell and even though he doesn't come to town to drink often, when he does, it's a lot. He can be ornery when he's sober and a real mean bastard when he drinks. He beat the hell out of a couple of truckers. It was right here, one night when they looked at her. That fight cost us our liquor license."

"You lost your license over one fight?"

"No, there were others before the road changed. This was once a wild place and a popular watering hole for a lot of people. I guess that fight was the last straw."

"And it all started with a catalog, huh?"

"Yep, and I didn't even know such things existed. I wish, oh well, you've met Maude."

"Yeah, but you should be happy. You might have gotten one who's mean as hell."

"I did that, without a catalog. Well anyway be careful up there Remember, keep your eyes off the wife, which isn't easy. You don't need to take my word for it, but if she's in the room, you will find it's damn hard not to look at her."

"I will, and thanks for the food, gas and the advise. I'll be back to finish filling up as soon as I can."

"Okay, I'll be here. One more thing. While you're up there, keep your eyes open. If you see that catalog, ask if you can borrow it. I sure would like to see what they're selling."

# CHAPTER EIGHT

I pulled up close to the only mail box, in the area. The name was faded and before I could read it, there was a gun shot. It was close and from the sound, I judged it came from a rifle. My instincts took over as I accelerated the truck up the road to the top of a small rise. A man stood looking into a dry aqueduct. He held a lever action 30-30 at the post position. He nodded to acknowledge my presence as I stopped beside him. I stepped out and followed his gaze into the storm drain. There was two horses, a buckskin colt and a bay filly. The bay's head was against the concrete wall and the right front leg had a compound fracture about 6 inched above the fetlock. The hoof and leg was bent backwards exposing the protruding leg bone. Her chest was inundated with elongated deep lacerations. There was a large accumulation of blood under her neck, but the bleeding had slowed to drips. The dripping was probably due to gravity or possibly she was bled out. The top of her skull was blown away verifying the euthanasia shot ended her misery. The buckskin was several feet on the other side of the bay. His head was twisted back toward us, while his body was facing away. The left front leg was extended to the front and to the left of the body. There was blood seeping along the left side of his neck. I looked to the rancher, hoping for some explanation. His eyes were moist, and suddenly, he started sobbing and handed me the gun. His voice broke as he said, "You do it, Please, you do it. Make sure they're dead. They're cut and tore all to hell."

I hesitated and looked closely for signs of life. The bay was obviously dead and as I watched the buckskin moaned and his left back leg jerked. The rancher pled for me to hurry, stating, "Don't let him suffer. Please shoot."

I raised the rifle and shot twice into his brain. Then lowered the rifle as I automatically levered another live round into the barrel. We stood without words for several minutes, until we were sure they were both dead. Then he wiped his eyes as he motioned toward my truck. I kept the rifle, took the live shell from the chamber, and placed the gun muzzle down between us.. He nodded and quietly said, "Thanks." He blow his nose and again wiped his eyes with a large bandanna. I followed his hand signals to a ranch house located in a small valley. I noted it was just out of sight of the roadway. We approached the dwelling and was met by an woman standing on the porch. Her blond hair was uncombed, her face devoid of makeup and her blue eyes were red rimmed and full of tears. She looked like she was going to ask a question. Her mouth opened, but two quick sobs covered any words. A look from the rancher conveyed the answer. She lowered her head and covered her face with her hands. She quietly asked, "Both of them?," then looked up at me. I had moved closer but barely heard her words I nodded my head and mumbled, "Yes." The tear drops fell freely down her cheeks as she turned and walked into the house.

The rancher took the rifle from my hands and motioned for me to follow while explaining. "That's my wife, Johanna. The buckskin was her favorite."

I nodded, as we walked, then said, "By the way, I'm Dutch Evans."

Without breaking stride, he said, "I figured as much. I saw the California plate when you drove up. The Sheriff told me you were coming. My name is Jim and I need a drink. Come on, I have some whiskey in the house."

We entered the kitchen and he motioned for me to take a seat. He quickly placed two glasses on the table. His hand was steady as he filled each with at least an ounce and a half of bourbon. He raised his glass in a toast. I nodded and raised mine. We click the rims together, smiled, and tossed the whiskey down in one gulp. The burn was instantaneous. My eyes watered as the heat in my throat intensified and then spread downward to the pit of my stomach. I caught my breath and whispered just loud enough to be heard. "You pour a stiff drink, Jim."

He nodded, and showed me the label, which read 100 proof. I noticed his eyes were wet as he gasp and spoke. "The Sheriff brought me this bottle when he came up here yesterday. I don't guess I ever had a 100 proof bourbon before. Maybe I had it once in a mixed drink, I don't know."

"Yeah, I agree. Some whiskey needs to be mixed or at least served with a chaser. A beer probably would have helped."

"I'll tell the Sheriff to only bring me the weak stuff, or bring a case of beer with it."

"You said the Sheriff told you I was coming. Did he drive up here just to bring you whiskey, or to tell you I was going to visit."

"No, to each. It was a good excuse for him to come up. I don't have a phone so he could call me. Oh I have one of those cell phones, but I don't have anyway to keep it charged. The only time I use it is to call out. Then, I have to plug it in to the lighter hole in my truck."

"Did he say how he knew I was coming?"

"He said someone called his office looking for information on my ranch. He got curious and called the Sheriff in your area and they knew about it. They told him you were heading this way."

"Yeah, Sam has away of smelling information, Then he probably convinced Dr. Healum to change his mind. The question is how much did Healum tell him?"

"Hell, I don't know anything about that, but that's not the real reason, the Sheriff showed up here with whiskey."

"It isn't?"

"Naw, He comes up here with his dogs about once a month. I let him hunt pheasants or quail down on the other side of the hayfields. He did say your Sheriff spoke very highly of you."

He reached over and poured both of us another drink. He was careful to limit it to less than half of the first shot of fire. He leaned back, rubbed his finger across the glass thoughtfully, then downed the drink in one gulp. He noisily exhaled, shook his head and said. "You know when I lose a calf or send one to market, I have a feeling of regret. I guess most of that feeling goes away when it comes down to money. A horse is different, They're like a member of the family, or at least a friend. I don't know how to explain it. Both of those horses were born here. My wife raised the buckskin as if he was her child. I knew she would take this hard. She wanted me to call the vet, but hell he couldn't get out here until tomorrow. I couldn't stand to see them suffering. I was glad to see you. You were welcome help, She needed someone, other than me, to tell her, they couldn't be saved."

I swallowed my drink before responding. "I knew they were hurt bad. What happened? I mean how did they get cut up? Why they fall into that culvert? It looked like they both had at least two broken legs. Yeah, you didn't have a choice. You had to end their suffering. I would have done the same thing."

He poured another drink with an extra measure even exceeding the first. I considered refusing, but thought better of it, since I needed to gain his confidence. He pulled out his bandana, wiped his eyes and dropped another shot. He gasped a couple of short breaths, then exhaled before speaking. "Yeah it had to be done, but damn it hurts."

I fingered my glass, without speaking, as Jim once more filled his own glass and continued. "We have more work to do. So drink up and lets get it done."

"I'm with you. What do you want me to do.?"

"I want to get those horses in the ground. I have a 6 cat with a back hoe attachment." He stopped speaking, looked at me, took a deep breath then quietly said. "I guess we should take the cat up and pull them out of the ditch first."

I tossed down my shot of whiskey, waited for the throat burn to subside, then asked. "Where are we going to bury them?"

Jim nodded before replying. "I want them down by the barn. That's where they were born. I guess it's just fitting, they end up there."

I wanted a chance to carefully examine both horses. I offered an alternative plan. "I have 4 wheel drive on my pick up and a good chain. I can drag them down to the barn one at a time while you use the cat to dig a hole. It will give us both something to do and save time."

"Yeah, that makes sense. Are you sure your pick up can pull them out of the culvert?"

"I'm sure," I replied, as we rose from the table.

# CHAPTER NINE

I tied the back legs of the bay together with my lariat rope. Then hooked one end of the chain to the rope and the other end to my bumper hitch. The truck in low gear easily pulled the carcass onto the roadway. I repeated the process with the buckskin and stretched the two of them out side by side. The sound of the diesel engines acceleration told me Haystack was busy. It gave me a little time as I methodically examined every inch of their bodies. They were both about a year old and the buckskin had not been gelded. The lacerations on their neck and chest appeared to have been the result of crashing through barb wire fences. I found no external evidence that could explain their behavior. My conclusion, something or somebody had spooked the hell out of them.

My thoughts were frequently distracted by remembering Johanna's reaction. I was thankful to be working out of her sight. Gus had not exaggerated. She was, for a fact, a real looker. Her youthful beauty had not been diminished by an outdoor life. In fact, the darkness of her skin added to her attractiveness. It wasn't any mystery with Gus's reaction, when you compared Maude's wrinkled sun dried hide to Johanna's alluring flesh. I had to wonder what she was afraid of. Jim was a big strong man and had all the characteristics of someone who had worked hard all his life. He could hold his own in a violent confrontation. He was tough, but not without compassion. Hell, I saw him cry, without shame, over a suffering animal.

None of these thoughts solved my next problem. I had to drag these horses past the house. Maybe I would get lucky and she wouldn't be looking through a window or worse be outside. I considered waiting until dark, but

Jim might misinterpret my reasons. No, I had it to do and I needed to get it done. The cat's engine had toned down to an idle. He was waiting.

I drug them one a time to the deep hole Jim had prepared. If he was feeling any effects from the alcohol it didn't show. I was impressed with his expert operation of the cat and back hoe. I watched, as he placed each horse side by side and covered the hole. He drug the back hoe over the dirt and leveled the ground while my thoughts again returned to Johanna. I was beginning to think like Gus. If there's a catalog I wanted to see it.

Jim shut down the cat and said. "It's dark and we can't do anything more tonight. Bunk here and tomorrow we will try to figure it out. I know for a fact they spooked and went through three barb wire fences. It cut the hell out of them. Each fence, as they hit it, increased their fear. Anyway they ended up breaking their legs jumping into that damn cement ditch."

"Any loco weed around?" I asked.

"Loco weed! Nope, none around. Someone or something scared the hell out of them. We'll try to find out tomorrow, if you will stay over?"

"I'll stay. Where can I bunk?"

"We have a spare room. I'll show you after supper. First we need to find something to eat. I don't want my wife to fix us anything tonight. I guess we'll have to rough it. I can whip up a couple of baloney and cheese sandwiches, Do you think they might take care of the problem?"

I looked down to hide my smile and said, "That would be fine and I like a lot of mustard."

# CHAPTER TEN

It was still dark when the rattling of pots and pans coupled with the sound of bacon sizzling signaled the beginning of a new day. The aroma of coffee filtered the air as Jim opened the door and announced, "Breakfast's ready."

I hadn't slept as my thoughts alternated between the two dead horses and Johanna's tears. At least we ended the horses suffering by shooting them. There wasn't anything we could do for Johanna. I did wonder why Jim didn't at least take her into his arms and try to comfort her. I rapidly dressed in the dark and hoped maybe she would be cooking breakfast. I looked forward to seeing her again without the disheveled appearance.

"Good morning," Jim said, as I entered the kitchen. He turned back to the stove as he motioned to take a chair. He wrapped his hand in a towel and grasped the handle of a large pot of boiling coffee. He poured us each a cup and replaced the pot before continuing. "My wife is still under the weather, but I still remember my bachelor days. I can whip up a pretty good meal."

The air was permeated with the scent of pine. I glanced over at the stove as he shoved another chunk of wood into the fire. He had his back to me as he flipped the eggs and placed a couple of slices of bread into a slightly greased skillet. I was mesmerized by the aroma as the wood popped and crackled in the stove. I wondered if his wife was really indisposed or was he just keeping her out of my sight. He broke my trance when he asked,

"How do you like your eggs?"

"Over medium," I replied.

"Good, I forgot to ask, but that's the way I fried them," He said, as he put the plate in front of me.

I was even hungrier than I realized. I'd eaten very little since leaving my ranch. I took several bites before slowing down to enjoy the taste. Then, I said, "You're a good cook. This bacon is delicious. It has a unique flavor I've never tasted before."

"It's an old family recipe. I have my own smoke house and I take my time in curing my bacon and hams."

"Well, it really works. This is great."

He got up and refilled our coffee cups before replying. "Thanks, I have a new ham down in the spring house and I will fix us a couple of sandwiches for lunch."

"Oh wow, that sounds good" I replied, while breaking off a piece of toast and sopping up the egg yolk. A couple of bites later, I said. "So, you have a spring house, a smoke house and I suppose a root cellar."

"You're right. The Sheriff said, I'm living in the 19th century. I guess he's right. But, I'm use to it. Hell, It's the way my family has lived for generations. Besides I can't get the electric, nor the phone company to string wires up here. They have both in the village, down by Maude's, but they want a fortune to extend it up here."

"Well, it seems to work for you." I said, as I glanced around the kitchen.

"Oh, yeah, water. Well we do have indoor plumbing for the bathroom. I put it in when those big stores quit sending out catalogs. I figured if I had to buy toilet paper I might just as well put the toilet inside. We ran out once and I tried to use an old gun catalog. It plugged up the pipes something awful. Now I keep a large supply in the back room. We have a big basin out the back door that we use for the kitchen. Someday, I will put the sink in here."

I laughed, as I replied, "Yeah, catalogs don't work well with modern plumbing."

He opened the topic of catalogs, but I didn't know if his wife could hear us or not. I decided the time and place was not right. I excused myself with the explanation. "I have a roll of toilet paper in the truck and I am going to take it up to the outhouse. I need to spend a little time relaxing."

"You're welcome to use the indoor toilet," he quickly said.

"No, thanks anyway. It has been a long time since I used an outhouse and I think I need a refresher course."

He laughed, "Suit yourself. I will go down and bring in a couple of horses while you take care of business. Do you want to ride bareback or my wife's saddle?"

"I shook my head and answered. "I have my own saddle in the truck. If it's all right with you, I'll use it."

He laughed and said, "That's fine, but you'll still be riding her horse."

# CHAPTER ELEVEN

It was just first light when we walked up to the ditch fence. The top two strands of wire were snapped. The third wire was pulled loose from the posts. The bottom wire was taut and intact.

Jim put loops in the ends of the broken strands of wire and laced bailing wire through the loops. By placing the wire into the claws and using the barrel shank behind the head of a hammer he wound them tight. A few wraps of the loose ends around the taut wire, completed the task. I stapled each wire to it's respective post and made sure they were secure before I spoke.

"It appears they tried to jump the bottom strands, but didn't make it. It's my guess they tripped and were airborne when they hit the ditch. Dropping the eight feet into the concrete would account for the fractures and the positions you found them in."

He quietly listened to my theory while pulling hair and flesh from the barbs of the fence. He stood with his back to me and seemed reluctant to allow me to see his face. He pulled a bandana from his back pocket, blew his nose and wiped his eyes before responding.

"Yeah, I don't know what would make animals act that way."

We fixed the fence leaving ourselves on the road side. We had to walk down to the gate to return to the barn. I talked as we walked.

"You know, my animals went crazy the night we found those dead calves. First, Ralph took out one of our best horses and had him ground tied. In his entire life he had never moved over a few feet while ground tied and that was only to graze. Ralph said he saw the blackness move and his horse spooked and ran back to the barn. Then my dog barked, whimpered and acted scared while my stud horse raised hell in his corral. This was about two o'clock in the morning, mind you. About this time the coyotes found the dead calves. Ralph fired some shots and believed the noise scared them off, but now when I think about it, I don't know."

"Yeah, coyotes don't scare easy anymore." Jim said without breaking stride."

"There's more. The following night I rode out to guard the dead cattle until an investigation could be made. The coyotes never came back. I sat on a rock and had to hold my reins all night because the horse was skittish. Then when I rode in the Deputy Sheriff shined a light on us. She spooked and by damn, she tried to buck me off."

"Weird, I never would have believed a coyote would be scared off of a free meal."

We picked up the horses at the barn and rode out due West. We passed several pig pens and then rode through an immense garden. We picked up the dead horses tracks on the East end of the garden. In addition to the hoof prints, there was a heavy blood trail. I pointed out several places where the blood had splashed to the side and commented this was an indication of blood spurts from arterial bleeding. Jim nodded and remarked.

"Yeah, they were bleeding to death. I am surprised they made it as far as they did."

It was over a thousand yards to the next fence and we rode in silence. Jim remarked, as we stepped down.

"Well at least they both went between the posts on the same side. They sure tore hell out of the wire, but we have to only splice each strand once."

I nodded, and went to work making loops on the broken ends. Jim busied himself making bailing wire splices when he asked, "Are you married?"

"No, I'm divorced and widowed."

"Oh! Married twice. Two women?"

I finished making a loop and managed to cut the palm of my hand on a barb, before answering. "No only one. She divorced me then died."

"Divorced huh. What happened?"

I was taken aback by his questions, but answers might open the door for some questions. I hesitated for a moment, took a deep breath and replied. "Well, to make a long story short. She thought bartenders had more fun than police officers and she ran off with one. They went to Los Vegas, she got a quickie divorce, and he pimped her out on the streets of New York. I heard she caught every disease known to man and died."

"Damn, ran off with a bartender. Was she pretty'?"

"Yes, very pretty."

"Well, that's what happens. Ugly men, like you and me, who marry pretty women, have to watch out for those things."

"Ugly?" I questioned.

"Yep I have been meaning to ask, what happened to your nose?"

"Well, it has been broken. The first time, a saddle bronc rared up in the chutes and his head caught me square on the nose. The second time, a bull slapped me with a horn. The third time, a rope with a bull on one end and my horse on the other snapped tight across my face. The last time, I got the hell beat out me by two gargantuan men who used me for a punching bag."

He laughed and resumed tying the last wire as he remarked,

"That would do it and I guess it explains the rest of the scars. Myself I can only blame being born ugly. Then the normal wear and tear from years spent out in all kinds of weather, doesn't help."

The third fence was the worst. The two horses had each hit between alternate posts and broke them off near the ground. The individual barbs were encased in flesh and hair. The blood trail was heavy and started about 20 feet from the fence line. There was evidence they both had fallen and were momentarily entangled in the wire. I shook my head and remarked.

"They had hell here. Then to get up and run damn near a mile. Well it's amazing, but they must have really been terrified."

Jim stood silently then walked over and took a seat on a nearby rock. Both of our horses started a nervous dance and tried to pull away. I grabbed both sets of reins and tried to settle them down. Jim jumped up and took his horse away from me and we walked them down the fence line until they quieted down. I mentioned, "Damn, they are acting just like my stud. He was skittish the night we found the dead steers."

We entered a gate and started across the pasture when Jim remarked, "Maybe they didn't like the smell of horse blood. I don't know, but there isn't anything I can do there. I have to bring up a shovel and two new posts. So for now, I will show you where I found my dead heifers."

Jim pointed out an area 50 feet from a Northern fence and 100 feet in either direction from the East or West fence. He gave a verbal narration as we walked and I listened without interruption.

"It was right here, but as you can see this area is heavily sodded. I couldn't find any tracks. We have thick woods North of here and the fence line marks the end of my property. Beyond that is federal forest land and it goes over the top. I don't know how far North it does go. There really isn't anything over there for 50 miles. Then you run into a federal prison. There aren't any roads from this side and it is a hell of a long trip if you want to go around to get to the prison."

He stopped and looked at me and I took the opportunity to speak.

"The other three sides are encompassed by several barb wire fences and the only access is through your driveway. Right?"

He nodded and answered "Right, and nothing came in that way."

I thought for a minute and then asked. "Was it cold that night?"

"Damn cold, even that ditch over there had ice."

I glanced over at a small ditch with six inches of slow running water. Then continued. "This grass was probably frozen down and if somebody walked on it there may have been tracks. Tell me, when you found them what did they look like? I mean how were they situated?"

"Well it was kind of funny. They were both year old Black Angus heifers and they were stretched out face to face. Their legs were touching and when I first saw them, it appeared like they were dancing. You said you had an investigation. Did it tell you anything?"

"Yes, it told me I missed a lot. The investigator was Doctor Healum, a veterinarian with experience. He found the blood had been replaced with normal saline and the brains, jugular vein and carotid arteries were missing."

"Well, I didn't see any blood and I don't know anything about those other things. There was one really weird thing though."

"What was that?"

He hesitated, took three deep breaths and said. "Like I said they were Black Angus heifers and their hides were very black. Well they both had blonde scalps sewn onto their heads."

"What?" I asked, "You're saying they were wearing wigs? Are you kidding?"

He sighed, shook his head, and looked directly at me without a trace of a smile and said. "No, not wigs. human scalps. Long flowing blonde hair scalps. The Sheriff said, they did not have black roots and they came from naturally blonde young women. Women who took good care of their hair.

"Good lord, It might not be too late. Doctor Healum needs to see those bodies."

Jim turned away as he said. "Well, then it's too late. The Sheriff cut off their heads and took them to some lab. The bodies, well, I can't say anything about what happened to them."

# CHAPTER TWELVE

A small opening surrounded by tall pine trees. Good shade, with a spring fed creek running down the draw. An ideal choice of surroundings for our lunch.

"A great place for a picnic," I remarked, as I bit into a ham sandwich. Then added. "God, this ham is good. Another family recipe, I guess."

Jim stopped chewing as he answered. "Yes, an old family recipe and a lot of slow curing in the smoke house. I'm sorry I forgot to put any mustard on it. I just remembered you wanted a lot of mustard on your horse cock sandwich yesterday."

"Yeah, but there is a world of difference between baloney and this ham. I wouldn't do anything to change this flavor." Damn the words were out of my mouth before I realized it. I guess I'm a hypocrite. I've used the term horse cock many times. but somehow I couldn't today. It just didn't seem proper to use slang in the presence of this great ham. I changed the subject as I continued.

"I saw a lot of empty brass lying around the pastures. They all seemed to be 30-30 caliber. Do you do a lot of shooting up here?"

"Yeah, quite a bit. My wife doesn't like shooting, so I come up for target practice."

"The brass is spread out. What do you use for targets?"

He again stopped chewing rearranged his bread and then laughed as he spoke. "Oh, various things and if a coyote gets in the way. Well that's just to bad. Did you know if they are in a pack and you hit one, they will turn on him. They are a bunch of damn cannibals. Those bastards."

I asked, "They're protected, aren't they?"

"Yeah, they say they keep down the varmint population, like rats, mice, gophers and prairie dogs. They forget about fawns, calves, lambs and chickens. There is a loophole I rely on and so far it's worked."

"What is that?" I asked between bites.

"A rancher can kill a coyote if it is threatening his stock."

"Good law, you can say they are getting your chickens."

He laughed, shook his head and replied. "Hell it's the skunks that get into my chickens. I have a hell of a time with them. My wife doesn't want me to kill them, so I have a 22 rifle and only shoot shorts. It doesn't make much noise and I tell her it only stings them. Then I bury them when she isn't looking. It sure stinks for a couple of days. I tell her it's because I didn't kill them."

I finished my sandwich and looked up into the timbered forest, then remarked. "It is quiet and peaceful here, it's hard to believe there is anyone within a hundred miles. I guess there is some people around. Maude told me she has seen lights up here at night."

Jim leaned back against a tree and placed his hands behind his neck before he spoke. "Maude would talk your leg off if you would let her. The problem is you can only believe half of what she says. In this case She's right. There is a lot more people up here at night than in the daylight. Most of them are poachers. Some hunt for meat and some for reasons I don't understand. The game wardens tell me they kill deer and only take the antlers. Sometimes they will kill a bear and only take his gall bladder and paws. You suppose that's what we are dealing with? Hunters who kill cattle and only take the insides."

I shook my head and replied. "I don't know what we are looking for, but hunters have to leave tracks, and I haven't seen any."

Jim kicked a small rock and watched it roll down into the water before saying "One forest ranger told me he run into a fellow up here, not too long ago, who said he saw big foot. I haven't found any of his tracks either. If he was roaming around in this thick timber you would think some of his hair would snag on the tree limbs. I hear he is a big hairy beast."

"Maude said she believed it was flying saucers. Gus told me he thought she was crazy. They both agreed there are a lot of lights. I would hate to think they are all poachers."

Jim kicked another rock and watched it stop short of the water. He cleared his throat and said. "There are some prospectors up there all the time, then you have game wardens and forest rangers. They all have lights. Sometimes at night I hear shooting and my wife pokes me to see if I'm there. This makes me believe she hears it and wants to make sure I'm not involved. Maude can believe what she wants, and she will say so. It doesn't matter whether you want to hear it or not.. Gus will only talk if Maude is not there, If she is, he will only open his mouth to agree with her. I haven't seen any crop circles, bright lights or strange creatures. I believe if I was going to see them, it would have been yesterday, after a couple of slugs of that 100 proof liquid fire we drank."

I nodded in agreement, Then said. "I don't know if that stuff will make you see creatures or fix it so you don't see anything. Maybe there is only one drink difference between the two. I'm sure glad we stopped when we did. By the way does any one live in the village, or are Maude and Gus the last survivors?"

"Well, yeah, Maude's wacko son and some of his friends bed down there sometimes. There is probably 400 houses there and they will move into one. Stay until they trash it and then move to the next one."

"400 houses. That was a large oasis out here. Where did everybody go?"

"Just disappeared. There was a lumber operation in the national forest and it shut down. A couple of mines went bust and everyone left. I hated to see it go. We had a real nice little community. There was a one room school house. It was a dance hall on Saturday night and a church on Sunday. All we had to do was shuffle chairs and benches in and out."

He stopped and seemed thoughtful and I said. "Your school house was a church on Sunday. I thought I saw a church up on the hill?"

He laughed and said. "You did. They had a real preacher up there. The school house only had a guy who preached. You'd be surprised how many people seemed scared to go into the church, but seemed okay to go to the school house to hear preaching."

I nodded and said. "Some people are like that. I guess it's good they had a choice. The school house seemed to have served everyone's needs."

He smiled and said. "I went to school there, grades 1 thru 6. Only one teacher, but 6 grades." He hesitated, then continued. "Then, there was a country store and meat market. We even had a Sheriffs sub station and lockup. The Deputy Sheriff only came out on weekends. He was suppose to keep the peace at the dances. He usually was better at watching fights than stopping them. The butcher doubled as a Deputy Sheriff during the week. He could call and get a Deputy to come out if it was an emergency. Most of the problems were put off until the weekend. Some would solve themselves before the Deputy would get here."

"It sounds like the butcher was a busy man."

"Yeah, he was also the deputy coroner. Maybe they figured he was the one who would know it somebody was dead. More likely, I think he got that job, because no one else wanted it."

I laughed as I spoke. "I'm surprised they didn't make him the Justice of the Peace."

"Nope, Maude was the Justice of the Peace." He shook his head and smiled as he continued. "She lost he job right after she lost her liquor license. I always figured she should have been the Sheriff instead of the Judge. She has a left hook and a round house right that could deck a mule."

"How did she lose her liquor license?"

He kicked another small stone into the water, then stood up as he spoke. "Well, the restaurant first had a beer and wine license. Then they expanded with an off premises package store. They could only sell the hard stuff by the bottle and outside of the cafe. Hell, they couldn't even sell it from the gas station because of some law designed to stop drinking and driving. They stored it in one of the cabins behind the place. It was well stocked, beer by the case, whiskey and wine by the bottle. If you wanted a bottle, Gus would walk you back and make the sale. You couldn't drink it on the premises. Well, no one paid a whole lot of attention to that rule. There were beer parties in the parking lot. No one seemed to care and felt they were just bending the law a little. Then they started bringing the hard stuff into the cafe. Maude was selling soda pop for mixing and beer for chasers. Maude got greedy and started pouring drinks in the cafe. A man and woman came in, ordered a meal and watched the action. They ordered an after dinner drink. When it was served, they pulled out badges and Maude was out of the liquor business."

I said. "Yeah, I guess if a law is bent, it's pretty easy to go ahead and break it. I thought they lost their license because of fights."

He said, "Naw, they only say that, so they don't have to admit it was their fault."

I said, "When I was down there it seemed they were going to be out of every business before long. They said their supplies hadn't been delivered. They didn't have any food, even if someone wanted to eat. Maude tried to feed me a sandwich on stale bread, no lettuce, a piece of rubber, masquerading as cheese and one piece of over the hill baloney. The only thing edible was the mustard."

He knelt down at the stream, cupped his hands and scooped up two drinks of waters before speaking. "Yeah you're right. They went bust when the road changed.

They just don't have sense enough to figure it out. Then again a hell of a lot of it's their own fault. They give, that worthless son of theirs, money to buy supplies and he disappears. He always comes back when he's broke. He's in and out of jail and he keeps company with a bunch of bastards, who are capable of anything. I think it's only a matter of time before he gets into serious trouble or somebody kills him."

I moved down to the stream, quenched my thirst with a couple of handfuls of water. Then pulled out my handkerchief, wiped my mouth, smiled and remarked. "So you felt sorry for them and that's the reason you gave your dead heifers to Maude."

Jim's head snapped up, his mouth opened and closed without speaking, as I continued. "The way you feel about coyotes you wouldn't leave two good carcasses out for their food. You didn't bury them and without a freezer you couldn't keep them for your self."

"It was good meat." Jim exclaimed.

"I'm sure it was, and with their business they probably still have a freezer full."

"Maude probably thought you were a government inspector trying to trap her. Otherwise you could have had a good black angus steak."

"Yeah, and I will bet Maude had some private stock of beer hid away."

# CHAPTER THIRTEEN

It was early afternoon as we were riding out the north edge of his property. There was a commotion in a stand of pine trees. We both pulled up our mounts and strained our ears to identify the noise makers. It sounded like several birds yapping at each other. There was the distinct call of crows notifying the flock of new found food. Several magpies were adding their voices to the clamor. I pointed toward the trees as Jim nodded and kicked his horse into a gallop. I followed until we crested a ridge. We slowed the horses to a walk. Then stopped, just before approaching a secluded knoll encircled by evergreen trees.

We dismounted and walked to the gate of a fenced in cemetery. Jim stood silently outside the gate as a huge flock of crows and magpies took flight. He waited until they settled in the surrounding trees before entering. I quietly watched as his shoulders slumped and head bowed as he began a slow reverent walk up the pathway.

I stood at the gate, wondering if I should enter. It appeared to me he considered this sacred ground. I didn't want to incur his wrath by an uninvited trespass. The birds were strangely silent and the only sound came from his boots crunching the gravel as he moved slowly forward. He suddenly stopped and stood motionless for a moment, then tell to his knees and cried out. "Oh God, oh God, my God, why, why?" His shoulders shook and his words intermingled with uncontrolled sobbing as he continued,

"Those Son of a Bitches, those Son of a Bitches, damn those Son of a Bitches!"

I rushed through the gate and arrived at his side just as he slumped face down to the ground. I knelt and placed my hands on his shoulders as

I caught a whiff of dead flesh. I quickly looked up and saw a disemboweled hog stretched out, belly down, length wise on the mound of a grave. The entrails were spilled out equally on each side from underneath the body. The surrounding dirt was stained dark red from the seepage of blood. Ants were a crawling blanket, as they competed with the hordes of flies for the free meal. I gasped and then gagged as I grabbed the hind leg of the pig and pulled the carcass from the grave.

Jim raised up to his knees, looked at me, rubbed the back of his hand across his wet, half closed eyes, and muttered, "That's my wife's grave."

I nodded and said, "I will get my rope and drag it out of here."

He muttered, "Thanks." Then started to rise, but stopped and pointed as he exclaimed. "Look at the head, look at the head. My God, look at the head!"

I had rolled the pig over when I pulled it from the mound and the head was now snout up. I walked forward until I was abreast of the front shoulders it was then I noticed the white hair protruding from the back of the skull. I pushed the snout over with the tip of my boot. There was a blonde scalp sutured to the pigs head. I knelt down and found the stitches were continuous and securely attached to the scalp of the hog. They were even, but not tied off. There was an inch of thread hanging loosely from the entrance and the exit points at the rear of the skull. The sewing material appeared to be fishing leader of about 6 pound test. I decided against removing the scalp until I could talk to the Sheriff.

I explained this to Jim as I attached my lariat to the hind legs and then mounted my horse. I started to move toward the cemetery gate when I had the sensation of my horse dropping out from under me. Just as I realized we were falling I heard a loud report of a gunshot. I instinctually released my hold on the rope allowing it to pull loose from the saddle horn. We fell to the right, but my evasive actions were too slow. My leg was pinned to the ground by the horses collapse.

I turned my head just as Jim cried out and started to fall. His shriek was instantly followed by the sound of a second gunshot and then a third..

There was the laughter of several people in the woods above us. A loud voice yelled. "How about that Haystack? Just try to dance now, you son of a bitch." There was another outburst of laughter, then the voice continued. "You can still dance at the end of a rope, you bastard, and that's where you belong."

I waited until the laughter subsided, before trying to pull my leg free. The gravel from the pathway was biting into my flesh. Finally I managed to untie the cinch allowing just enough slack to move the saddle and free my leg.

Jim was sitting up, creating a tourniquet, by twisting a tied bandana on his left thigh "Don't do that," I said as I pulled the stick from his hand.

"Why not? John Wayne always does it that way." he replied.

I loosened the wrap while explaining. "Yeah, but his wounds are not for real. You not bleeding that bad and we only need pressure on each side of your leg. Now stay still until I find something to use for a splint. We'll have to use the bandana for compresses."

"A splint?"

"Yes, a splint. You have a wound completely through your leg and it appears it may have broken your femur."

He said, "I'm going to crawl over there and get in the shade."

I put both hands on his shoulders and said, "No, damn it. You're to stay still. Look, I am going to scare the hell out of you. You have a bullet wound that probably shattered your thigh bone. You as a stockman know it's a marrow bone. Well, marrow is fat and when trauma or a fracture occurs it destroys fat cells. They, in turn, release a quantity of liquid oil. The trauma also tears some of the veins in the leg. This allows fat to enter your blood stream. Now, with fat running through your system, when it hits your lungs and heart. Bingo, you're dead from fat embolism."

He looked puzzled and then concerned as he replied. "I never heard of anyone dying from a broken leg."

I released my grip as I said, "Well they do and I want to completely immobilize the leg before you move. Understand?"

"Okay, you didn't tell me you were a doctor."

I laughed and replied. "I'm not. I'm just a medical school drop out, who continued studying."

He looked up and asked, "A drop out? Bad grades?"

"No."

"Lack of money?"

"No."

He smiled and said. "Ah ha, a woman then?"

"Yes, a woman." I agreed, as I pulled a board from the fence.

He raised his voice to make sure he could be heard over the noise as I broke the board into splint size pieces. "A pretty woman?"

"Very pretty."

"Yeah, like I said. Those are the ones, ugly men like us have to be careful of. Do you know what ever happened to her? I bet she run off with somebody else. Right?"

I knelt down and using my lariat, tied a make shift splint on his leg before answering. "You're right. It turned out she was married to a crime syndicate boss. In the end, he killed her." I moved back to a sitting position and continued. "Now, either the slug or a bone fragment from your left thigh is embedded in your right thigh. Fortunately it missed the artery and didn't reach the bone. It doesn't seem to be causing any immediate problems. Lets see, we had three gun shots, your horse is dead up by the trees, my horse is dead by the gate and you're wounded. The question is, How in the hell do we get out of here?"

He thought for a minute, pushed himself backwards until his back was resting against a headstone. He used his shirt sleeve to wipe the sweat from his face then replied. "I don't know, but I sure could use a shot of that 100 proof firewater right now."

# CHAPTER FOURTEEN

I knew, I had to stall for time, since I wanted to watch, Jim in case he went into shock. I pulled him into the shade of a large pine tree that gave me the advantage of resting beside him. I used the time to catch my breath, while surveying the landscape. There was a lot of open ground between our location and the ranch house.

He broke the silence. "I hope you're not going to try to be a hero and carry me out of here on your back. Hell I am a good 6 inches taller than you and outweigh you by 50 pounds."

I laughed, "No I'm not going to try to carry you. I was just trying to come up with a plan. I'm going to have to walk to the house and it's across open areas. I estimate it's close to a mile. I believe I can bring my truck right up here. I don't want to get shot when I walk in or when I drive back."

He shook his head and remarked, "Hell, if you were going to get shot you would be dead by now. Think about it. Those shots came from the woods to the right of the cemetery. We were facing downhill and both horses were struck in the left chest and I was hit in the left leg. That was good shooting and you were a sitting duck."

"You're right Jim. Three shots, three hits and all fired from a long distance. My horse was hit and falling before I heard the sound. Since we know bullets travel faster than the speed of sound. We have to assume the shooter was beyond the ridge. Damn good shooting and they could have picked me off anytime."

He took off his hat and wiped his brow before responding. "You know, you only arrived yesterday and since you got here I have lost, 1 sow, 4 horses, a couple of fence posts and I have a broken leg. I'm beginning to think you're bad luck."

"Wait a minute, just a damn minute." I said, as I turned to face him and then continued. "Don't forget you lost two heifers before I even knew about you. We don't know when the sow was killed. The weather is hot and when the blood quits circulating the bacteria multiplies like crazy. The fact her entrails were dumped out slowed the decomposition process. The created gasses caused the odor and signaled the birds to their feast. I would hazard a guess who or what ever spooked your horses probably killed the sow. Besides it seems to me it was your friends who did the shooting."

"My friends? My God, I hope I don't have any friends who would shoot me."

"Well, they did mention dancing. I heard you beat the hell out of a couple of truckers. Was that over them wanting to dance with Johanna?"

He shook his head while looking directly into my eyes before he answered. "No, that was partly my fault. I told people I got her from a catalog."

"And that wasn't true?" I asked.

"No, and it caused the problem. You see, they figured any girl who was bought out of a catalog was for sale. They asked her how much? She said how much for what? They replied, all whores have a price and that's when I stepped in and beat the hell out of them."

I nodded and said, "No one could blame you for protecting her and maybe they were the shooters." I hesitated then continued. "I am curious, why did you make up the story about the catalog?"

He sighed and said, "I guess you probably heard I bought both of my wives, Maddalena and Johanna, from a catalog?"

I nodded and replied "Yes."

He took a couple of deep breaths, sighed again and continued. "Well, somebody should know the story in case they do kill me. So far you're alive and kicking. Maybe they don't want to kill you."

I smiled and with a little impatience in my voice replied. "I hope you're right, but please get on with the story."

"Okay, well to begin with they're sisters." He hesitated and I spoke.

"And they were both natural blonds."

"How in the hell did you know that?"

"A lucky guess. Now go on."

He studied my face before answering. "Look, damn it, if I tell you, promise me you will keep their secret. I believe if word gets out they may be in danger. So promise."

I shook my head and replied. "Look Jim, Maddalena is dead and Johanna may be in danger. In addition there maybe a common denominator between what's happening on your ranch and what's happening on mine."

He looked confused and asked, "A common what?"

"I'm sorry, a common denominator. It means a common trait, or in our case something indicating we have mutual problems. Didn't you learn about denominators in math?"

"Nope, I told you I only went through grades from one to six."

"That's too bad, with your size you would have made one hell of a high school football player. It's a shame you missed that experience."

He smiled as he said, "I missed more than high school football,"

"Oh, like what?"

"High school girls."

"Get serious, I have to go for help and you are stalling to keep from telling me the story."

"I know, but I am serious. You know I never even had a girl friend until I got Maddalena. I think, maybe it's why I fell so hard for her. Not that I don't love Johanna, but damn, I sure miss Maddalena."

There was tears in his eyes as he finished and he looked away from me. I started to get to my feet with the words. "I'll go for help."

A loud voice stopped me with the command. "Freeze right there, mister, and keep your hands where I can see them." I started to turn and the voice continued. "Don't turn around."

Jim, called out, "Where in the hell are you?"

"I'm in the timber just behind you. Don't move."

"Next question, who in the hell are you?" Jim asked.

"Is that you, Haystack?"

"Yeah. If that's you Hollis, quit playing cops and robbers and get down here. We need some help."

I lowered my arms and turned around as the crackling of dry leaves signaled the approach. Jim looked at me and said, "Relax it is just Hollis Woodman. He is the game warden in these parts."

A tall gaunt man came into the clearing from a stand of thick pine trees. He was cradling a lever action carbine in the crook of his left arm. His right hand swung loosely near a holstered pistol on his hip. The large pistol rested in a tied down holster and he eyed me suspiciously before nodding and turning his attention to Jim. I thought, this guy isn't playing cops and robbers, Hell, he thinks he's Wyatt Earp and he's not kidding.

Jim motioned for Hollis to take a seat in the shade and waited until he was seated. Then he began telling him what happened. I stood quietly for a moment, until it became apparent that Jim was not going to bother with the formality of an introduction, I squatted down next to a large rock to wait for the stories end, Hollis didn't interrupt and listened intently until Jim stopped with the words. "Well that's it, and here I am with a broken leg and a couple of dead horses."

Hollis nodded, and carefully examined the compresses without removing the splints. Apparently satisfied he stood and walked over to the dead sow. He looked her over very carefully and then spoke. "Been dead for a least a day, I'd say. The coyotes would have been here if you hadn't killed so many of them."

Jim's voice rose as he protested. "I didn't kill that many and you know it."

A smile crossed Hollis's mouth, then quickly disappeared, as he responded. "Yeah, there's still plenty around, but they're dining up above here. I found two dead bucks just up the ridge and a fresh killed boar bear. The antlers were cut off the deer and the meat left to rot. The testicles and the gall bladder were missing from the bear as well as his paws. The deer were probably killed yesterday, but the bear was still warm when I found him today. I heard some shooting and worked my way down the hill and found you."

Jim shook his head and responded. "Great detective work, since we're a couple of sitting ducks on this open ridge. I guess you thought we were the poachers."

Hollis looked directly at me before speaking. "It occurred to me that you might be, but then I thought you might be shooting coyotes again."

Jim quickly answered. "Damn you Hollis, forget the coyotes and tell me who was shooting at me."

A faint smile again crossed Hollis's lips before he spoke. "Well, I don't know. If it was the same people who killed your sow. They would have to been hiding in the woods. Yeah, patiently waiting for you to find her. A long wait and I doubt that happened. I believe we would have found them if they stayed overnight. You see we have been out here every night for the past week. Night before last, we caught Maude's son and a couple of his cohorts with a doe, I guess Maude was going to cook up some venison chili. I did hear the yelling about your dancing. This was after the shots, but I never saw anyone. I guess they went over the top since no vehicles came out this way. By the way, who is this quiet fellow sitting next to the rock?"

I spoke up. "My name is Dutch Evans and I'm a rancher from California. Now can you help me get Jim to a doctor?"

"Yeah, I will have to go back to my truck and use the radio. It's up on the road a couple of miles from here. I have a government issue cell phone.

It can't get a signal from here. It works everywhere else, but never on this side of the hill. They tell me it has to go though a rely station at the federal prison. That makes this side a total blackout. I have complained only to be told we have a contract for another year. So sit tight I will return as soon as possible."

# CHAPTER FIFTEEN

I watched Hollis disappear into the woods. I resumed my seat as Jim looked toward me and said. "I guess it'll take a while."

I nodded, and replied. "Yes, now we have time and nothing to do. Tell me about your wives."

He hesitated, picked up a stick, broke it, throwing each piece separately to the ground before answering. "Well it's a long story."

"We have time." I assured him.

"Yeah, okay. We have to go back to 1938, Katharaina was a 16 year old girl, living with her parents in Germany. She had an older brother, who was a doctor and her father was a high ranking gestapo officer. Her mother was a devout follower of Hitler and a leader of the aryan social circle in Berlin." He stopped, seemed thoughtful, for a couple of minutes, then continued.

"Katharaina had reached puberty and was selected for breeding. You know, where she was destined to contribute to Hitler's plan of creation. This meant she was to have children for the fatherland. She was attractive and there was no shortage of volunteers. Most of them from the ranks of the gestapo. Her brother, on the other hand, was pulling for his friends. He introduced her to a select few he considered suitable candidates. He even told her she should be proud so many were willing to sire her children. She steadfastly refused all offers. Her mother was secretly reluctant and offered solace. Her father felt she was still too young, but didn't dare speak out. They ignored the warnings of friends that she would be taken against her will. It seemed if they did not accept any of the local stallions. She would be sent off to a stud farm. There to be bred by any german solider, who was next in line. The pressure for her to breed increased. Finally in desperation they quietly sent her to Argentina.

Once safely there, she lived with distant relatives on their cattle ranch. She changed her name to Kemena Aznar and became very rich from the money sent to her by her family during world war two."

He stopped, looked at the ground and wiped his brow before saying. "My leg is throbbing and it hurts like hell. Damn I wish I had a shot of whiskey. Can't you loosed the splints?"

I checked his pulse on the top of his foot before replying. "No it's not cutting off your circulation and it has to be tight for two reasons. It has to keep your leg from moving and it needs to hold those compresses tight against the wounds."

He nodded and mumbled. "Okay, but it still hurts."

"I know," I replied and said. "Hollis will be back soon. Maybe he will bring a first aid kit or some whiskey. In the meantime, grit your teeth and go on with the story."

He shrugged and continued. "Okay, lets see now. Kemena had a young nephew, the son of her older brother, who had been sent to live with her. He grew up, married a girl whose family had also fled to Argentina during the war. They had two children, a boy and a girl. The girl married and became the mother of Maddalena and Johanna. You see they were actually forth generation from the family in Germany."

He stopped talking and using his hands pushed himself upright and backwards to a different position. I offered to help, but he shock his head no and squirmed around until his shoulders were braced against the trunk of the tree. He was swallowing hard and gasping for breath before he again spoke. "Damn, oh damn that hurts. Where in the hell is that Hollis?"

"He will be here in a few minutes." I said trying to reassure him even though I wasn't sure myself of how long he would be gone.

He nodded and said. "Yeah, I guess all we can do is wait."

"That's true, but you still haven't told me how you found your wives."

"Okay, I have to back up a little. In 1946, right after the war, a big hereford ranch up in Colorado sold their entire herd. It was a gigantic, well advertised sale. It was large enough to attract many purebred cattle buyers. They even flew in from several countries. My grandfather went there and soon realized he didn't have the money to buy anything, In fact, he ended up working for the seller. I think his job was driving a limo and chauffeuring the big spenders around. Kemena arrived from Argentina. She was dressed in furs, had rings on every finger and bracelets up to her elbows. Well you could say she was young, naive, and with an impressive line of credit. Grandfather helped her make buys and arranged for the shipment of her purchased bulls. Being always the gentleman, he took care of any other problems as they came up. She offered him a big tip when she left and he turned it down. I believe that cemented their friendship."

I laughed and remarked, "He went from chauffeur to squire. Not a bad move."

Jim gave me a dirty look and continued. "Grandma was there and she would have killed him if he had any romantic ideas."

"Sorry, I just couldn't resist. Besides squire doesn't necessarily mean anything romantic, It is just that in the hierarchy of being I think it is a couple of steps up from chauffeur. You know one is a servant while squire is a friend or escort. So again, I'm sorry. Please go on."

"Oh hell, I thought you said sire, but you said squire. Now that's a big difference."

I shook my head, as I replied, "Yeah a huge difference and you know the difference. Damn it Haystack I never know when you're putting me on."

"I wouldn't put you on, but I couldn't let you get by with a smart ass remark." He laughed and then continued, "Well, back to the story. She wrote often and told grandpa about her ranch on the Pampas in Argentina. She asked him about his ranch and wondered how many gauchos he had working for him. Her letters were usually upbeat, but one wasn't. It was a letter from 1947 when she mentioned neither her mother or father had survived the war. Then she added her brother had been convicted of being a war criminal in Dresden and they executed him by hanging. In the same letter she explained why she changed her name from German to Spanish. It seemed even though Argentina had many Germans, some people didn't like them. She never married and once in a while she needed a shoulder to cry on.

After both grandpa and grandma died she continued to write to my dad. After his death, she wrote to me. Now I'm no great shakes at writing, but I enjoyed her letters, so I wrote back.

Then one day she wrote that several masked men had broken into the girls home. It was in the middle of the night and their parents were drug out into the yard. In spite of their pleas, they were both shot Maddalena and Johanna managed to escape out of a window and hid in a nearby haystack. She was now hiding the girls in a remote area on her ranch. Everyone was scared and she needed to get them out of the country. She also added that she hoped a Haystack would become their means of salvation for a second time."

He stopped and took a deep breath and I said, "I guess that explains why Johanna hates shooting." He nodded, as I continued, "You figured, she was hoping you would be the second Haystack?"

He lowered his head and replied. "Yeah and I sure turned out to be a lousy protector for Maddalena. Right now, it doesn't look like I will be much better for Johanna."

I was quietly thinking it would have been better if it had been a catalog. I replied. "I don't know Jim. I believe the jury is still out. How hard was it to get them to the states?"

"I had to get help. The Sheriff knew a local attorney, who would work with an attorney in Argentina. We managed to get Maddalena here on a visa. Once here, she had to marry a citizen to stay. I was more than willing and in spite of the difference in our ages she said she loved me. You see I was five years older then her, which wasn't a big difference. We were warned if we were just getting married to get around the law, we could both be in deep trouble. Well, that was not the case. We were damn happy and she was a great wife.

Johanna was a different problem. She was an underage orphan living with an aunt who had changed her name. You can see the legal hurdles we had to cross. We needed to have Kemena named legal guardian. It was almost done when she took sick and died. That made Maddalena Johanna's only living relative. We started an adoption procedure and the family connection helped by cutting through lots of red tape. It still took time, but finally she received a visa and was on her way. She arrived and we were a happy family, until Maddalena was murdered."

His eyes were moist and he stopped talking as his voice choked up. I took the opportunity to speak. "My God, and you said I was bad luck. Compared to what you have been through, I brought you good luck. What happened next."

He wiped his eyes on his sleeve before answering. "Well, with Maddalena gone the adoption was stopped. I talked to Johanna and she begged me to keep her here. You see she didn't have anyone left in Argentina. I was the only one she could turn to. To be truthful, I didn't know what to do. My attorney was trying to keep immigration away. They wanted to revoke the visa and send her back. We talked about making me her guardian, but the attorney said it wouldn't protect her from being deported. Fortunately she had brought her records with her and I kept her out of sight until the day she turned 18. On that day we went to town, stayed at the Sheriffs house and had our blood tested. Three days later we were married. The Sheriff and our attorney were the witnesses. My leg is throbbing like hell. What does that mean?"

"It means it's broken." I replied, as I patted him on the shoulder. He gritted his teeth and rared back against the tree. I waited as he took several deep breaths and seemed to relax. I said, "I guess you took her out to meet Maude and crew only after you were married."

"Yeah, You're right. I guess, I wanted to show her off, or maybe I just wanted to brag. You see I am 10 years older than her and I wanted to make Gus jealous. They all seemed surprised and wanted all the details. I had already told them I met Maddalena through a catalog. When they asked about Johanna, I just said, same place."

"Why did they think they were Russian?"

He laughed as he said, "I didn't lie. I just said they were from a town in Europe. I added, it was a small town, whose name I couldn't pronounce but it was near Moscow. I still don't want their German background known."

"I won't tell." I said as a spot appeared in the sky and the increasing noise of a helicopter approached. I reached over and put my card in his pocket as I said. "Here's my card. Give me a call when you get settled in the hospital."

"What hospital?" He yelled, and then asked, "What in the hell is that thing?"

I shouted. "It's a medical helicopter. They are going to fly you to the hospital."

I saw his face turn white and then a bright red as he yelled. "No, by God they're not. I have never been higher off the ground than the back of my horse. I sure as hell am not going to start now. Besides I'm not going to any hospital. You said you were going to get a doctor and he had better be in—."

His last few words were drowned out by the noise of the chopper landing 50 yards away.

# CHAPTER SIXTEEN

"Ben, Ben Bartholomew. I'm the Sheriff in these parts." he said as he stuck out his hand.

I accepted his offer and engaged in a firm handshake as I replied. "I'm glad to meet you. I'm Dutch Evans. You know with all the hollering and yelling. I didn't think you were ever going to get Haystack into the copter, let alone make him stay."

"Well it wasn't easy." He laughed, and then continued. "I'm damn near as big as he is, but only half as strong. That's why I brought two of my biggest deputies. They can handle him and secure him for the trip. I'll bet you could still hear him as they took off. Even though those helicopters sure make a noise and kick up a hell of a dirt storm, don't they?"

"Yeah, they do for a fact." I agreed, as I wiped the dirt from my eyes.

Ben smiled as he said. Jim will quiet down and might even enjoy the ride. I slipped him a pint of whiskey and told him it was a bon voyage gift."

"Hey, I'll bet he thanked you for that." I said, then added, "He's been wanting a drink."

Ben's smile broadened as he replied. "As a matter of fact he didn't say thank you. What he did, was cuss me out for taking so long in giving it to him. If I cut out all the obscenities his words amounted to, A man could die of thirst, if the pain didn't kill him first." He hesitated then added, "He told me to keep an eye on you. Said you have a thing for married women."

Hollis came out of the timber before I could reply and Ben yelled. "Did you find anything?"

Hollis spoke as he moved toward us. "Yeah, I found where they stood when they fired. My range finder puts it at 372 yards. The timber opens just enough up the slope to make it a dear shot." He stopped walking, looked back up the slope then said. "Damn good shooting though. All things considered. I don't know how they got out of there. It's rocky as hell up there and a couple of rocks were kicked loose, but I didn't find any tracks. They also were very careful and picked up all their brass before leaving. They left the deer and bear, and I did recover the slugs from each animal."

Ben and I watched as Hollis walked over to my downed horse. He carefully laid his rifle muzzle up across the neck. Then facing the rear of the animal he placed his left knee on the shoulder. Without looking up he pulled a knife from a concealed sheath in the boot of his outstretched right leg. He moved with the deftness of a surgeon as he methodically opened the chest cavity and started probing into the shattered lungs.

I quizzically looked at Ben as he shrugged his shoulders and answered my unasked question. "Army Special Forces. How do you like the knife?"

"I don't know. It seems sharp as hell and the serrated edge seems to slice through those ribs without any effort."

Ben laughed and with a smile added. "Yeah, it's a winner. Not so pretty, but hell for stout. He had it made specifically, by a knife maker in Texas. As far as I know it's one of a kind. He spent four years in the Special Forces and didn't like any of their knives. He had his own ideas and this is one he designed."

I nodded and said. "Well it's not only a great knife, but he handles it like an expert."

"Oh, he's an expert all right. Don't make no mistake about that. Hell he could cut out your gizzard and be home eating breakfast before you knew it was gone." Ben said, as he looked at me with just a trace of warning in his eyes.

I shook my head and replied. "I believe it, and I wouldn't want him to cut out my gizzard, even if I had one. I don't imagine many people around here try to push him."

Ben laughed again and said. "You're right again. I can sometimes disagree with him, but not without caution. Oh I'm not afraid of him, but he's married to my sister and she can beat the hell out of both of us. So I watch my step, but he's on his own."

Hollis held up his hand with something clutched between his thumb and forefinger. We started towards him as he spoke. "It is a small caliber, copper jacketed soft point, the same as the others. I would guess a 25-20 or at most a 25-35. Not a hell of a lot of shocking power. Plenty though, when you can shoot as straight as the deadeye who did the shooting."

I walked over and looked at what he was holding. I was still pondering the expanded fragment when he pointed up toward the ridge. He said. "Look up there where the trees cross above the rocks." I nodded, as he continued. "That's where they were standing and your horse was hit first. When she went down she pinned your leg, didn't she?"

"Yeah, it happened so fast my right leg was pinned under her."

He nodded and continued. "Well. kneel down here and you'll see you were out of their sight line. I think maybe a dead horse saved your life. Then again, maybe not. Think about it. If they wanted you dead, they would have shot you first, and then the horse."

I shook my head as I looked up the hill and then toward where Jim had been standing, before saying. "You're right, they could have killed me first." I hesitated then added, "That was damn good shooting though. I'll bet both horses were busted through the lungs. I can see where I dropped out of their sights, but Haystack was only a leg shot."

His laugh, was without humor, as he responded. "That's right, they didn't intend to kill him and they didn't intend to shoot him in the leg."

"What?" I asked.

He smiled as he pointed toward Maddalena's grave, then spoke. "Jim was standing by the grave, facing the shooters when your horse was hit. His reaction caused him to turn toward you. The triggerman fired at the same instant catching him on the left leg. Think about it. The wound was crouch high and if he was facing forward he would be singing soprano now. Hell, it just missed him anyway. The bullet entered at the right altitude. They were shooting down hill and the exit wound was about two inches lower Nope, they didn't want to kill him. They only shot to emasculate and put an end to his manhood. In plain english they were going to shoot his balls off."

I stood silently for a few seconds then said. "I believe you're right, but that would be one hell of a shot."

He looked up the hill and said. "I have known some who could do it."

"I imagine you have, but they also mentioned dancing."

He grinned as he replied, "Dancing can have more than one meaning."

I nodded in agreement and turned to find Ben standing at the head of the dead sow. I moved closer as he pointed to the scalp and commented. "It's the same as the other two. Notice the running stitch with the untied ends."

"I wondered, if it would be the same. Did you run any tests on the scalps?" I asked.

"Yes, and we found the DNA was completely different. They both had type O blood, and were natural blond females. They each apparently took excellent care of their hair. The pathologist estimated their ages as mid twenties and that's about all we could tell."

I nodded, and said, "I would bet this scalp will fit right into the same pattern. I don't suppose you're missing any blond girls in this area?"

He shook his head no, as he motioned me to follow him over to the shade.

I took a seat under a pine tree and asked. "How do I contract the coroner? I would like to get copies of the pathologists report."

He replied. "I'm the Coroner and I will send you the reports, including the one on our new scalp. You won't find much in them other than what I just told you, Maybe you will stumble on something. God knows, we need anything that may be a lead."

"Hey, I would appreciate it. I didn't know you were both the Sheriff and Coroner. I suppose you have all the records on Maddalena."

"Yes, but that's an open case, with a body, and I can't give you any of those records."

I smiled and replied. "Can't or won't. You know the circumstances of the dead sow. As well as the shootings might be the break you need to close her killing."

Ben said, "I forgot for a moment. When we checked up on you, they did say you were one of the best homicide detectives they ever had. However the District Attorney demands that any release of records has to come from his office."

I said, "I understand, but maybe you could answer a couple of questions?"

He wiped his brow with a handkerchief before answering. "I might, what are the questions?"

Hollis walked over holding the second slug in a bloody hand and before I could speak he said. "I got them both and they look like they are the same. I will mark and package them. To protect the chain of evidence I will turn them over to your deputies. What about the pig scalp?"

Ben answered, "Leave it for now. I have two men on their way. They will photograph everything before taking the whole head in for examination." Hollis nodded and started to speak, but Ben had not finished and continued. "They have horses and when they finish with the scene they will drag all of the carcasses down into the draw. There is a big pile of brush just around the ridge and with a little help they can burn them."

Hollis replied, "I have a can of gas in the truck. I will bring it for the barbecue. It'll take me a while to get up there and back, besides I want to go by the stream and wash up."

I was glad, I had already quenched my thirst and finished my meal. Maybe the coyotes wound enjoy a blood and guts cocktail, but I wouldn't. He started to walk away and then stopped and turned toward me, as he said. "Oh, I'm glad to have met you. I guess you'll be gone be the time I get back." He moved away before I could answer.

We watched as he moved off into the timber and Ben spoke first. "Yeah, we will have a big bon fire tonight. Jim always insists on burning his dead animals. He says it's neater and saves a hell of a lot of digging. That is what he did with those two heifers you wanted to know about."

I tried not to act surprised as I said. "Oh, I guess that's why no one could tell me where they were buried. I thought maybe the coyotes got them."

He laughed and replied, "Nope, the coyotes can dig up a grave but even a pack of coyotes can't get rid of a big carcass before it starts to smell, Besides it's against the law to feed the coyotes. No, I agree it's better to burn them."

# CHAPTER SEVENTEEN

"Two riders coming." Ben announced and then added, "And they'll want to talk to you."

"Me, why would they want to talk to me?" I asked.

"Well they're members of my posse and they brought some mares at the wild horse sale in Nevada. We found out they were captured with the bunch your stud was running. I bought a couple myself. They're all good looking mares and it turned out they were all pregnant."

"So, what's the problem?" I asked.

"The problem is, we think your stud is the one who impregnated our mares."

I laughed as I replied. "He sure is good at that. I hope you are not going to start a flock of paternity suits."

Ben laughed, shook his head and replied. "By damn, we should. Everyone of those foals has a wild streak."

"How did you know about my stud?"

"Easy, Our vet traced the possible family tree and came up with your stud. It seems he's a legend in the wild horse world and we would like to know how you captured him?"

I sighed, nodded my head, then said. "Well, as you probably know my stud had been named public enemy number one. He had been stealing mares for a couple of years and they were going to kill him. I have a veterinarian friend whom I rode with in our younger days. He talked them into letting us take a crack at catching him. Hell, we had nothing to lose even if we killed him. It was what was going to happen to him anyway. We had a map of where he was running and we chartered a helicopter to help chase him down. Well, let me tell you, I have been on many wild rides, but that was the worst. I don't believe I took a deep breath during the entire time. Hell I was hollering louder than Haystack did today. You know, I didn't have any whiskey to help me. When I tried to get them to let me out, they just made believe they couldn't hear me. I completely lost interest in horse hunting and was clutching a hand hold with both hands. I kept my eyes clenched shut and yelled my head off. It was terrible. We zigged, zagged, and bounced up and down, while violently swaying in every direction. Then I had a sinking sensation and thought we were crashing. It turned out it was just a soft landing. When I opened my eyes I saw we had the stud down. The vet had nailed him from the air with a tranquilizer dart. We put a sling on him and he rode back to my place via an air lift. They lowered him into the corral and Ralph unhooked the sling. We landed and the vet gave him a shot, to wake him up. Let me tell you he was one mad horse."

Ben laughed and replied, "I'll bet, but how did they get you to ride back in the chopper?"

"Oh hell, going back was a snap. I watched out the door and actually didn't even notice the ride. I was just happy to see the horse swaying below us and knew he wouldn't remember any of it. Now quit stalling and tell me about Maddalena."

"I'm not stalling." He said while looking toward the two approaching riders.

"You said you would tell me the story and then we were interrupted."

"I never said I would tell you anything. What I said was I might answer some questions."

I shook my head and said. "Yeah, okay, Where was she found?"

He pointed to the cemetery and said. "She was hanging from a limb in the big pine tree. The one just up the hill from the graveyard. She was in plain sight and 14 feet off of the ground. If you look closely you can see the cut off limb. We sawed it off and left her intact. We took it with her to town for examination."

I followed his gaze and replied, "Yeah, I can see the cut off branch from here. Did you check it for marks?"

He nodded and said. "Yes, she was hanging with a one half inch sisal rope around her neck. The branch did not have any marks or embedded rope strands to show if she had been pulled up or down. It seems the rope was just draped over the limb. The noose was attached to her neck with a hondo loop. The other end, attached to the tree, with a girth hitch. Strange Huh?"

"Yeah, even weird. Did the tree trunk have any marks showing a climber."

He shook his head as he replied. "Nope, no broken bark and no hook marks, like from a lineman."

"Damn," I muttered and then asked. "How did you get her down?"

"Hollis threw a rope over the branch, climbed up hand over hand until he could straddle the limb. He pulled a chain saw up on the end of a rope. He tied the limb behind himself, then sawed off the part she was hanging from. The way he had it rigged he could lower her while she was still attached.. He is stronger than hell and has had all that special training."

"Yeah," I said and then remarked. "He seems to be very perceptive, in addition to his other talents. I'm surprised he is not a detective on your department."

Ben laughed as he spoke. "Well, he should be, but I don't want to be accused of nepotism. Besides, I've talked to him about it and believe it or not he wouldn't change his position for anybody. He is happier sleeping up here under a pine tree than home in bed." He hesitated then added, "No cracks about my sister now."

I laughed and replied. "I wouldn't dream of it. Lets get back to Maddalena. Did she choke to death?"

Ben hesitated then answered. "No, she was dead when they strung her up. She died of shock."

"Shock?"

"Yeah, shock and loss of blood."

I thought for a moment and then asked. "Was she scalped."

Ben shook his head as he replied. "Nope, and before you ask her blood type was A positive."

"Yeah, and the others were type O.

"Right."

Ben was looking off into the distance and scratching the ground with a twig as I asked the next question. "Was she mutilated'?"

He didn't alter his gaze and said "Yes, she was mutilated. Look Haystack doesn't know any of this. He only knows she was found dead. Just dead, while hanging on the end of a rope. We want to keep it that way. Okay?"

I didn't hesitate as I answered. "Fine by me, I won't tell him. I would like to know though, how was she mutilated?"

The riders were getting closer and I feared I would not get an answer when he lowered his voice as he said. "Her entire reproductive system was missing."

"What?" I asked.

"Yeah, she was opened up and everything was gone. The ovaries, the uterus, the vagina and the fallopian tubes, all missing."

"Jack the ripper lives." I muttered, then hesitated for a few seconds and continued. "That's why you won't release the records. It really has nothing to do with the D. A."

He looked embarrassed, as he replied, "Okay, I thought it would just sound more official if the D. A. made the order."

It made it sound more ridiculous. I thought, but no more ridiculous than saying Jim always burned his dead stock. I remained quiet, as the two riders rode up.

Ben turned away and started to brief his deputies. I picked up my saddle and started to walk away. Ben yelled at me, "Remember, mum's the word."

I turned as I said, "You got it," and then as an after thought, I asked. "Who found her?"

Ben yelled back. "Hollis, he saw her swinging when he was up on the ridge." I nodded, and continued my walk.

# CHAPTER EIGHTEEN

It may have been a mile as the crow flies, but I'm not a crow. When you're stumbling across rocks and staying close to the tree line it's a hell of a lot longer than a mile. I started to wonder if it might have been better to stay in the open and risk being shot. Then again, that didn't seem like much of a choice. I continued on while cursing the unseen son-of a-bitch, who might be trying to shoot me.

"A horse! a horse! my kingdom for a horse!" I mumbled, then wondered, where did that come from? Talking to myself was bad enough, but now I was quoting Shakespeare. "I wondered if King Richard was carrying his saddle when he uttered those words? Naw, probably not. Hell he was a King. He must of had at least two men to carry his saddle. Maybe a pretty maiden to carry his bridle. Now, that would be something." Damn it, I thought, I have to shut up. Here I am sneaking through the trees as quiet as possible and verbally ranting away. Well hell, another hundred yards and I can keep the barn between myself and the woods. A loud whoosh stopped me in my tracks. I looked back to see flames encased in black smoke shooting skyward. Damn, they must have used at least five gallons of gas to ignite that blaze. I hurried across the open pasture and slowed only when I came abreast of the barn.

The Sheriff's pickup with a two horse trailer attached was parked next to the corral. I hesitated long enough to notice the newness of the painted logos on the door panels and trailer. The tack door was open and I pushed it closed as I passed.

A cowboy shouldn't have to carry his saddle and blanket over twenty feet. I thought, as I dropped mine into my truck bed. I stopped, caught my breath, then started toward the house to get a drink of water. I noticed an envelope taped to the outside mirror of the truck. I cautiously looked around and seeing no one, I moved back and removed the letter. I stood with my back leaning against the bed of the truck as I read the contents.

"Mr. Evans. Please, please take me with you when you leave. I believe I'm in great danger and fear someone is trying to kill me. Please don't say anything to anybody. I think my husband may be involved. He warned me, not to talk to you. So we need to do it quietly. Please! Please! Please, I beg you, please, take me away from here." It was signed, "Johanna."

I folded the letter and shoved it into my back pocket then looked toward the West. The sun was going down and the light from the fire was fading into the dusk. I was confident the Sheriff and his two deputies were still there. I didn't see any sign of life from the house. I moved toward the back door. It suddenly opened and the entire doorway was filled with the largest man I'd ever seen. He was wearing a Sheriff's uniform and before I could speak, he stepped out and said. "Johanna isn't here."

I looked up and realized, because of his size, I couldn't even see the doorway. I suddenly felt uncomfortable and backed away several feet before speaking. "I just wanted to check to see if anyone had informed her about her husband."

The leviathan bulk was ten feet in front of me and I still had the feeling he could reach out and slap my head off. His voice was gruff as he spoke. "I don't know. I have looked everywhere for her, but she's gone."

I nodded, as he continued. "I guess you're leaving. When I find her I will tell her you were asking about her. Okay?"

There was an implied threat in the tone of his voice and I stepped backward as I answered. "Thanks. I do have to go, I want to get down the hill before dark."

I watched him in my rear view mirror as he entered the house. I fired up my truck and was well on my way, when I vowed to return after dark, and have a look around.

# CHAPTER NINETEEN

Maude's chili was hot enough to injure, but mild enough, not to kill. I was on my third spoonful when she leaned across the counter and in a low voice asked. "How do you like the chili?"

"Fine!" I answered and took a big drink of ice tea before continuing. "Venison always makes good chili."

She rared back from the counter and folded her arms across her breasts. Her cheeks tightened, as she starred at me. There was a prolonged silence, then in an indignant voice responded. "I will have you know that is grade A beef."

I put the tea glass down and motioned for a refill, as I said. "Yeah, sure it is. I believe you would call it the Kings beef. Believe me, I know the difference and I prefer venison every time."

She put both hands on the counter as she leaned forward and whispered. "Okay, okay. Keep your voice down." She pushed herself upright, while maintaining eye contact. Then poured my tea, as her lips curved into a slight smile.

I laughed, as I spooned another shot of the liquid fire into my mouth and quickly reached for the now refilled glass. I gulped down half of the tea and said, "Besides, that bunch in the back booth is making so much noise, no one could hear me anyway. What are you serving them?"

We both looked over toward the corner booth where six obvious intoxicated males were all trying to talk at the same time. Their words were slurred, exaggerated, loud and barely coherent. We listened as one yelled, "My God, I tell you she's a beauty. When she smiles I just melt. I can." He was still talking when a louder voice drowned him out. "Yeah, she is damn pretty from the waist up, but she's two ax handles and a plug of chewing tobacco across her hip pockets." A third voice chimed in. "I don't give a damn about her big butt. In my opinion each time she smiles another inch or two drops off. Then if she bats her baby blues her ass shrinks into a thing of beauty."

Maude turned back to face me and with a tone of defiance said. "I only sell them seven up and coke. They brought in their own bottle."

I laughingly said, "Whiskey has sure loosened their tongues. I wonder who they're talking about?"

"I don't know." She answered, and then continued, as she wiped the counter. "Now I suppose you're going to tell me that only women gossip."

I motioned for more tea before responding. "Oh, I don't think they're gossiping. I always believed that nothing nice is ever said in gossip."

"And what nice things have they said?" Maude asked.

"Well, for starters, she has a nice smile and big blue eyes. Put them together and it adds up to enough sex appeal to excite those young studs."

"Studs! Studs indeed, those pecker necks don't have enough peter to piss over their zippers." She waved her towel toward the booth and continued. "Take a look, at least half of them have pissed their pants."

I shook my head, swallowed a mouth full of chili and started to speak, when Maude yelled. "The Sheriff just drove in."

There was a moment of complete silence from the back booth. Then a few mumbled cuss words, followed by a rapid disorganized rush through the door. The noise of their frantic footsteps on the gravel was dying out when the Sheriff entered with the words.

"Have you been pouring whiskey again, Maude?"

Maude frowned and started to speak when he interrupted. "Hi Dutch, bring your bowl and join me over here in a booth. I need to talk to you." I turned to look at him as he seated himself and continued speaking. "Maude, bring me a bowl of chili and a glass of ice tea. On second thought bring the pitcher and a glass of ice." He turned his head towards me and in a lower voice remarked. "I have eaten her chili before and she doesn't spare the hot."

I nodded, and took the seat opposite him. He looked up as Maude arrived with the food and drink. She smiled at me and placed a large glass of ice next to my small one and said. "You may need this before you're though."

I mumbled, "Thanks," as she turned to face Ben and in a defiant voice said. "I wasn't pouring whiskey, Sheriff. I just served the soft drinks for the mix. Besides, what if I did pour the hard stuff? What could you do to me? You already took my liquor license."

"I didn't take your license. The alcohol board took it and you damn well know it." His voice rose as she hurried away doing an excellent job of ignoring him.

I poured myself a large glass of tea, before taking my next spoon full of chili. Ben returned his gaze from Maude's departing form to his chili and took the first bite. "Wow!" he exclaimed and went for his drink. Maude rapidly returned to our booth and her angry voice drowned out his gulping.

"And another thing, How in the hell do you think we can control things when you closed the sub station?"

Ben swallowed hard and replied. You know I had to shut it down when everyone left. Hell, with so little to do, I couldn't afford to keep it open."

Maude put both her hands down on the table and leaned forward before speaking. "Yeah and every one wouldn't have left, if they hadn't built the freeway ten miles South of here."

Ben looked up and was so close to her face that their noses almost touched. His voice was soft as he spoke. "I didn't have anything to do with it. You know it was all politics."

Maude moved her face closer and said. "Yeah, it was all politics. I have always said, if it wasn't politics it would be illegal. Now I am convinced it is politics and it is illegal. Why don't you do something about it?"

Maude pulled her body up erect as he answered. "You know we always roll when you call. It's not like you don't have any law out here."

She scoffed with the words. "Law! Law out here. Hell the only law out here is, you can do what ever you're big enough to do."

Ben didn't answer, but slowly shook his head. Maude stood starring at him for a moment and then asked. "Do you want more Cayenne in your chile, Ben?"

"Hell no Maude. It's close to battery acid now."

She smiled, flicked her towel at him and said. "Don't eat it then."

"What do you mean, don't eat it? You know I love it." He yelled and smiled as she disappeared into the kitchen. He starred at the kitchen door for a moment then turned toward me and continued. "We fight all the time, but it isn't serious. We really like each other."

"I would have never guessed." I said as I spooned another mouthful and reached for the tea. It was a dark brown and at first sight appeared to be coffee. I drank half a glass and then stopped for air. I said. "The tea is strong, but anemic compared to the chili."

He gulped two spoonfuls, wiped his mouth and said. "Johanna is missing. What do you know about it?"

I thought for a moment before replying. "I heard she was gone. That big deputy of yours told me he couldn't find her."

Ben looked confused and quickly asked. "What deputy?" Then continued before I could speak. "The only two deputies I have here, were the ones up at the fire. They're still there. Hollis went down to the house to tell Johanna about Haystack, but couldn't find her. You were gone, she was gone, and we thought maybe she was with you."

"Bad guess." I said, and then added. "There was a huge man there in a Sheriff's uniform. I mean big. seven feet plus and four to five hundred pounds. He told me he had been looking, but couldn't find her. He came out of the house, talked to me and then went back in. He was nowhere in sight when I left."

"Did he have a badge?"

"I don't know. Hell, I would had to stand on a chair to see it."

"That big, huh?"

"Yeah, and it was getting dark. The only vehicles there was Jim's pick up, mine, and your pickup and trailer. Come to think of it, your truck is not an extended cab. Your two deputies would fill the front and the two horses wouldn't share the trailer. Hell, if he came with them he had to ride in the truck bed."

Ben stood up and stated. "I'll be back in a minute. I have a cell phone and I have to go outside and attempt to reach Hollis. A lot better reception out there. Sometimes we have to call the station and they radio him. I'm going to give him this information and ask him to take another look around. Finish your chili and wait for me."

I nodded and watched him take out his phone as he exited the door. In a few minutes he returned and yelled for Maude.

She came into the room from the kitchen and asked in an annoyed tone. "What do you want?"

"The Flaxen Fillies bus is parked out back. How many cabins did you rent?"

Maude kept her annoyed tone as she replied. "All four of them. Why do you care anyway?"

"Just say I'm curious, Okay. How many Johns are there?"

She wiped her hands on her apron before replying. "I don't know. Two or three carloads and six big rigs with sleeper cabs that pulled in about dark. You know when the CB's announce a party, everybody shows up. I only rent the cabins. It's none of my business what goes on as long as they don't tear things up. I will say, that none of them have shown any interest in coming in to eat."

Maude closely followed Ben as he returned to the booth. When he was seated he looked at her and said. "Fix me a pot of Chili to go. Make sure there's enough to feed four people and throw in some crackers." She nodded and turned to leave as he added, "While you're at it, my chili is cold, heat it up." He handed her the bowl and warned, "I want it stove hot, not pepper hot." She gave him a sarcastic smile and laughed as she walked toward the kitchen.

"What are the Flaxen Fillies?" I asked.

Ben shrugged as he replied. "Whores on wheels. all blonds. They take call girls to a different level. You set up a party, give them a call and they roll."

"Huh." I replied and then asked, "Are you going to make a raid?"

"Nope, they're legal and there isn't a damn thing I can do about it. I'm going to alert the deputies at Haystack's to be available, just in case of trouble."

I reflected on this for a second and then remarked. "That bus must have been modified, but still there wouldn't be much chance for privacy."

Maude placed the steaming bowl of chili in front of Ben as she spoke. "Hell, with that bunch, there ain't no need for privacy." She wiped her hands on her apron, smiled and added. "Besides those trucks all have sleeper cabs and they'll be rocking."

Ben crumbled a cracker into his bowl as he remarked. "Yeah, between those trucks and the cabins there won't be much wear and tear on the bus"

Maude turned toward the kitchen and suddenly stopped as the sound of a large vehicle crossed the gravel driveway. Ben looked up with his spoon halfway to his mouth and asked. "What is it'?"

Maude laughed as she spoke and said, "The party is growing. The Roan Trotters just pulled in."

Ben lowered his spoon back into the bowl and exclaimed. "Damn!" Then looked at me and said, "All redheads."

I nodded and shrugged my shoulders.

Maude laughed and remarked. "Bella will make a fortune tonight."

Ben's face turned red as the sound of several cars crossed the gravel. In a low voice he uttered. "Damn that Bella. Damn CB radios. Everybody within three hundred miles knows about this party. There's bound to be trouble." He pulled the napkin from his lap and threw it on the table before continuing. "Now all we need is for the Night Mares to show up."

"Don't tell me." I said, and then asked, "Brunettes?"

He nodded and said, "Yeah, and they also have what they call the Remuda, It's a mixture of all."

"Why don't you go talk to Bella?" Maude asked.

Ben clinched his fists as he replied. "Talk to her! Hell, you know I can't talk to her. To begin with, I can't stand her."

Maude smiled as she said. "Bullshit. If she smiled and wiggled her butt, you would break your ass climbing into her RV."

Ben shock his head from side to side as the muscles in his jaw tightened. I almost asked if he needed a tetanus shot, but thought better of it. He didn't seem in the mood for any of my humor. I broke the silence by asking. "Who's Bella?"

Ben slammed his right fist on the table. The impact caused the spoon to fly from the bowl splattering chili in my direction. I instinctively reared back to avoid the spicy shower and thought maybe he needed a rabies shot instead of a tetanus. Maude walked over and started wiping the table, as he replied. "Bella is the head whore. That's who she is."

Maude turned and headed for the kitchen with the soggy towel as she said. "She is not a whore, she's the Madam. Ben can't stand a woman who is both pretty and smart."

As soon as she was out of sight Ben leaned closer to me and looked toward the kitchen. Satisfied she wouldn't hear, he spoke in a low voice. "Let me tell you, she is a real beauty. She has fantastic calves, A smile that will knock your soaks off and breasts. Oh, Yeah those breasts. They'll make your mouth water. I'm telling you, every ounce of flesh on her body screams sexy." He suddenly stopped speaking and straightened up. Then glanced at me, with a sheepish grin, as Maude returned with a pan and fresh towels. She didn't speak before continuing to clean the table.

Ben mumbled, "I'm sorry Maude." She only nodded, as He placed his napkin in the pan and continued. "Yeah, I remember telling you, She is a real looker and it is a shame she's a hooker." He stopped and studied his hands for a moment and then added. "I meant every word of it. Damn it, I still think she is the prettiest woman I've ever seen."

Maude picked up the pan and stood watching him. When he quit speaking and lowered his head, she spoke. "Yeah, and she's smart." Ben nodded without speaking as she continued. "I hear she has a Masters Degree in business."

Ben looked up and added. "Hell, she might even be an attorney. She incorporated her own whore house business. Then ever time I get into an argument with her, she quotes me the law. To make matters worse, she's always right."

Maude nodded, smiled and returned to the kitchen with her wet towels.

Ben stood up and walked over to the counter. He yelled. "Maude where's that chili to go?" She answered without entering from the kitchen. "I put it in your truck. I didn't want it to spill, so I even strapped it in with the seat belt. I figured you had spilled enough for one night, but just in case, I threw in a bunch of extra napkins."

He tossed some money on the counter and turned toward me. He cocked his head as he put on his hat. Then he said, "I'm going back up to check with my crew and Hollis. Are you going to hang around?"

I nodded, as I spoke. "Yeah, I'll be here for a while."

He was mumbling in a barely audible voice as he walked out the door. "If only, she wasn't a whore."

Maude, shook her head as she wiped the counter and then spoke in a quiet voice. "I think the Sheriff has a problem, only he doesn't know it."

I laughed and said. "Oh, I believe he knows it and it's driving him crazy."

# CHAPTER TWENTY

I finished my second bowl of chile and gulped the last swallow of tea. Maude approached the table just as I pushed the empty bowl away. She started to wipe up and clear the dishes before she spoke. "I'm glad you're staying. I feel better when someone is around."

"Where's your husband?" I asked as her wide wiping motions caused her stomach to brush against my arm.

She raised up, dropped the towel into the dish pan and replied. "He went to town for supplies and probably will be gone for a couple of more hours."

I nodded and asked, "Is that why you have that 45 tucked in your belt?"

Her mouth opened and closed a couple of times before she spoke. "How in the Hell did you know? I have it under my apron."

I laughed as I answered. "I felt it when you bumped my arm. Damn, for a minute I thought you had hit me with a hammer."

She put both hands on her hips and assumed a defiant stance as she said. "Well, you see, I don't really want to shoot anyone. So, I don't carry a smaller pistol. I figure if I just point it at someone it will scare them to death. Now you take Bella she has one of those little flat 2 shot jobs. She carries it in a holster strapped to her right thigh. I think it is only a 32 or something like that, but make no mistake, she would shoot you and it would hurt."

"Yeah, No doubt about it. I'm surprised the Sheriff hasn't arrested both of you for carrying concealed weapons."

"He wouldn't dare." She smiled and moved her hands down her thighs as she spoke. When she was satisfied the apron was smoothed out she continued. "Besides I don't carry it when he's around."

"Good idea." I replied while looking at the bulge under the apron. Then I asked, "How about Bella. Does she carry her hide out whether he's around or not?"

"Yeah, I think so, and believe me it's the only flat thing on her." she replied, as she disappeared into the kitchen.

I was alone and deep in thought when the rattling of the dishes from the kitchen was suddenly interrupted by a voice from the doorway. "Hi cowboy, where's Maude?"

Startled, I quickly looked up into a vision of feminine beauty. She was standing just inside the doorway. Her lips were parted, allowing a full display of the pearly whites. I had to take a deep breath before mumbling. "She's in the kitchen, I think."

She slowly moved toward me as I thought, "The Sheriff didn't lie. She's a knock out and if, like he says, her smile can knock your soaks off. Well, the rest of her will knock your cock stiff."

She gracefully slid into the booth across from me and then asked. "Do you mind if I join you?"

"Not at all," I replied, trying to keep my voice at its normal level.

She slightly titled her head toward me and asked. "Why aren't you at the party?"

"I wasn't invited." I replied.

She titled her head away from me and in a quizzical voice asked, "Don't you like parties?"

"Not really, but if it was a party with you, I would make an exception."

She laughed and replied. "Not with me. I only drive the bus."

I shook my head as I said. "I hear you own the bus."

Her smile turned into a cute pout as she remarked. "Maude talks too much."

I nodded without speaking, as she continued.

"Seriously, though, I do have some great girls. I know one in particular, who would love to entertain you. It would also be a good treat for her, since I'm sure by now she's tired of drunk adolescents."

I shook my head and said. "No thanks, It's you or nothing. Besides I have an aversion to paying for sex. You just said she would love to entertain me. Now, why should I pay to make her happy?"

"Good for you, Dutch," came a voice from the kitchen, We both looked toward the swinging door as Maude entered the room and continued. "As for you Bella, I do not talk too much."

Bella looked indignant as she replied. "You do too! What else did you say about me?"

Maude laughed and said. "Not much, just that you have a pea shooter strapped on your right thigh. I didn't mention that you own a brothel as well as the traveling party girls."

"Damn it, Maude." Bella retorted, why did you have to tell him all my secrets, including my secret defense?"

Maude shook her head and said. "Oh, Bella, Bella, you have a lot of other defenses. And I might add, a hell of a lot more secrets. Why did I tell him? I will tell you why. I look at you two and figure nature might take its course. I didn't want him to be surprised. Besides, wearing a short dress like you do, only invites him to peek. Anyway, I'm sure he would discover it, one way or another."

I instinctively cringed as Bella's lime colored, seductive, eyes became an icy cucumber green stare. She angrily chewed her lower lip before speaking in a surprisingly low voice. "Maude, have you been drinking?"

"Your damn right." Maude responded, hesitated, and then continued, "I've had a couple and if I listen to you two any longer I will need several more. Hell, you're acting like two stray puppies. Both of you are afraid to move for fear of being bitten by the other. I've seen better approaches between a pair of bashful teenagers."

Bella looked at me for several seconds before speaking, then said. "Now, I need a drink." She reached into a bag and took out a sealed bottle of Jack Daniel's and placed it on the table between us.

I grasped the bottle with my right hand, then used the left to reach for my pocket knife. She smiled as she placed her hand over mine and quickly split the cap seal with her thumb nail. She maintained her grip as we lowered the bottle to the table. I didn't make any effort to pull away, but I did feel the need to say something. My voice quivered as I asked, "Is this a pint?"

"No, it is more than a pint, but less than a quart. 750 something or other." She slowly removed her hand as Maude appeared carrying three water glasses. They were half full of ice cubes.

"I like mine on the rocks." Maude said, as she placed them on the table and then continued. "Pour me a stiff one, and I'll take it into the kitchen. I still have work to do."

I poured until the ice cubes were covered before she said. "Enough, this sure is a hell of a lot better than the wine I was drinking." She picked up her drink and started for the kitchen. I was pouring the whiskey into the remaining two glasses when Maude stopped and looked back at me. She raised her glass, grinned, and said. "By the way Dutch, try not to piss your pants." I opened my mouth to answer, but, before I could speak, she disappeared into the kitchen.

Bella's head snapped up as she asked, "Would you like to explain that?"

"No, not really." I shook my head then continued, "I could, except it is a long story and has absolutely nothing to do with me. Lets just say Maude has a crude sense of humor."

She smiled before responding. "Yeah, I have to agree. especially after the things she said about me. Shall we just call it even."

I nodded and replied, "Good idea. I thought her remarks were uncalled for and very rude."

She giggled and said. "That makes her rude and crude." She hesitated and then continued. "That's funny, but true, and it rhymes. On top of everything else I don't know why she thinks she's a match maker."

"The wine." I said, and then added, "Lets go back to square one. I'm Dutch Evans and I'm glad to meet you."

She extended her hand, which I willingly accepted. Her smile broadened as we shook. She said. "I'm glad to meet you and I'm Bella. Is Dutch your real name?"

"No, it's Eugene, but I have always been called Dutch. Is yours Bella?"

She giggled and said, "No it's Viveca. I have been told it means life. I haven't been called by my real name for a long time. The name Bella seems to fit me better for now. I guess it is because of my profession." She hesitated then said. "I think I prefer we stick to Dutch and Bella. Agreed?"

I raised my glass to toast and said. "Agreed, and the name Bella sounds good. Viveca is a pretty name, but it sounds snooty. Not like you at all." She giggled and raised her glass to click mine, as I continued. "I hope it's not your intentions to get me drunk enough to join the intoxicated adolescents."

There was a loud crash of pots and pans in the kitchen, followed by a string of obscenities from Maude. We both looked toward the kitchen as I remarked. "I hope her husband gets back soon with the supplies."

Bella looked puzzled as she said, "He isn't getting supplies. He was out on the parking lot, directing traffic, when we drove up."

I hesitated, then thoughtfully asked, "Are you telling me he never left?"

Bella shrugged, but didn't answer. I continued. "Maybe, what you're saying is, he was first in line for the party?"

She giggled and replied. "I never said that. I only said he was telling everyone where to park."

I nodded and said. "Wow, maybe, that's why Maude is heading for a binge?"

She glanced down as she fingered the rim of her glass, then softly said. "I'm beginning to regret giving her the bottles of wine."

"You gave her the wine?" I asked.

"She looked up and replied, "Yes. Two bottles. I always give her two bottles every time we come here. She usually rations herself and they last a couple of weeks. Today I believe she might have killed both bottles. Damn it, sometimes married people act so stupid." She took a big swallow of her drink and then asked. "Are you married?"

I took a small drink before answering. "No, I was divorced and then became a widower."

Two wives?" she asked.

I shrugged my shoulders and said. "One wife. She ran off with a bartender, divorced me, and ended up as a street walker in New York. She died of an accumulation of diseases. Some social and a couple of others."

She took a sip from her glass, looked up and half smiled as she said. "I don't believe you can become a widower after a divorce."

I laughed and replied, "Don't get all legal on me. Anyway you look at it, it comes out the same. I'm not married."

"And the bartender?"

I shrugged and answered. "Damn if I know. He probably dumped her after the money was gone."

"She had money?"

"Yeah, She maxed out the credit cards. Most of the charges were for expensive clothes and jewelry. Then she emptied the bank accounts, picked up the money laying around the house and took off." I hesitated, than added. "Hell, all she left me was bills, the dog and a short note."

She bit her lower lip and appeared concerned as she asked. "A short note?"

I nodded and said, "Yeah, a real short, Dear John. It simply said. The money is spendable, and you are expendable. Goodbye."

I was so preoccupied socializing with Bella, I didn't hear Ben drive up. It was only when he yelled, that I noticed his presence.

"Maude, what in the Hell are you doing? You know you can't serve alcohol in here."

A slightly slurred voice came from the kitchen. "I'm not serving alcohol. I am drinking it. You know where the ice and glasses are. Help yourself, but you will have to ask Bella to get a drink. It's her booze. If you don't want any, you can."

He interrupted in a loud voice. "Maude, are you drunk?"

She hesitated then answered, "Probably, yeah, yes, I think so. Now, join the party or shut up."

He shook his head as he approached our booth. Bella was the first to speak.

"Hello Sheriff, please join us?"

He didn't speak as he slid in beside her. He placed both hands on the table. Looked down at them for a few seconds, then asked. "Dutch have you been here the whole time since I left?"

I shrugged and replied. "Yes. In fact, I haven't even moved."

He nodded, then asked. "Did anyone else come in?"

I shook my head and said. "Just Bella."

He placed his right hand onto his left wrist as he turned his head toward her. He hesitated then said. "Hello Bella."

She smiled and replied. "Hi."

He nodded, then asked. "Did any of those gigantic, peace keeping, bus drivers of yours, leave since you arrived?"

She smiled and said, "No, why do you ask?"

He ignored the question and continued. "How many of those steroid freaks do you have out there tonight?"

She frowned as her voice became loud and stern. "Stop calling them names. In answer to your question. There are four drivers outside. Three are now, either roaming or standing by. Jack is making arrangements and collecting the money. Now tell me why you want to know?"

Suddenly Maude shouted from the kitchen. "It's ten o'clock, Bella. I won the bet and you owe me two bottles of wine. This time make them the big bottles. After all, this was a big bet."

Bella yelled back, "You'll get paid."

Ben asked, "What bet?"

Bella answered. "It's none of your business. Oh, what the hell, She bet me that I couldn't get Dutch to join the party by ten.

I stuttered, as I placed my drink down. Then asked. "What?"

Maude shouted, "Don't forget the second bet, Bella."

Bella gulped her drink and pushed her glass toward me. She motioned for a refill and yelled back. "No decision has been made on that one. The bet's still on."

I poured her drink and asked. "What was that about?"

Ben raised both hands in a defensive mode and said. "I hate to break this up, but I have more important things to discuss. Bella, I believe you have always told me the truth. I also believe you haven't told me some things that are important"

Bella took a sip of her drink and ran her finger along the rim of the glass, before asking. "Like what?"

Ben looked directly into her eyes and said. "Like three of your blonds bimbos have mysteriously disappeared recently."

Her voice snapped as she answered. "Don't call them names. And, yes, three of my Ladies of the Evening have left without notice."

Ben nodded and continued. "Did they, by chance, leave all their worldly possessions in their rooms?"

"Yes. Now tell me how you know this?" She asked.

Ben said. "In a minute. First do you have their things?"

"Yes, and before you ask, their possessions are all in separate bags. That has nothing to do with you. It's just when they send for them or come back, their things will be ready,"

'Good, good. Now next, were they all natural blondes?"

Bella sighed and in an exasperated tone answered. "I don't know. I think so, but I really don't know. Why is it so important?"

He looked at me as he spoke. "Lets just say, I believe they had a bad hair day."

She looked at me, then at him and said. "What in the Hell are you talking about? I mean really, what has being real blondes have to do with anything?" She hesitated, then with a tone of concern, she said. "Wait a minute, just a damn minute. Are you saying they had a bad pubic hair day?"

Ben rubbed his hands together and smiled before speaking. "No, that's not what I meant. We will talk about it later. For right now, Bella this is important. I need their personal belongings and I need them now. I want you to call the brothel."

"You mean the ranch," She interrupted.

He looked at me and then back at her before speaking. "Yeah, ok, the ranch. Anyway tell whoever is running things to get them ready. I will send a deputy to pick them up."

She straightened her back and raised her head in an indignant gesture. Her voice was angry as she spoke. "You will, like Hell. It's a busy time right now. The last thing in the world I need is a uniformed cop walking in. You know half of my business would run at the sight of a badge."

Ben nodded and replied. "Ok, Ok, no uniforms. I will send a detective instead."

"That would be better." She said. Then she seemed thoughtful and continued. "Tell him to leave his gun and badge in the car. He doesn't need to advertise his presence. Tell him to walk in, like any other John."

He nodded, exited the booth and said. "Lets make the calls." She slid out, paused and stood at the edge of the table. Then busied herself smoothing out her blouse and skirt. Her profile was one of female perfection and I envied those lucky hands. Satisfied with her efforts, she turned her head toward me and said. "Don't go away. I'll be back in a few minutes." I watched her as she moved toward the door. First the calves, then the thighs and finally the butt. I unconsciously picked up my napkin and wiped my mouth. Maude's voice broke the spell. "By damn, I knew it. You're salivating like the famous dog,"

# CHAPTER TWENTY ONE

B en returned and resumed his seat. Maude appeared from the kitchen with three half full glasses of ice. She placed one in front of me, then looked at Ben. She shrugged and placed one in front of him without speaking. The last one she held in her left hand. She indicated with her right, a request for a three finger drink. I obliged, as she spoke. "Bella left her booze, Lets drink it, before she comes back."

I freshened my drink as Maude made her way back to the kitchen. I held out the bottle toward Ben and he pushed the glass toward me and remarked. "What the Hell. Bella owes me a drink." He was silent as I poured and then said. "Every time I get into a conversation with her I come out second best." He hesitated then added. "You know, she is madder than Hell at me. She says I had no business telling you she has a brothel, as well as the whores on wheels. Like it makes a big difference."

I smiled and said. "It seems to me you tried to push her buttons."

He swallowed a large swig of whiskey, followed by an exaggerated sucking in of air. He hesitated then exhaled with a loud whooshing sound. "That's good booze." He remarked as he wiped his mouth with the back of his hand. He seemed thoughtful, then licked his lips and said. "That's true, but it holds her attention, and It keeps me on the subject."

I nodded and asked. "What happened to her?"

"Oh she is checking the outside action. I wired a couple of her bus drivers to keep her busy. I wanted to talk to you before she returns." He looked toward the door and then asked, "Do you know what the name Bella means?"

I shook my head and replied, "No."

He nodded and said. "Beautiful. Yeah, can you believe it. Beautiful in Latin. I looked it up. Boy it fits. Doesn't it?"

"Yeah, it, for sure, fits. Now that I think about it, I believe it means the same in Spanish. Is that what you wanted to talk to me about?"

He leaned forward and lowered his voice. "No, there are several things. It has to be just between us for now. Do you understand?"

I whispered back "Ok, but how can you be sure she will be kept busy?"

"I just know. I have a twist on two of her drivers. They each have a couple of outstanding warrants. They cooperate and I don't push the issue."

I nodded and asked, "Big warrants?"

He smiled and replied, "Big enough. How do you think I found out about the three missing whores? You know I'm betting we find their DNA is a match with those scalps."

His voice had become a whisper. In order to hear I had to lean forward until we were only inches apart. He started to speak when Maude interrupted. "If you two start kissing, I'm calling the cops."

We both looked over and found her standing behind the counter. Ben said, "Damn it Maude. Why don't you make some noise. Sing, whistle or something. It's the least you could do. Better yet yell, if you're going to sneak around."

She laughed and said. "Me, sneak around. It's you two. Whispering secrets like a pair of school girls. The only thing missing is the giggling."

She was retreating to the kitchen when Ben asked. "Have you heard anything about Junior?"

She stopped and said. "No, Have you found out anything?"

He answered. "Nothing, but we have an APB out for any info." He looked back at me and continued. "Maude's son, Junior has been missing for three days now. He has been missing before, but we always found him in jail or just indisposed. This time nothing."

"I knew they had a son, but I didn't knew he was a Gus Jr."

"He's not. His name is Junior." He leaned toward me again and in a low voice added. "He looks like Gus, but acts like Maude. He is a damn rebel and is constantly in and out of trouble."

"Is Johanna still missing?"

"Yeah. I know what you are thinking. But there doesn't seem to be any connection. Junior can't seem to hold onto a job. This time he did tell Maude he was hired to deliver oxygen tanks to some company. He doesn't have a truck and all the local oxygen supply companies deny he ever worked for them. Johanna has class. I can't see her going for a bum like him."

I took a sip of my drink before saying. "Sometimes different types of people attract each other."

He picked up the bottle and freshened his drink, then said.

"You might be right and I have considered that angle. The best source of information would come from his buddies. We checked with them and got the same story. He's working for some oxygen company. They did say it was a secret operation and he wouldn't tell them anything else. As far as Johanna is concerned they all denied knowing anything about her."

I sipped my drink, then asked. "Do you think it's a government project?"

He shook his head and replied. "Damn if I know. If it is they are playing it close to the chest. I do have contacts and they say it is not a government project."

"Would they tell you the truth?"

"Yes, I believe so. In the past when I asked. They would say, they couldn't talk about it. I appreciated their position since they just admitted it existed. In this case I get a quick, we never heard of it."

I considered this and said. "There is the possibility the company furnished the delivery truck. It would make a difference if the oxygen tanks were the large cylinders or the small tanks used by individuals. If he was delivering the small tanks the locals would be aware of it. My best guess, would be, the large cylinders, like those used by welders or hospitals."

Ben nodded and said. "Good theory, but where would he get the cylinders? The locals would be aware of a major competitor, wouldn't they?"

"Yeah and would probably be mad as Hell. Especially if someone was cutting in with a large volume. Lets consider it may have come in as part of a large load. Say, maybe fifty cylinders with others on a big rig. Maybe delivered in an isolated area."

Ben sipped his drink and appeared thoughtful. Then said, "Of course, and we know everybody believes this is a secret. I think I will go out and talk to a couple of big rig drivers."

# CHAPTER TWENTY TWO

Bella and Maude simultaneously arrived just as Ben left. Bella with a big smile, Maude with a fresh glass of ice. Bella spoke first. "I've been standing outside waiting for him to shut up, or leave."

Maude divided the ice between our three glasses, then she said. "I told Bella the Sheriff was telling secrets and we shouldn't interrupt."

Bella motioned for me to pour before saying. "The Sheriff always believes he knows secrets. The truth is, everybody knows before he finds out anything. We humor him and act like everything he says is news."

I looked at Bella and asked. "Why were you waiting outside?"

She laughed and said. "I know he told my drivers to keep me busy. So I decided to play along and just watch through the window. Maude came out periodically and kept me posted on what you were talking about."

Maude spoke up. "Yeah, and if he thinks Junior ran off with Johanna, he's crazy." She steadied herself by grabbing the edge of the booth before continuing. "Wow, the room was rocking. Must of been an earthquake." She hesitated until she regained her balance then said. "Junior would never have anything to do with that snooty little bitch. So there, you can tell the Sheriff, what he can do with that secret."

She moved slowly toward the kitchen leaving a trail of spilled whiskey in her wake.

Bella laughed and remarked. "She won't have a drop of whiskey left when she gets to the kitchen."

"She isn't doing bad. So far no ice cubes have bounced out." I said, then continued, "I don't think she needs anymore anyway."

Bella bit her lower lip and her eyes showed concern, as she asked. "Is Johanna really missing?"

"It seems like it. I was looking for her and a big deputy said she was gone. Since then, others have looked and no one seems to know where she might be."

She furrowed her brow before saying. "The Sheriff told me he was worried." She sipped her drink then continued. "He has told me so many wild stories. I never know when to believe him. Sometimes I tell him I'm not a proverbial dumb blonde. I'm a smart redhead. It doesn't seem to make any difference. He still tells me unbelievable things."

I looked into her eyes and said. "You're a redhead with green eyes"

She smiled and said. "And I am smart. So what does that make me?"

I smiled and replied. "A very attractive and desirable woman?"

She shook her head, but kept smiling as she said. "Baloney, that's just the whiskey talking."

I shrugged and replied. "it's not the whiskey. This is only my second drink."

"Yeah, your second drink all right. How many times has it been freshened?"

"Oh, maybe once or possibly twice. Always just a touch to negate the water taste. You know from the melting ice cubes."

"More baloney." she said as she held up the bottle and continued. "It's almost gone."

"Hey, I had lots of help."

She nodded, then said. "I know you did and if I didn't know it, I would believe you were as big a liar as the Sheriff."

I took a sip of my drink before saying. "Thanks for the vote of confidence."

She reached over and patted my hand and said. "I'm sorry, I didn't mean it that way."

I smiled and said. "If it means you will hold my hand, you can call me all the names you can think of. In fact, it you run out of names I might be able to give you a few."

She gave my hand an extra pat and then pulled it away. She took a sip of her drink before saying. "Lets get back to Johanna. Did you know she was Haystack's second wife?"

"Yes."

"Did you also know his first wife was found hanging in a tree?"

"Yes."

"The Sheriff told me, if she had hung herself it would have pulled her head off. Do you believe that?"

"Yes, she had a small diameter rope around her neck and she dropped over ten feet. In all probability her head would have snapped off."

Her eyes narrowed and her mouth had a determined looked as she asked. "Has anything like that ever happened before?"

I smiled as I answered. "Yes, It happens frequently. The rope may have been misapplied, the drop too long or the person too heavy. It probably don't happen much anymore, since we stopped hanging criminals."

Her face seemed to lose the determined look and became one of disbelief. She hesitated, took a drink and said. "The Sheriff has a picture in his office of such a hanging. There are two men kneeling beside a headless body. It has the caption, "BLACK JACK KETCHUM LOSES HIS HEAD OVER HANGING." It looks like an old picture and they may be under a gallows. Do you think it happened or is it from a movie?"

I nodded and answered. "It happened in New Mexico in 1901. I never have seen the picture with the caption you described, but I have seen a similar photograph. There actually are three men in the photograph. Two are kneeling and a man is standing just outside the structure looking in. The men are not identified, but one was probably the Sheriff."

"Well, Ok. Maybe, but The Sheriff told me his Great Granddaddy was there and when they picked up the head, Black Jack said "Ouch." Do you Believe that?"

I started to laugh, but stopped and answered, I don't know if his Great Granddaddy was there or not. I do find it very hard to believe Jack's head said "Ouch."

She giggled and said. "Yes, I found that part a little hard to swallow."

"So would Jack." I answered.

"God, you're sick. Have a drink," she said as she emptied the bottle into my glass. I looked at my half full glass and then at her near empty one. She smiled and said, "Don't worry, I have another."

She produced a bottle from her bag and refreshed her drink. "You're a traveling distillery." I said, then asked. "How come it's been opened and is half gone?"

She replaced the cap and put the bottle between us before answering. "It's a bottle we keep in the bus. A couple of the girls need a shot or two before the party starts. You know to get in the mood."

I was quiet for a moment then said. "I just never thought about it. I guess it was a surprise to realize your girls have moods."

She indigently replied. "Well they do. They are people like everybody else." She hesitated and then asked. "How come you know so much about hanging?"

"In the past I was a homicide detective. Now let me ask you a question. What were you doing in the Sheriff's office?"

"Every time a street walker is arrested for rolling a drunk, or involved with drugs, he calls me to come in. He says since they give phony names, he needs to know if they belong to me. I keep telling him, my girls don't walk the streets. It doesn't matter though, he still insists I come in. I think he does it just to harass me."

"Maybe it's his way of flirting with you."

She seemed stunned for a moment, then said. "Flirting, flirting. No way. Me and Ben, the Sheriff, not in a million years. Wow, how did you come up with such an idea?"

'I'm sorry. Tell me, do you know Johanna?"

She took a large drink and seemed thoughtful before speaking. "If he thinks for one minute that I."

I interrupted "Hey, take it easy. I'm sorry. Tell me about Johanna."

She looked at me and said. "Do you think Jim Haystack murdered his first wife?"

"No, and her name was Maddalena. Did you ever meet her?"

"I only heard about her. They say she was very pretty. Did you know her?"

"No, I didn't know anyone around here until this trip."

She sipped her drink then fingered her glass before speaking. "She was younger than Jim. I heard he found her in a catalog."

"Yes, I heard the same thing."

"Then she dies and it isn't long before he marries Johanna. Who, by the way was even younger."

"Yes, and also very pretty."

Her eyes narrowed as she spoke. "She was barely 18 when they married. They say she was a catalog bride. The same as Maddalena."

I sipped my drink and waited without speaking.

She crossed her arms across her chest as she spoke. "Don't you think this is suspicious?"

"It appears to be, but he didn't kill Maddalena."

She chewed her lower lip then said. "Maybe he did something to Johanna."

I shook my head and replied. "He didn't. I was riding with him this morning and she was there when we left. She was gone when I came back."

She continued biting her lip before speaking. "I know she was scared."

"You sound like you know her."

She nodded and said. "I do, we have talked a couple of times. She told me she was afraid of someone in her past. but she never said who."

"When did you talk to her?" I asked.

"The first time in the Sheriff's office. It was a couple of days before she got married. It was kind of funny and I felt she knew about Maddalena. It was never mentioned, but there was something. Her hands were shaking and she looked scared. I felt she just had the before marriage nerves. You know being so young and all." She hesitated, smiled, and continued. "We were getting along fine until she asked me if I was the Sheriff's wife."

I had been putting off making a head call and this seemed like a good time. I excused myself and resolved to be careful. Lest, I join those on the bottom rung of Maude's ladder of masculine endowment. I even carefully turned on the faucet to avoid any splashing while washing my hands. I started to exit then self consciously ran my hands down my fly. Failing to detect any sign of moisture I returned to the booth. Bella looked up and greeted me with a large smile. I started to speak, but she interrupted.

"The next time we met, she was in town. Haystack was at some ranchers meeting and she was shopping. She saw me first and came over to say she was sorry. I asked what she was sorry for and she said she felt she had upset me. I laughed and told her to forget it and we had lunch. We mostly talked about girl things. She still seemed uneasy and I asked her if something was bothering her. She remarked, living is for the young, but death is for everybody. I asked her, what do you mean? She shrugged her shoulders and quietly said she couldn't talk about it. I asked, if Haystack was abusing her. She said she had to go and walked out. I was mad at first, but then I remembered our first meeting. I guess we're alike. I walked out that time. If it's something we don't want to talk about we just leave. She did stick me with the check. Which is okay, since I'm the one who invited her."

She stopped talking as the Sheriff walked in. We both remained quiet as he approached the booth. He spoke first as he slid in. "I didn't find out a damn thing. I find it hard to believe that none of them knows anything. They can be chattering like a women's club meeting, until I walk up. They see me and instantaneously become a conglomeration of clams."

Bella smiled and remarked. "Maybe it's your charming personality?" He looked at her without responding and I felt the need to chime in. "Well, if it's oxygen tanks, trucks have to be involved. Furthermore tanks take up a lot of space. I mean it's not like hiding a bucket of oats."

Bella said. "Why a bucket of oats?"

"Then we could just turn the horses loose and they would find them." I said.

She smiled as she fingered her drink and said. "Don't be silly." She hesitated and added, "Are oxygen tanks those big green cylinders?"

"Yes," I said.

She grinned and said. "I saw some. A whole lot of them."

Ben quickly asked, "How many? Where?"

She ran her finger across the nm of her glass and he again asked. "Where?"

She licked the tip of her finger and then said. "On the road." She returned to running he finger around the glass rim.

"Damn it Bella. Where?"

She grinned and looked at me. I said. "It's important Bella. Where did you see them?"

She looked back at Ben and asked. "Real important?"

He raised his voice as he said. "Very damn important. Now where did you see them?"

She shrugged her shoulders and replied. "You don't need to shout. He opened his mouth, but before he could speak she continued. "You know the deserted gas station just west of the Haystack turnoff. The one with all the tumbleweeds piled up next to it."

"Yes, I know it."

"Well, you know, if they ever caught fire, it could spread and be very dangerous."

He said in a very low voice. "Bella, please."

She smiled and continued. "I drove out here, day before yesterday to make arrangements for this party. The driveway area of the station was full of those tanks. I thought it was strange, since no one was around. I was going to tell Maude, but I forgot."

Ben asked. "How many, would you say?"

"I don't know. The driveway was full. Maybe a hundred, I don't know. Funny thing though, I didn't notice them on the way back. Did you see them when you drove out?"

"I didn't drive. I flew in to Haystacks ranch. Damn it, I have his truck and no radio. I have to get a unit to check this out and the closest one is at the ranch. I guess I can use my cell phone and try to call Hollis. Then he can get in touch with them on his radio."

Bella picked up the bottle and offered it to him. He shook his head and said, "I have to make a call." He pulled out his phone and headed for the door. Bella watched him go and removed the bottle cap. I placed my hand over the mouth of my glass and said. "No more, I've had enough." She pulled her hand back and replied. "Really, it's going to be a long night."

I nodded and explained. "There's a war going on in my stomach. I believe the whiskey is fighting with the chili. I don't know who is going to win. I'm sure, no matter who wins, if I drink anymore I'm going to be the loser."

She recapped the bottle as she said. "The Sheriff is too busy for a drink. You have had enough. Maude spilled enough, and drank more than enough. That leaves me and suddenly I don't want anymore. Can you tell me what's so important about oxygen tanks?"

I thought for a moment then said. "I don't know."

"But you said they were important."

"Yes I did. Well, Junior is missing. He told his friends he was working on a secret job. One of them said he heard Junior was hauling Oxygen. The Sheriff suspects, if Junior is involved, it's an illegal project. Then to add fuel to his suspicions, Johanna is missing. There was three vehicles at the ranch. One a Sheriffs unit with two deputies. The others were Haystack's pickup and my truck. Ben is using Haystack's pickup and I have mine. Her horse is dead. If she left on her own, she had to walk."

She chewed her lower lip and then asked. "Why are you here?" Before I could answer four men entered and headed for a booth. She spoke up. "Sorry fellows, the kitchen is closed." They stopped, looked around and started to speak. A large well developed man stepped through the door and said. "You heard her, The kitchen is closed." There was some mumbling and one said. "How come, the restaurant seems to be open, they're here?"

The man at the door replied in a stern voice. "They're here because they belong here. Now the restaurant is out of bounds for this party. Please leave." He nodded to Bella and held the door open as they filed out.

She smiled and said. "Thanks Bill."

We watched him as he closed the door. Then she turned her head toward me and said. "Well?"

"I had some cattle business with Jim Haystack and when we finished. I came down here. It was my intention to grab some supper, then rent a cabin for the night. I did get supper, but the party preempted me on the cabin.

I was killing time when I met some charming female company., She had a bottle of good whiskey. So, here I am."

She listened attentively then said. "Maude told me you're a rancher. The Sheriff said you're a private investigator. You told me you were once a homicide detective. You know a lot about hangings. Maddalena died by hanging. You said you had cattle business with Haystack. Now, let me ask you again. Why are you here?"

"Wow, I guess there aren't any secrets around here. Let me assure you, I'm not here because of Maddalena. I had two Red Angus cattle mutilated, one heifer and one bull. Haystack had two Black Angus heifers mutilated. I'm trying to find out who did it and why?"

"Why is it a secret. I'm sure you knew everything about me before I walked in. Why isn't Haystack looking for Johanna, or is that a secret?"

Before I could answer, the Sheriff walked in and said.

"Hollis doesn't answer his phone and his dispatcher can't raise him on the radio. I called my office and they can't raise the deputies at the ranch. I told them to keep trying. I guess I have to go look for those tanks. Do you want to ride along Dutch?"

I nodded as Bella said. "I want to go with you. I'm the one who knows where they are."

Ben smiled and said. "Good. There's room in the truck and I need the company."

We moved from the booth as Bella said. "I will bring the whiskey. There might be snakes out there."

# CHAPTER TWENTY THREE

Three adults in a pickup seat can usually ride comfortably. This trip was different. The Sheriff drove, Bella was in the middle and I was next to the passenger door. It was night time and very dark. The dash board lights illuminated her very short skirt and the protruding bare legs.. I tried to look away, but her breasts were like magnets. Her tantalizing thighs consistently brushed against my leg. I tried to think of other things as her presence was creating a barely manageable desire. It was only my herculean restraint of common sense, over impulse, that was keeping both my eyes and hands, under control. The only distraction occurred when her hide out pistol pushed against my leg. Ben commented the rough ride was due to Haystack's shocks being shot. I thought, thank God, pleasure sometimes comes from strange circumstances.

At Bella's direction we parked just off the roadway. The deserted gas station was just ahead and on our right. I had my mag light from my truck and wanted to first check the area alone. I asked Ben to talk to Bella for a few minutes.

I moved slowly, illuminating the area for several feet. I scanned the ground carefully both to the right and left. When I reached several feet beyond the driveway I doubled back and rechecked the ground. Only when I was satisfied, did I motion Ben to join me.

When He stepped from the cab he stopped and yelled. "Can Bella come?"

"Yes of course." I answered, then added. "Just stay close to me until we finish. Then, if you want, you can look around, but only where I tell you to walk"

She yelled back. "We have to stay with you. You have the only flashlight."

"Good." I replied and waited until they joined me.

Ben said. "I told Bella you homicide detectives see things other people just walk over."

"Maybe, but there is one difference. Some people only look at what they believe is important. We believe everything is important until proven other wise."

I flashed my light onto the driveway as I spoke. "There are dual tire tracks running from the road into the driveway. Then, there are single tracks running at an angle to the others. It appears a big rig came from the West, stopped and backed into the drive way. The single tracks show the turning of the tractor to maneuver into an unloading position. I believe this means his rig couldn't clear the over hanging roof. These old gas stations were not designed to give clearance to semitrailers. That's the reason the dual tracks end just this side of the drive. Once they unloaded they pulled out and had to back up once. Then according to those tracks in the weeds, They went back West."

Ben commented, "They didn't stay for the party, did they?"

"No, but it was a couple of days ago. Of course they might of come back." I flashed my light down the driveway and said. "There were two of them. The boot tracks show where one walked down each side of the truck. The prints are large, maybe size twelve's. They each had different traction design soles and were probably heavy work boots. Then we have the same boot tracks returning to the cab."

I motioned for them to follow me and I led them to just under the overhang. I ran the light over the area and said. "Those same boots were all over this area. There are two bar marks on the ground showing what appears to be the supports from the bottom of a hydraulic lift platform. The cut marks in the dirt show where the cylinders were spun into position from the truck. I count ten across and eight deep."

Ben looked closely where I was shining the light, then remarked. "Eighty cylinders and the gouges are deep. They were full and heavy. I would say the men were strong and accustomed to handling oxygen."

I nodded and said. "I agree, as I recall a full cylinder is five feet tall and weighs one hundred eighty five pounds."

We moved to the other driveway area just outside the overhang. I flashed my light onto the roadway, and said. "This was a smaller truck, but it did have dual wheels on the back. The driver was not an experienced trucker. He tried at least four times to back into the driveway." I flashed my light on the corner of the building. Several boards were busted and caved in. I remarked. He missed the driveway by three feet Then he pulled forward and tried again. This time he only missed by a foot. He hit it hard each time. This corner is close to being totally wiped out. The next time he missed the corner, but he struck the overhang with the top of the truck." I illuminated the structure showing the broken boards and paint transfer. I continued. "Apparently he underestimated the needed clearance. In the event you see this truck, you will have plenty of paint transfers to make an identification."

"I wonder why he backed into this end?" Ben asked, hesitated, then continued. "The oxygen would be closer to the truck on the other side."

I nodded and stated. "I wondered about that, but the drive area is broader here. You can see he was off into the weeds and then backed up onto the hillside. I think he was having trouble turning around. It appears like he came in from the West Turned around and backed in for loading, then drove out East."

Bella said, "I hope he didn't go to the party. With his driving he would wreck all my buses."

I said, "I don't believe he drove out. He drove in but someone else may have driven out. We'll get to that in a minute. Lets look at the tracks. When he finally got parked, he stepped out of the cab." I flashed the light on the ground and continued. "These foot prints were made by a small person. They look like cowboy boots and about size seven. Ben, you said Junior was short. He might wear boots to make himself appear taller?"

Ben replied. "Yes, he always wears boots. I never thought much about it, but I don't believe he has ever been on a horse."

"Well there's more." I said. then walked back under the overhand and continued. "There are bar support marks, which I again believe were made by a hydraulic lift. Then we have numerous two wheel tire tracks. It seems he was using a hand truck to move the cylinders. Those boot tracks were the only ones in this area. It appears he was alone during this time."

Bella asked, "If he was alone why did you say he didn't drive out?"

"I think some people joined him. "I replied as I moved along the driveway. I stopped just shy of the road and pointed at some tire tracks. "Those were made by a jeep." I said, and when Ben and Bella came along side of me, I continued. "I have an early military jeep and my tire treads are the same. This jeep must be in better condition than mine, I won't drive mine out on the highway. These tracks drove over the truck tracks. Then over here the truck ran over the jeep tracks. It seems the jeep arrived after the truck and was here when the truck left. The jeep parked next to the weed patch and three people got out. They walked over to where the truck was parked. All four of their footprints are there. One person from the jeep was wearing shoes. There isn't any design evident are either the sole or the heel. A second subject was wearing work boots with a distinctive tread. Both of these people wore size ten or eleven footwear. The third person wore a boot that was at least a size eighteen, The work boots and the size eighteen walked back to the jeep with the cowboy boots. It looks to me like the shoes drove the truck, when it left."

Ben nodded and said. "They probably changed drivers for the truck. Considering the paint transfers, I don't blame them. I'll bet the truck has significant damage."

I nodded and said. "If it was my truck, I would be mad as hell."

Bella's voice was slurred as she said, "I'll bet it's not their truck."

Ben turned toward her and asked, "What?"

I added, "Why?"

She hesitated, looked at me, then at Ben. She let out a deep breath, stumbled forward, then pulled her shoulders up erect and said. "Well, the paint is all white. We know it is a big truck with a boxed in cargo space. I think it might be a rental truck."

I said. "You may be right. That's good deductive reasoning. It also could be why the local dealers don't know anything."

Ben added, "Very good. If true, it could solve the puzzle. Then again we still don't have a crime."

I said. "That's partly true, but you have to admit we have an interesting set of circumstances. Maude's drinking herself into a stupor. You both say this is not like her. Gus is partying like a twenty year old and Junior is missing. There seems to be a covert operation. It involves oxygen and Junior may be implicated. Someone shot a horse out from under me this morning. Jim Haystack was shot and is in the hospital with a broken leg. Johanna is missing. There are crimes, but we can't seem to tie them together."

Bella said, "Jim Haystack was shot? My God, When, I mean why? How could it happen? Do you think Johanna is all right? Oh my God."

I said, "Calm down. Ben is the Sheriff and he will explain it to you. I'm going up behind the buildings and look around. There are a lot of sage bushes, tumbleweed plants, and bunch grass. Tracks may be hard to find, but I want to make sure all three left in the jeep."

I carefully moved toward the hillside, making an effort not to obliterate any tracks. I heard loud voices and then Ben saying. "I am doing all I can. Hollis is looking for her." This was followed by loud sobbing. I hoped it was

Bella sobbing and not Ben. At this distance I couldn't tell. I thought, if it's Ben, so much for the hard case lawman image. If it's Bella, so much for the stone hearted whore stories. I reminded myself that Bella was not a whore. The sobbing brought back the memory of Johanna's tears and my urge to hold her in my arms. Like then, the crying suddenly brought tears to my eyes. I moved faster up the hill seeking rapid distance while cursing the crack in my tough guy armor.

I was moving the light from side to side illuminating a large half circle area. Suddenly I caught a whiff of an obnoxious odor and stopped in my tracks. At first it seemed I might have steeped into an patch of mutilated Jimson weed. Then I slowly proceeded upward, while allowing my nose to seek the smell. It became stronger and I recognized it as the smell of bloated decaying flesh. A few yards ahead the foliage appeared to have been disturbed. I cautiously moved forward and caught sight of a brown padded blanket. It blended in well with the background, but was identifiable when close up. I recognized it as the type used in moving vans.

I could still hear their voices and I considered calling out. I reconsidered and didn't because of the fear Bella would insist on coming. I didn't want her to witness what I feared was under the blanket. No doubt it was a body and maybe it was Johanna. I moved in and lifted up one end releasing the captive odor. I gagged and moved back. I remembered, no matter how long you're in homicide you don't get accustomed to this smell. The odor quickly added to the tears in my eyes. I thought, oh good, now I have an excuse. The light only penetrated to the bodies knees, but it clearly illuminator the cowboy boots. I moved to the other side and repeated the unveiling. It revealed a very bloated torso with the head so distorted it was difficult to recognize as human, I took note that the only footprints in the area was the size eighteens.

I moved upwind, composing myself and breathing fresh air for a couple of minutes. I dreaded my next move, but it had to be done. I took my time backtracking to the pickup. Bella was still sobbing while wiping her eyes. She looked so vulnerable I wanted to hold her and kiss away her tears. The spell was broken by Ben's voice. "Did you find anything?"

I motioned for him to get out of the truck. When he stepped out and approached me, I turned and walked away. He followed until we were on the other side of the building and out of Bella's sight. I said in a low voice. "There's a badly decomposed body up there. I believe it might be Junior. At any rate it's time you called your homicide team out."

He said, Junior, did you recognize him?"

TED KNUCKEY

I shook my head and replied. "I have never seen Junior, but the body is so bloated I don't know if anyone can recognize him. I'm only going by the fact he's wearing the cowboy boots we've been tracking."

He nodded and asked. "How about identification, Did you find a billfold?"

I shook my head and replied. "Hey, you're the Sheriff/Coroner, that's your job. Not mine. I didn't touch anything."

He shook his head and said. "It's not my job. Hell, I hire people to take care of those things. I will call my office and start the detectives rolling. I'm willing to wait for them."

"How about Bella. Are you going to tell her?

He hesitated then said. "Damn, I think she's on a crying jag. This is going to open the flood gates." He stood quietly for a moment then continued. "You know, I happen to have an opening in my department. If you want the job it's yours."

I motioned him toward the truck while shaking my head. As we moved I said. "You know, she will want to see the body. Believe me, two or three days covered with a warm blanket has not created a spectator scene."

He nodded and said, "And it has been hot as Hell, which doesn't help."

# CHAPTER TWENTY FOUR

B ella was asleep in the truck. Before She dozed off she called one of her drivers and said to fold the party. She then told them she had a ride and not to worry about her.

Ben and I were sitting on the cement platform that was once a gas pump island. He spoke first. "How much did she have to drink?"

"I don't know. She may have drank some wine with Maude. When she came into the restaurant she had a bottle of Jack Daniel's and we all sucked that up. While you and I were talking she was outside. When she came back she had another bottle, but it was only half full. She explained she gave some of her girls a drink to get them in the mood."

"That's the one she brought with her. Right?"

"Yes."

"Since we came, she had a couple of slugs from it, She ought to be a stockholder. She issues a small bottle to her girls before every party, They each get one and it's about a half pint bottle. I suspect she was into the second bottle herself."

"Does she have a drinking problem?" I asked.

"No, and neither does Maude. I don't know what's happening. This whole damn area has gone haywire." He was quiet, for several minutes. It was like he was trying to decide before continuing. Finally, he nodded and spoke. "You and I both know it's Junior up there under the blanket. Do you have a theory on why?"

"Maybe we should wake Bella and asked her. She came up fast with her last idea, and it was a good one. I, for one, believe she was right. Junior was hired to rent a truck in his name. The oxygen is a big secret and cannot be allowed to surface. They waited until Junior did all the heavy work, then they didn't need him anymore. The truck is probably scrap iron by now and can only be traced to Junior. A dead end. Oh, Hell, sorry, poor choice of words."

He nodded and said. "Yeah, that makes sense. My intel boys tell me you use to be a rodeo rough stock rider. Was it broncs or bulls?"

"Both. They must of talked to Deputy Sam Brown. He loves to tell everything he knows, to anyone who will listen."

He laughed as he said, "Yeah, I've talked to him a couple of times. It's strange every time I call your Sheriff I end up talking to Brown."

"Well, there is a reason for it. He was born and raised in the area. He has been on the Sheriff's department longer than anyone else. In fact, six times longer then the present Sheriff. He knows a lot of people and their history. Those people who think they are important, he calls Mr., Mrs., or what ever title is appropriate. Those who are important he calls by their first name. Everybody likes him and if you want good information he's your man."

Ben laughed and said. "He is a talker, but he strikes me as having a cowboy attitude. If it needs doing, do it, and don't bitch about it until you get it done. Now as a rough stock rider you have an additional outlook. I think the rough stock riders of today have the same mentality as the gun fighters of the old West."

I scratched my head before speaking. "I don't know, if that is a compliment or an insult."

He laughed, "It may be a little of both. It's just my observation. I wasn't kidding when I offered you a job."

I nodded and said, "It will be light soon and this will be an easier scene to work. When I found the body I took a quick look around and only saw the size eighteen footprints. Your investigators will want to double check for other prints."

Ben asked, "Are you saying they killed him at the Jeep. Then the big guy carried him and the blanket up the hill?"

"Yeah, It's a possibility. He took him far enough away from the road so it wouldn't be seen. The blanket would not only hide the body but would keep the odor down. It might also deter the birds and coyotes."

"How about blood. Wouldn't that smell attract the wildlife?"

"I didn't see any blood. My bet is Mr. Big broke his neck."

Ben was silent, then rubbed his forehead with his fingers. Finally he spoke. "You know, you said a big deputy was up at Haystacks."

"Yes."

"Well, I might know who that was. I fired a deputy a month ago. He would still have his uniform and Hell you can buy badges at a novelty shop. They might say Junior G Man or Chicken Inspector, but they look authentic at a distance." He hesitated and I asked.

"Was he big, I mean huge, big?"

"Yes, I guess you might say huge. On his employment application he's listed as six foot eight and two hundred eighty pounds. He was long on muscle, short on brains."

"You fired him?"

He nodded, and said. "Yeah, every time he touched someone we got sued. He slapped a drunk to wake him up. Broke his jaw. He grabbed a guy to stop a fight. Broke three ribs. A young waitress was fooling around with him and he playfully grabbed her arm. Compound fracture of the humerus. He didn't have any idea of his own strength."

"Wow. It doesn't sound like it. Is he still around?"

"Don't know, I did get an inquiry from an Oregon Sheriff. So I believed he was up there. He did a lot of bad mouthing around here. You know about the department, the brass and me. I called him and told him to be careful and not burn his bridges. He didn't listen and kept on jawing. You know I believe when you burn your bridges the smoke trail follows you forever."

"What kind of recommendation did you give?"

"I said he was a good man, but a liability risk. Then I laid it all out for them. Hell, I wasn't going to lie."

"This guy, a body builder?"

"No, even though his name was Charlie Atlas. He got his muscles the hard way. He started working at a young age as a lumberjack."

"He sounds like a good possibility for what we have here. Although, I don't think he was the man I saw at Haystacks. Hell, the guy up there was well over seven foot tall. Weight, somewhere in the neighborhood of five hundred and wasn't a damn bit fat. If his shoes match his body, those size eighteen's could be bronzed and used as his watch fobs. In fact I don't think he could ride in a jeep with two other people. No, I don't believe we're talking about the same guy."

Ben pushed some buttons on his cell phone. He shook his head and started walking away from the building. His back was to me, but I could hear him mumbling. "Damn reception." He wandered back and forth for several minutes and went several feet up the hill. He was out of sight for awhile then I saw him walking back to resume his seat.

"Everything okay?" I asked.

"I can't raise Hollis on his phone and the station can't get him on the radio. The two deputies don't respond to their phones and they are away from the radio. Damn it, they're probably asleep by the fire."

"Could be. If we had a fire I would be catching forty winks myself."

He laughed and said. "Yeah, me too. Damn it, if I tell you something will you promise to keep it just between us."

"Yes."

"Well, Johanna told me Maddalena was with child."

"Did Haystack know?"

"No, and it wasn't his, nor was it Maddalena's. I asked her whose it was and she said, It's nobody's baby."

"Whoa, hold on, just a minute. Are you saying she was a surrogate mother?"

"Maybe, but even a surrogate would have somebody's baby."

"Yeah, it had to be from someone."

"I did ask her and she said the same thing. Under the circumstances I didn't push it. She was very vague and uneasy about talking to me. I was afraid if I asked her to explain she would clam up." He hesitated then continued. "She did say they knew a doctor in Argentina. He supposedly was a friend of their family. Recently, he showed up here and implanted a fetus in Maddalena's womb. He told Johanna he was going to do the same to her as soon as she was married and old enough. She is very scared and felt she had to tell someone. I'm the law and a friend of Haystacks, so she reluctantly confided in me."

I was silent for a second and then said. "Did she say fetus?"

"Yeah, that is what she said. I told her she must mean egg. She said maybe, but whatever it was it was a baby. She went on to explain she knew about artificial insemination of cattle and it wasn't anything like that. Remember I was talking to a seventeen year old girl. One, who had led a fairly sheltered life. I felt she was very smart about some things and naive as hell about others. To make matters worse, she was very emotional. Damn, I can't stand to see pretty girls cry."

"I have the same problem with crying females. In fact I don't even draw the line at pretty." I sighed, and continued "Well, even with the tears, it might give us a clue to why Maddalena's body was mutilated."

"You said us. So you're interested in more than mutilated cattle."

I smiled and said. "Call it professional curiosity. My interest, for the record, is solely on the cattle. My instincts tell me your problems and my problems are all connected. So, I'm not going to close my eyes to any information that might come my way."

"Good, I'm glad to hear it." He hesitated then added. "It sure helps a lot if they're pretty."

"That's for sure, but any crying woman brings out the Sir Galihad in me."

"Yeah, me too. You know I think pretty women cry more than the others. Have you ever noticed?"

"No, can't say I have. To tell the truth I never gave it much thought"

He rubbed his chin in the thinker fashion, then said. "I believe, the pretty women are not afraid to be seen crying. The others are embarrassed and sneak off to be alone."

I nodded and said. "Bella was crying. Does she cry often?"

"No, this was the first time I've ever seen her cry." He hesitated then continued. "She is very pretty. The crying was not pretty."

I asked. "How often does she hold these parties?"

"Oh Hell, she holds parties regularly all over. Here she parties about once a month, sometimes twice. There isn't a set schedule. When the people ask for a party and send money, she rolls. She can mobilize a couple of bus loads of whores faster then you can say, let's dance. The military could take lessons from her on mobilizing. Come to think about it, I have seen a lot of military at her parties. I don't believe they were studying battle plans though." He laughed and continued, "I think the ones here are her biggest. She always draws a crowd."

It was light enough to see across the road when the truck door opened. Bella stepped out, smoothed out her skirt, and announced. "I need coffee."

I started to speak, but stopped as she asked. "What's that noise?"

Ben and I stepped out from under the overhang and looked upwards. The chopping whir of a helicopter was growing louder. The flying dust made us turn our heads as it landed in an adjacent field. A uniform deputy and a investigator climbed out. They quickly approached us and the deputy handed Ben a large thermos of coffee.

He said, "We heard you were here all night. Figured you might need this." Before Ben could answer the detective spoke up. "The rest of the crew are bringing the equipment and the vehicles. I came to get started. What do we have?"

Ben pointed at me and announced. "This is Dutch Evans a homicide detective. He will fill you in." He turned, held the thermos out toward Bella. She smiled, took a couple of unsteady steps. Ben held up his hand signaling her to stop. He moved to her, took her arm and they retreated to the truck.

# CHAPTER TWENTY FIVE

It was breakfast time at Maude's, even though it was just past noon. Maude and Gus had been notified of Junior's death and were in seclusion. Bella had showered and changed clothes. She looked great and if she was suffering from a hangover it didn't show. She was all smiles and running the management like she owned the place. Two of her drivers had turned into fry cooks. Three ladies of the evening had become proficient waitresses. Hot coffee was poured, as the bacon and eggs with hash browns was served with rapidity.

I was enjoying the hot breakfast when my waitress lingered for a moment. I glanced up and did a double take. She was by all standards pretty. Long flowing brown hair, complimented by warm brown eyes. A soft, heart shaped face, with a fair, unblemished complexion. I allowed my eyes the pleasure of wandering over her body. My gaze, even though moving, lingered longer than it should. I thought, such a perfect figure, would aroused jealousy in the likes of Marylyn Monroe. Damn, whores shouldn't be pretty. They should be like brood mares with a broad unattractive ass. A hard unemotional face. Yeah, built for service, not extreme desire. Then again, my ex wife was pretty. They said, before she died, she was not pretty. I guess I just believed, if they become whores they're no longer pretty.

I took the opportunity to ask if she had restaurant experience. She stopped me with her answer. "We weren't born in a whore house you know. Most of us worked at something else in our lifetime."

I felt she took offense to my inquiry and to correct the matter, I said. "I'm sorry I haven't been to bed since yesterday and I wasn't thinking."

She started to untie her apron as she spoke. "Well, we can fix that. Every man should get into bed at least once a day. I just happen to have the time."

Bella spoke up. "He means he was working all night, Jill."

Jill remarked. "So was I, but I don't mind a little overtime."

Bella said. "Stop it, He is not a John. Don't treat him like one."

Jill turned toward Bella and said. "Oh, I get it Private property. Hands off. Okay." She looked back at me, winked, then wiggled off toward the kitchen while relying her apron.

I watched the rear end action as she disappeared from sight. I glanced over at Bella just as she diverted her eyes from me. Her face was very red. Was it anger or possibly embarrassment. I wondered if a Madam could be embarrassed. A whore probably can't, but a Madam, Maybe. She looked up as I started to speak, but she spoke first. "She thinks she's so cute." I thought, she is cute, but there are times when anything said, shouldn't be. I decided my eggs needed a little more Tabasco.

Ben slid into the booth across from me. Looked around, and motioned a waitress for food and coffee. I was putting the cap back on the Tabasco as he asked. "What's the matter with Bella?"

I glanced over at her now redder face, then whispered. "I don't know. Maybe it's a hangover?" I thought this is the time for candy and flowers, both of which, are in short supply around here.

He nodded and said. "Wow, I think her blood pressure has gone off the charts. I thought her hair was as red as red can get. Now, her face has added a new definition for red."

A waitress, other then Jill, brought him his eggs and coffee. He said, "It's a little late for breakfast." She stood there without speaking, as he continued. "I suppose it's all you have." She tossed her head as she turned and walked off." He reached for the Tabasco and remarked. "Another hangover, no doubt."

"No doubt." I said as I forked another fork full of eggs into my mouth. I wasn't about to tell him Bella caught me with my eye balls out on a six inch stem. Yeah, caught cold, staring at an attractive female butt wiggling out of sight.

He looked thoughtful as he said. "Both Bella and the waitress are redheads. I guess maybe it's true, redheads have bad tempers." He stopped speaking, started to pick up his coffee, then put it back down as he spoke. "Oh hell, I'm sorry. You're a redhead, aren't you?"

"Yes."

"Do you ever get mad. I mean real mad?"

"I used to. Then it dawned on me. Every time I got mad, I got hurt. When you get hurt often enough and bad enough, you learn not to get mad."

He took a big drink of his coffee and asked. "If you don't get mad, what do you do."

I noticed Bella had moved toward us and was listening. I took a drink of my coffee, carefully wiped my mouth with a napkin and said. "I cry a lot." Bella laughed and I hoped it meant we had made peace.

Ben shook his head and said. "I asked for that, didn't I?"

Bella was walking away and said. "Yes, you had it coming."

He nodded and said. "By the way Bella, you were right. My office checked and found a rental truck company had rented a truck to Junior. It was four days ago and he rented it for two. He used his driver's license for identification and gave a hundred dollar bill for deposit. They said the hundred has been forfeited and they want their truck back."

I spoke up. "Was anyone with him when he made the rental?"

"They said no. One employee thought he saw a car drop him off. The only thing he could remember, it was green. He didn't see who was driving or if anyone else was in the car."

"Big help." I said.

Ben nodded and said. "It might not be all bad. Now we have a license plate number. Unless they changed plates. I have the copter flying around Haystacks to find Hollis and maybe Johanna. I haven't heard from anyone and I need sleep. I'm going over to our closed sub station. There is a cot there and I am going to crash for a couple of hours. Dutch, there is a bunk in the holding cell. You're welcome to use it if you want to."

"Thanks for the offer, but I don't like to wake up behind bars. I think I will just take my truck and find the shade of a pine tree."

Bella moved over to the booth and said, "I'm sorry, I should have mentioned this before. We have all the cabins and the girls were using them to shower. They're through with cabin tour and it has been cleaned up. The linen been changed and everything. Dutch why don't you take this key and use it. You can take a hot shower, then catch some sleep."

I looked at Ben and said. "That's a Hell of a lot better offer than you made." I slid out of the booth and said, "Thanks Bella, A hot shower sounds great and I do need some sleep."

I was moving toward the door when she said. "Sleep tight and I'll make sure Jill doesn't bother you."

# CHAPTER TWENTY SIX

I stretched in enjoyment of the hot caressing water. I washed, rinsed, and stood until my hands wrinkled. I stepped out and dried off while trying to see my image in a fogged over mirror. I noted the one luxury item missing, was a complementary bathrobe. Since I was alone, I felt no need for modesty. I causally draped the towel over a hook, opened the door and stepped toward the bed.

A female voice startled me as she said. "My, you are a real red head."

I stopped and said. "Bella, You scared the hell out of me!"

She laughed and asked. "Why, were you expecting, Jill?"

I shook my head and said. "I wasn't expecting any one."

"Don't kid me, you were secretly hoping for Jill. I saw the way you looked at her."

"I was not. How did you get in here? I thought I had the only key?"

She giggled and replied. "This is the only cabin I have two keys for. Now come here and I will take your mind off Jill. In fact, when I am through with you, you won't ever want to look at another woman."

"Whoa, you're scarring me again."

"Why are you scared?"

"Call me a coward, but I fear castration."

"Okay, maybe you will still want to look, but it's me, you will want."

"I've already been in that state of mind."

I quickly slipped into bed beside her. My arms encircled her body as our flesh met and bonded as one. Time and fatigue ceased to exist as we moved in an synchronize union. There were sounds and noises that equate only to those heard at night in the nocturnal areas of the zoo, The only recognizable words spoken were mine as I exclaimed. "Wow, you're also a true redhead."

Our bodies were entwined as we slept in exhausted contentment. Time had passed without notice, until someone raped on the door. We didn't move and no voice demanded our response. I ran my hand through her hair and mumbled, "Wow." She nuzzled my neck and snuggled closer, while Her throat emitted a low purr. she whispered, "I'll say, wow, wow!" She hesitated, slowly raised her head, then asked. "Now do you wish it had been Jill?"

"Jill, who?"

"You know Jill who. She may be better than me. She's had a lot more practice and I mean a lot more."

I laughed and replied. "If she was better than you, I couldn't live through it. There was a couple of times today, I thought I was going to die."

She giggled and said. "I didn't feel any signs of your dying. I will have to ask Jill if she ever had anyone die."

"Jill only deals in a service and she may be very good at it. I personally believe it is a lot better, when both parties have lust."

She looked at me accusingly and asked. "How did you find out the difference?"

I shook my head and said. "Every time I open my mouth I get into trouble."

She giggled and said. "Not every time."

"Is Jill as ornery as you?" I asked.

"Probably, more so. She also charges and I don't. If I did you couldn't afford it."

"Maybe I could open a charge account?"

She pushed me back on the bed and said. "We'll talk about it."

I started to speak, but was interrupted by a hard knock on the door. We ignored the intrusion until it was followed by a loud voice. "Dutch, Dutch Evans are you awake?"

"I am now. What do you want?"

"The Sherif needs to talk to you. He's in the restaurant."

"Did he say needs or wants?"

"What?"

"Oh hell, tell him I will be there in a few minutes. I have to get dressed."

# CHAPTER TWENTY SEVEN

I don't imagine I had over thirty minutes sleep. In spite of that, I felt refreshed. I could say it was the hot shower and not be lying. It certainly did it's share. On the other hand, Ben looked like he had aged several years since this morning. I took the seat across from him and asked. "Did you get any sleep?"

He sighed and said. "No, I have been busy as Hell. The copter spotted Hollis's truck, but there is no sign of his whereabouts. I drove up there and checked the house. It's one big mess. Someone or something devoured three big hams. Some of the bones are on the table and the rest on the floor. I'm telling you there are teeth marks on the bones. They were gnawed."

"Human or animal?"

"I don't know, It's hard to say, but they're big."

"Johanna?"

"Still missing and so are the two deputies. Their horses are there, but they aren't."

Jill brought me a cup of coffee and refilled Ben's. She smiled, but didn't speak. She turned to walk away and Ben asked. "Jill, where's Bella?"

She spoke, over her shoulder, as she continued toward the counter. "She's sleeping."

He threw both hands up in a what can I do gesture, and said. "When she wakes up, tell her I have a truck bringing supplies. We need to feed anyone who is assisting. No charge, but have them sign a ticket."

She nodded and replied, "You know this is the third time you told me to tell her."

"I'm sorry, I have a lot on my mind."

I asked, "Who are you expecting to help?"

"Maude said all of Juniors friends are coming. Hell, I need help. They know these woods and they hunt. They can work from here and the posse can work from the top."

"The posse?"

"Yeah, they're on their way. Twenty good officers on horseback can cover a lot of ground. They will sit up their chuck wagon up at Haystack's. If you want a good steak there will be plenty there tonight."

"Okay, I'll keep it in mind, What did you want to see me about?"

"What?'

"Somebody about knocked my door off the hinges. When I asked what they wanted, He said you wanted to see me. So I dressed and here I am."

He shook his head before speaking. "I didn't send anyone to fetch you. Hell, when you walked in I thought you just wanted an update."

"Well the update is appreciated, but a couple more hours sleep would be more in order."

"Yeah, I read you, but it wasn't me who interrupted your siesta. There is one update for you. The Medical Examiner confirmed Juniors neck was broken."

"Then did he find it was the cause of death."

"Not necessarily. He says as a ex homicide detective you'll understand. I wrote down what he said and since I'm the only one who can read my writing, I'll read it to you."

I nodded, took a drink of coffee and said. "Read on."

He reached into his shirt pocket, pulled out a pair of glasses and without comment, hooked the frame behind one ear at a time. He adjusted them to fit his nose. Satisfied with the fit he reached into his right hand pants pocket and retrieved a wrinkled sheet of paper. He silently stared at the writing for a minute then said. "Well, here goes. The vertebrae was completely severed below the axis. The sternocleidomastoid and trapezius muscles were severely torn. The indication was a violent amount of force was involved." He hesitated, then turned the paper toward me and pointed to the words. I nodded, as he continued. "I made him spell those things."

"Yeah, okay, I don't blame you. But you did pretty good on the pronunciation."

"Thanks, but there is more and it's more complicated. I have these notes, but it's easier if I explain it the way he did. The assailant and victim were facing each other. The assailant, with his right hand, grasped the victims head. His thumb was on the right temple of the victim and the middle or ring finger on the left temple. The hand encompassed the forehead, then applied pressure. It fractured the skull at both temples. Result, bone fragments penetrated the brain. The Doctor believes these injuries were the first. It is doubtful that the assailant released the victim at this time. He believes he maintained his grip and twisted the head until the neck snapped. Any of these injuries would lead to death." He took off his glasses and looked at me as he continued. "Can you imagine a grip like that?"

I shook my head and replied. "Maybe size eighteen is your ex deputy. If so, he strikes again."

"Sounds like it could be. One other thing he said the trapezius on the right side of the neck was the most severely torn. What does all this mean to us?"

I thought for a moment then said. "Well, to start with, the assailant was facing the victim. He used his right hand to grasp the skull by placing his thumb and finger on the temporal bones. He twisted the head to the victim's left. This was the same movement as twisting the lid from a jar. The condition of the body probably won't show the grasp of the assailants left hand. My guess would be it was on the victim's right shoulder."

Ben said, "Wait, wait a minute." He put his glasses back on, looked at his notes and continued. "The doctor said, the right clavicle was broken. There's more. Yeah, here he said, something in centimeters, but changed it to three and a half inches from the acromial end of the clavicle."

"He changed it from centimeters to inches?"

"Yeah, he said centimeters and I said talk english, so he changed it."

"Okay, did he say anymore about the fracture?"

"Yes, he said, The clavicle was pushed inward and shattered. It appeared to be a pressure fracture."

I shook my head and said. "Our suspect is as strong in one hand as the other."

Ben was deep in though as I glanced toward the kitchen seeking a refill of coffee. Jill briefly stepped out, held her finger up to her lips, then motioned for me to come. I nodded and she retreated back through the door. I said. "Excuse me Ben, I need to make a rest stop."

His head snapped up as he came back into focus of the present. He said. "Yeah, okay I was just wondering why I can't get a hold of Hollis."

The kitchen door was behind him and I entered without his notice.

Jill whispered, "A man just opened the back door and told me to keep quiet. He dropped this note and left"

She handed me a sealed envelope, addressed in big black letters. "DUTCH EVANS PERSONAL." I asked, "Did he say anything else?"

She whispered, "No, and he spoke in a very quiet voice. He scared the Hell out of me."

I opened the envelop as she continued. "He was huge. I mean he was the biggest man I have ever seen."

"Is that why you're whispering?"

"Yes, he told me to keep quiet."

There was a one page note inside with red printing, It said, "Dutsh, we gat yure beli and if yu tell any budy we wilt kilt hre. we wil let yu nu wha to. stay har untel yu here." I turned to Jill and asked. "Where did he go?"

She whispered, "I don't know. I didn't hear him leave. The door just closed, and he disappeared."

I ran out the door and to cabin four. The door was kicked in. The bed clothes strewn across the floor and a chair knocked over. Bella's clothes were neatly folded on the night stand. I called Bella, and ran into the bathroom. There wasn't any answer, Bella was gone. My knees were weak and I sat down on the bed. I read the note again and thought, If size eighteen wrote this, his shoe size is higher than his I.Q.

# CHAPTER TWENTY EIGHT

In spite of the spelling the message was clear. They had Bella and there wasn't a damn thing I could do. Yeah, nothing, but follow their orders. No, I had a lousy cup of coffee, when I should have been here for her. I swallowed hard as a moment of nausea passed. My eyes teared up and I didn't bother to wipe them. Damn, the bastard who set me up for this. Ralph and Mary both said, I fall in love too fast. They were right. Fortunately it doesn't happen often, but when it does it hits hard. Yeah, that parts easy, falling out of love is a bitch.

Whoa, wait a minute. I had to quit feeling sorry for myself. Bella was in trouble and I wasn't thinking straight. This was a crime scene and I needed to treat it as such.

First the door. The locks were still in the locked position. The wooden door frame didn't hold. One well placed kick shattered the restraining frame. The door flew open throwing wood splinters half way across the room. A powerful son-of-a-bitch with big feet.

Then the note. The envelope was a standard business, size ten. I couldn't see light through it, so it' was a security type. The flap was narrow and uniform. Probably one of the newer self adhesive types. The kind you just peel and press. No chance for saliva tests. Damn new technology. It had crease marks showing it was folded from the end in thirds. Just pocket size. Then the writing, my name was spelled correctly. The letters were neatly printed in heavy black ink. They're broader than those made with a standard pen. Probably a chisel tip sharpie, the kind we used to mark evidence.

The note was on a sheet of white paper. It wasn't creased like the envelope, so it didn't ride in here in the pocket. My guess would be it was written here before being placed in the envelope. It appears to be a twenty lb. weight, computer paper. It was folded the same as a letter and may have prints. I should try to preserve it and have it run through a iodine fumer.

I needed to commit the facts to memory. I mumbled as I examined each item. The letters were a narrow red and don't appear to be ink. A red pencil is probably in the same place as the computer paper. Each letter is printed and not uniform in size or form. The indentations indicate they were drawn with a heavy hand pressing hard on the paper. It appears each letter was laboriously made with determination. Obviously the writer of the note was not the writer of the envelope."

I quietly moved toward the night stand and found two broken red tips. The pencil was just under the night stand. It had a tip capable of use, but had been sharpened by someone chewing off the wood. I opened the drawer to the stand and observed several blank sheets of white computer paper. I carefully wrapped the pencil and tips between two sheets paper and placed them in my pocket. I bent over to look behind the stand when Ben's voice startled me. "What the Hell happened?"

I took out my handkerchief and wiped my eyes before turning toward him and saying "Whoever wanted me out of here, did this. They waited until I left, then kicked in the door."

"He shook his head as he spoke. "Damn, what were they after?" I didn't answer and he continued. "Did they take anything?" I nodded, without speaking as he asked, "Anything valuable?"

"Very valuable?"

"What? Give me a description and we'll get it out on the air."

"I'll have to make a list. I'll get it to you as soon as possible."

We were both looking around the room and if he noticed Bella's clothes he didn't mention it. He was moving toward the bathroom when his cell phone rang. He said, "Hello, hello, hello. Hell, I'll have to go outside." He walked away and I could hear his voice, but not well enough to make out the words.

I picked up the bedding and shook it out. I noticed two small spots of blood on one sheet. I knelt down and checked under the bed. A ten cc syringe attached to an eighteen gauge needle was on the floor. They were just out of sight. It appeared to have been dropped, then kicked during a struggle. It was empty, but wet with a clear liquid. Damn, Bella didn't have a chance. She was over powered then injected. They wanted her to be in a state of unconscious submission. I checked the bedding again and realized the bed spread was missing. Yeah, her clothes are here. She was wrapped in the bed spread and carried off. My eyes teared up again. I was wiping them when he reappeared. "What's the matter with your eyes?" He asked.

I continued wiping as I said. "Oh, I keep getting dust in them or maybe there is something in this room causing my allergies to act up."

He said, "Yeah, I'm allergic to damn near all the weeds around here. I guess I'm like you, my eyes itch like hell and then I sneeze a lot." He looked thoughtful for a moment then continued. "Nothing seems to be bothering me today. Maybe it's because I am too damn busy to get an attack."

I started to speak as he headed for the door. "Ben, is there any news on Hollis?"

He stopped and said. "No, not a damn thing." He continued as he moved out the door. "I've got to find Bella. There's a lot of people headed this way and arrangements have to be made."

# CHAPTER TWENTY NINE

I didn't want to be seen as I moved behind the cabins to the kitchen's back door. The last twenty feet was without cover and I quickly crossed and knocked lightly. Several seconds passed before the door slowly opened. Jill's expression first showed fear then changed to uncertainty, before she spoke. "Dutch, oh God I was afraid he had returned."

"No, it's just me. I need a couple of gallon size, food storage, plastic bags. Do they have any here?"

She stood motionless for a minute then said. "Yes, I will get them."

I stopped her, when I said. "Wait, can you bring them to cabin four?"

She seemed doubtful, then replied. "Yes."

"Good, and bring a large trash bag with them."

She smiled and said. "Ooh, kinky."

I shook my head and replied. "No, nothing like that, but very important. Please trust me."

"Okay, you sound so serious. It will take me a couple of minutes."

"Great, and one other thing. Come from around the back of the cabins and try not to be seen."

"Sounds kinky again."

"It's not and I'll explain when you get there. Please just trust me."

She nodded and closed the door.

I was in the bathroom washing my hands when I heard her voice from the other room. "Dutch, where are you?"

I came out to find her standing just inside the door. She moved cautiously to avoid the broken door jam. Her eyes nervously scanned the splintered wood. She had the bags in her hand as she spoke. "I'm here, where do you want these?"

Her eyes widened and darted between me and the open door as I approached. I thought if I say boo, she will bolt. I kept my voice quiet as I said. "Calm down and come on in."

"I'm all right here." She hesitated then continued. "Am I going to end up in this trash bag?"

I shook my head as I assured her. "No, of course not. Bella's clothes are going in there."

She glanced at the folded clothes then asked. "Where's Bella?"

"Okay, that's the problem. Give me the plastic bags and you sack up her clothes, while I tell you."

She laid the two food storage bags on the chair just inside the door. She looked at me and moved cautiously over to the clothes. She started packing, as I explained.

I put the syringe with needle in one bag and the pencil and note in the other. I dated and initialed the bags as I finished bringing her up to date. I handed them to her and said. "You keep these and if anything happens to me, give them to the Sheriff."

She nodded without speaking and sat down on the bed.

I asked, "Are you okay?"

She looked down and quietly said. "I just need a minute."

I felt if I reached toward her, she would flee. I fought the urge to take her into my arms. I had to move away and I went into the bathroom. I waited for a few seconds then returned with a handful of tissues. Her tears were freely flowing as her breath was punctuated with uncontrolled sobs. I handed her the tissues and walked over to the doorway. I stood looking out over the deserted town and thought there is nothing sadder than emptiness. I heard her blow her nose, Then try to suppress a deep sob. These were followed by a couple of sighs and she said. "I'm all right now."

I didn't move and continued my vigil of the ghost town. I yearned for a sign, any sign, that Bella was in one of the buildings. Suddenly Jill ran to me, sobbing words. "Hold me, please hold me."

I eagerly let my arms encompass her trembling body. I thought even with a wet face, she was desirable. She felt firm but yet soft and vulnerable. A trembling, cuddly, female, whose body folded perfectly into mine. I searched for words to comfort her, while secretly hoping she would remain in my embrace. She raised her face and looked toward the door as she spoke. "See the white church at the top of the hill?"

"Yes, I see it."

She nodded and asked. "Do you see the brown house?"

"Yes, I see the brown house on one side and a yellow one on the other."
She sobbed and said. "Well, the brown one was where I was raised."
"You lived next to the church?"
"Yes, it was close to my father's work. Actually it went with the job." she hesitated then continued, "He was the preacher."

I thought, sometimes it's best to say nothing or to change the subject. I asked, "Did you go to school here?"

She released her left arm from our embrace. She wiped her eyes before speaking. "Yes, grade one through six. I was bused up through nine. That was as far as I got. I didn't graduate from anything." She crushed the tissues in her left hand, looked down and continued. "You see, I fit all the molds. You know, The preachers daughter gone bad. The small town country girl, who went to the city to make good. Failed as a waitress. Failed as a barmaid. Ended up working in a whore house."

Time for another subject change, I thought. "Are you and Bella good friends?"

"I guess so. She lets me pick my Johns. If I hear something she should know, I tell her. Does that make us friends?"

"I would say so. Plus you're a confidant and she left you in charge, so she must trust you."

She uttered a small laugh.

"What?" I asked.

She shook her head, smiled and said. I thought you were going to say I was a whistle blower. Then I could get indignant and say, you said we weren't going to do that."

I laughed and asked, "Would you have slapped my face?"

"I might, but it would all be in fun."

I smiled and said. "Yeah, we both could use a little fun, but it will have to wait. How long have you known Maude?"

"All my life. Why?"

"I'm wondering what brought on her big drinking binge?"

She pushed away from our embrace and moved to the bed. She sat down and seemed thoughtful, then spoke. "Damn, you're always so serious." She looked up, wiped her eyes and continued. "She and Bella had a big fight. It started a couple of days ago, when Bella drove out to set up the party."

"Is that the reason Bella got knee wobbling drunk?"

"Probably. They're really good friends and it was a nasty fight."

"Do you know what the fight was about'?"

"Well, you know three of the girls have disappeared. Bella found out Junior had set up a party for his friends. He was specific he wanted only natural blonds. He arranged it with one of our drivers and Bella wasn't involved. Now, they're gone and Bella thought Junior and his friends were holding them somewhere. You know, as sex slaves or something. They didn't take any of their clothes or personal belongings. Anyway, Bella told Maude and they had a bitter fight."

I asked, "Did the driver say where the party was to be held?"

"He never came back."

"So, three women and one man are missing?"

"Yes. Maude knows Junior and his gang are always in trouble. In spite of that, she is the typical mother and denies he could do anything wrong."

I asked, "Do you know Junior?"

"Yes, I went to school with him."

"What kind of a guy is he?"

"A rat, a bum and a thief. He's so dumb, he thinks he's smart. I don't think he has ever done anything honest. The strange thing is, he and his buddies always seem to have money."

"Are they dealing drugs?'

"I don't know. I do know they stole a truck full of medical supplies. It was headed for the prison and never got there. They were drunk and talking about it in a bar one night. A truck driver heard them and told me. Then once, they tried to sell Bella a truck load of whiskey."

"She didn't buy it, did she?'

"No way. The Sheriff is just looking for a way to raid the ranch. Bella runs an honest and clean business."

"Good. Do you know Jim Haystack?"

"Yes, but why is that important?"

"I don't know right now, but I want to find Bella and the more I know, the better chance I will have. How well do you know him?"

"I was raised here, remember?"

I nodded and asked. "Did he ever come to your ranch?"

She quickly looked up and answered sharply. "We don't talk about Johns."

"Oh sorry I asked."

"Well, I will say he was never at the ranch." She was quiet as I walked toward the doorway. I stopped as she said. "It might be important to know both of his wives once came to the ranch."

"Yeah, I think so. When did it happen?"

She sighed and said. "Well it was about a week before Maddalena was found dead. She and Johanna arrived and asked to see the person in charge. Bella thought they were looking for work and she called me to take care of them. You see part of my job is to screen new applicants."

I excitedly said. "Go on, Go on."

"Well, when I walked in, I introduced myself and noticed Johanna looked young. I asked her how old she was and she said seventeen. I told her she was not old enough to work for Bella and turned my attention to Maddalena. She laughed and said they were looking for advice, not work. I apologized and encouraged them to tell me their problem. Maddalena did all the talking. She said she was with child. Those are the words she used. I thought it was strange she never said she was pregnant. It was always I'm with child."

I repeated, "She was with child?"

Jill hesitated, then wiped her eyes and asked. "Do you think that was strange?"

I nodded and said. "Yes, yes it was strange. What else did she say?

"I asked, why did she come to the ranch? She said she wanted an abortion. I told her we didn't do abortions. She laughed and said she knew that, but considering the business we were in, we might know someone, who could help. I did know a couple of our women who had abortions. I called them in and they agreed to talk to her. I left while they were talking and don't know what was said."

"Did Maddalena ever say anything about whose child she was carrying?"

She shook her head and replied. "We did talk while we were waiting for our women to show up. Between the two of them I found out Maddalena was married to Jim Haystack. He believed they were on a shopping trip and he would probably die if he knew they were at the ranch. The child she was carrying was not his. When I asked the obvious girl question, She said she didn't know who the father was. I said, sometimes things like that happen. She said it wasn't like that at all. Then she said she couldn't talk about how she was with child. The other women arrived and I left."

I was quiet, as I wondered if her organs were removed to destroy any evidence of a pregnancy.

Jill asked, "Do you think she died from an abortion?

"I don't know. You've been a big help and I can't thank you enough. You have been up a long time and need to get to bed."

She giggled and said. "I thought we weren't going to do that."

I laughed and said. "Stop it, you know what I mean. Go find a bed and sleep."

# CHAPTER THIRTY

It was nearly dark when I left the room. I was walking toward my pickup when Ben's voice stopped me. "Dutch, do you have a minute?"

"Of course, What's up?"

He motioned me toward the restaurant. Several pickups, cars and suvs started to arrive. I had to hurry across the lot to keep out of the way. He met me at the doorway and said, "Dutch, we have one hell of a mess. They found Hollis up in the heavy timber. It was close to where the shooters hid when they shot at you. He's dead, tied to a tree and his necks broke."

"His neck is broken?"

"Yeah. They say it looks like someone tried to twist his head off. Been dead quite awhile. The deputy who found him said he was beginning to smell. We will know more before long. The homicide squad is on their way up there."

I looked around and asked. "Who are all these people?"

He smiled as he answered. "Some of them are from search and rescue. Several are volunteers and the rest are trusties from the county jail."

"They seem to be well armed. I see large caliber rifles and pistols of every shape and size."

"Yes, they own their own guns. Most of them are hunters and all are marksman. The trusties are not armed. You see, what I have done is called out the off duty jail cooks and the kitchen trusties. They will take over and feed these people. Bella's crew can be spelled off and get some rest. We cleared it with Maude, who doesn't seem to give a damn. The food situation is only temporary. We need our one chuck wagon up at Haystacks. The Sheriff in the next county is loaning me theirs and we will park it here. It should be here by tomorrow. I can't find Bella and Jill said she might have gone back to the ranch. Have you seen her?"

I quietly said, "No, not lately."

Several more trucks pulled in as Ben continued. "The agents from Hollis's department are coming to join the search. As soon as they arrive we will start." He hesitated before continuing in a loud voice. "Those bastards are holed up somewhere and they probably have Johanna. We're going to look behind every tree and turn over every rock until we find them. They're like any other animal, they have to eat, shit and leave tracks. The hunters will track them down and we have enough muscle to take them out. I don't give a damn how big, tough or how many, we're ready."

I stepped back to get out of the way. He moved forward through some still moving vehicles and directed them to a parking area.

I thought, Junior gets killed and it's handled routinely. Hollis gets it and he calls out the militia.

Confusion seemed to be the order of the day and I worked my way towards my truck, It required going around and through groups of loud talking men. I heard my name being shouted and I looked around. Ben was working his way toward me and in a loud voice said. "Wait a minute Dutch, I wasn't through. I need to see you."

He moved next to me and took my arm to direct us to a quiet spot. He didn't speak and seemed to be looking for someone. I broke the silence by asking. "You have any news of your two deputies."

He continued looking as he spoke. "No, not a thing." Suddenly he motioned to a large uniformed man in the crowd. The man nodded and moved toward us. As he approached, I noticed he was wearing captain's bars on his collar. We waited until he joined us and Ben said. "Dutch, I want you to meet Captain Savage from my department. He's in charge of searching this entire area. He will start with all the outhouses and vacant buildings."

I nodded, and extended my hand. We shook as Ben continued. "I told Captain Savage, I'm trying to hire you and he's all for it. So what's your answer?"

"I'm still thinking and haven't come to a decision yet."

Ben smiled and said, "Okay." He reached into his pocket and pulled out a Deputies badge. He reached over and pinned it to my shirt.

I asked, "What are you doing, Ben? I didn't say yes."

He laughed and replied, "You don't have to say a thing. I'm deputizing you under my powers and authority of posse comitatus. Captain Savage is a witness."

I looked at the Captain as he said. "You should have taken the job. This way you don't even get paid."

Ben said, "That's right, but it's not all bad. I'm doing both of us a favor. Your PI license only holds water in the issuing state. Oh yeah, I checked and know I'm right. Then the way you get involved in investigations, you need authority. The badge gives you authority, jurisdiction, and the right to carry concealed weapons. Here is your permit, all signed and legal." He handed me the folder complete with ID. I slipped it into my shirt pocket as he continued. "And, in turn I get a good investigator for free. We both win."

I opened my mouth to speak as his cell phone rang.

He listened intently then asked, "When?" He looked at me and said. "They found the deputies. They were in the fire with the hog. Both of their bodies were severally burned. There wasn't any evidence of burnt cloth adhering to the flesh. It appears they were naked and their uniforms and equipment are missing."

Captain Savage said, "Maybe the big guy Dutch saw now has a real badge?"

Ben said, "Maybe, I told the Captain of your encounter, Dutch."

I thought, since you are now short two badges, I could give this one back. A second thought told me this was not the time.

# CHAPTER THIRTY ONE

S till they came, more people, more guns. There was pistols, automatics and revolvers. Some carried both rifles and pistols. Others had one or the other. The choice of rifles ran from Carbines to one with a tripod on a long barrel. It suspiciously looked like a B. A. R. Two men dressed like Daniel Boone arrived carrying 50 caliber muzzle loaders. I wasn't sure if they were for real. To complete their ensemble each had a powder horn causally hanging from a raw hide strap over their shoulders.

A voice from behind me said. "The best of the black powder gun club is here."

Another voice said. "They're damn good with those things. Don't get into a shooting match with them."

Some one added, "Unless you want to lose money."

I noted their choice of artificial lighting was a little more limited. Most had flashlights and some preferred battery lanterns. So far I hadn't heard any shots. It was a relief to know they weren't a trigger happy mob.

The organized aggregations continued as they moved in and out in groups of twenty. All staying just long enough to eat and exchange greetings. There was uneventful discussions of fatigue, hope and boredom, While the emotion of excitement was conspicuous by its absence.

I re-parked my truck in order to watch both the area search efforts and cabin four. The mountains were inundated with darting lights simulating a gigantic fire fly hatch. It didn't give me a feeling of satisfaction, but it was entertaining to watch.

I thought, it's kind of like being in a drive in movie. I laughed, yeah, a drive in, by myself, watching a movie with a slow plot. It would be better if

Bella was here watching with me. Then it wouldn't matter if there was a plot on not. I hadn't seen a drive in for a long time. I wondered what became of them. No this is just an all night stake out waiting for something, anything, to happen. I yawned, stretched and suddenly wondered where Jill was sleeping. She certainly would be good company for a stake out..

# CHAPTER THIRTY TWO

It was midnight and no one had approached the cabin or my truck. The mounted posse was working the area around Haystack's. Meanwhile the deserted town was being canvassed by Captain Savage. He had adequate deputies with him and the woods were saturated with search and rescue volunteers. The Sheriff is somewhere asleep. At least I hope he is. The last time I saw him he was running on adrenaline, caffeine and optimism. Nobody seemed interested in the East. The truck load of oxygen went East, but how far East? They said the roads washed out just East of here. Near a wash, someone said. I needed to do something. They may be wrong. They're assuming the truck stopped in this area. I didn't want to fall asleep. Damn it, I'm going for a ride and hoped one of those volunteers wouldn't shoot me.

The current group leaving the restaurant continued their walk, seemingly without noticing my departure.

There wasn't any moon and the night was dark. The only light, other than my headlights, was from a drivers side spot light It illuminated the night sweeping over the landscape on both sides of the road. Driving slowly, I noticed the bar pits were overgrown, while tumbleweeds were solidly entwined along the fence line. Debris dotted the roadway and obviously maintenance did not exist. Broken barb wire snaked out in all directions and clung in pieces to broken and rotting fence posts. Deserted sheds had collapsed, while barns sagged from the wind and lack of repair. My light caught a pair of coyotes, who hesitated, then quickly scampered out of sight.

The dashboard clock clicked to two and I still hadn't found the washed out area. I stopped, cut the motor, and turned off the lights. It was quiet and the only sound came when I shifted in my seat. I was fighting fatigue and feared involuntarily falling asleep. I decided to check my pistols and reached under the dash only to find an empty bracket. A quick check with a flashlight confirmed my fears. My revolver was gone.

The empty space under the front seat told me the forty five Caliber automatic and three full clips were equally missing. The revolver, a three fifty seven magnum, was specially loaded. Chambers one, three and five held tracers. Chamber two, armor piercing while four and six held hollow points. I instinctively reached into my boot even though I knew my two inch thirty eight special was not there. I remembered I left it on the night stand and it would be under Bella's clothes. Jill would have seen it, when she moved the clothing. She didn't mention it, but what difference would it make, like the others it was gone.

I had to think this out. My truck was locked and I had the keys. How in the Hell did anyone get in and take the guns? The Sheriff, yeah the Sheriff. He could jimmy the doors. The son-of-a-bitch. He gave me a badge and permit to carry and then took my guns. What a bastard. Boy did I misjudge him.

The silence was shattered when I said. "Don't panic. Hell I'm not panicking. I have lost enough fire power to hold off an army and I shouldn't panic. All I have left is my pocket knife, If I had any sense I would panic. No, by God I'm mad. Damn Mad." I slammed my fist on the dash board and said, "Oh hell. It's bad enough to think these thoughts, now I'm talking to myself."

I stepped out into the darkness believing maybe a short walk would help. I really needed to clear my mind. I used the flashlight as I strolled along. I froze in my tracks as a sudden rustling in the brush startled me. Then let out a deep breath and felt silly as a rabbit scurried by.

I turned out the light and stood inhaling the freshness of the night.

I noticed, out of the darkness, there was a light. It was near the top of the ridge, it was very bright, considering the distance. I estimated it over a mile as the crow flies. By being confined to the ground it was closer to ten miles. A tough walk and all uphill. My truck had four wheel drive and aggressive off road tires. I could try it, but it would make more sense to wait until first light.

Suddenly the light exploded into a huge bright flash and the darkness became totally black.

# CHAPTER THIRTY THREE

It was cold. My ears were ringing with a steady loud, shrill and strident noise. Yet it seemed secondary to the thundering pounding inside my head. It increased and decreased with every heart beat. It was with painful effort that I managed to separately open each eye. Neither would focus and everything was a spinning blur. I quickly shut them in an effort to stop the resulting nausea. I realized my equilibrium was gone. I knew if I tried to rise or stand I would fall. In addition, I would probably faint. Maybe to lie face down and puke my guts out. Even that would be better than face up where I could choke to death on my own vomit. I had to stay still and hope this would pass. Yeah, it's a concussion for sure and maybe a fractured skull. In spite of the pain and my efforts to remain conscious, I succumbed to sleep.

"Wake up, wake up, you son-of-a-bitch," a loud voice commanded, as I was drenched with cold water.

I flailed my arms and tried to roll away. The spraying blasts of stinging water increased as I struck a wall. I pulled my knees up, tucked my chin down on my chest and folded into a fetal position. The peppering streams of water continued as the booming voice burst into raucous laughter. I tried not to move or flinch and just as quickly as the water started, it stopped. The laughter faded, a door slammed, followed by an uncomfortable silence.

I waited several minutes before unfolding and tried to orient myself. The room was shiny white. There wasn't any definition between the walls and the ceiling. The floor blended into the wall base and the effect was blinding. The water flowed to the center of the room and drained into an obscure hole. The entire area was devoid of furniture and conducive to instantaneous vertigo.

I was unable to stand. There was the sensation of uncontrolled falling. I tried to hold onto the floor, fighting to stop the instability. I needed to move and crept along hoping to find a corner to brace myself. Finally I realized the room was round. If there was a door, it blended into total concealment. Nausea took over and quickly emptied my stomach of all contents. It was followed with retching and dry heaves until my throat burned and my ribs ached.

Deep breathing hurt and I used rapid shallow gasps to get enough air. I was naked, wet and damn cold. Suddenly, without warning, warm water sprayed from the ceiling. I welcomed the warmth and watched with fascination as the room was cleansed. Then a voice resounded into the room. "Well, Dutch old boy, how you doing?"

I didn't respond and he continued. "Come, come, old buddy. Speak up. Don't you remember we're old friends?"

My voice was hoarse as I asked. "Where in the Hell am I?"

Laughter filled the room, before he said. "It might be Hell. That's for you to decide. By the way I love your pistolas."

"My what?"

"Your pistolas. I didn't know you were a pistoleer."

"A what?"

There was more laughter, then he said. "A pistoleer, or as you cowboys say, a gun slinger."

"What are you talking about?"

"Oh, come now. Don't play dumb with me. Bella had a little cute one. My man didn't think it was real. She shot twice at him as he came through the door. One missed and the second shot, hit his badge."

"Your man had a badge?"

"Hell yes, it saved his life. Fortunately he wasn't alone and when Bella picked up another pistola they grabbed her before she could shoot."

"Too bad."

He laughed and said, "Not really. We took your other pistolas from your truck when it was unlocked at Haystacks. We thought we had them all, but you had the little one in your boot."

"How did you know about my boot gun?"

"Oh, we know. You had a little pistola in your boot and Bella had one on her leg. You both left them in the cabin. People talk, we listen."

I said, "People like Junior talk and for money."

He laughed and said, "Wow, you got it stud."

"Where's Bella?" I asked.

A short laugh was followed by, "She's resting in similar accommodations."

I asked, "What does that mean?"

His tone became serious as he replied. "You know, she looks a lot like Lorraine. I mean the long flowing red hair. The green eyes and a figure that haunts you." He hesitated, then continued. "I can just picture her in a green sweater and black pants. Add a gold necklace and voila, we have Lorraine."

I didn't respond and he waited several minutes before continuing. "Oh, and we can't forget the luscious, seductive smile can we?"

"You rotten son-of-a-bitch. Who are you?"

The laughter returned as he said. "Now, now, don't be crude. I hated your ass in medical school and my feelings have at least doubled since then." He coughed, then said. "I'm hurt since you don't remember me. Especially, since it was you and that bitch, who got me thrown out of school."

I asked, "What in the Hell are you talking about?"

"You know what I'm talking about. I had a good business going until Lorraine got pregnant."

"What did her pregnancy have to do with you?"

"Don't play games with me Dutch. You know it's me, Abel Cutter. You remember you told the school about my abortion practice."

"Abel Cutter, Yeah, I remember you had the hots for Lorraine. She often told me you were harassing her. That explains a lot. I didn't know anything about any abortions. In fact, I didn't know she was pregnant when she left."

"Well she was, and it was your child. A student, I treated, confided in me. I called Lorraine and offered my services. She said no. I tried to convince her it wasn't wise to bring any off spring of yours into the world. She disappeared the next day. The following day I was informed I was no longer a student. I hadn't left the Dean's office when I heard the police were searching my clinic. It had to be you or her. One of you snitched on me."

"Well, it wasn't either of us. I am curious though. Why would anyone seeking an abortion tell you about some one else being pregnant?"

"That's simple, they talk to each other about such things. I had a good reputation and they would refer their friends."

I quickly replied, "That's bullshit. She wasn't referring anyone to you. She was referring you to them. The truth is you were paying for referrals."

He laughed as he said. "Yeah, maybe, but business is business and I prefer to think of it as the other way."

I hesitated for a moment then said. "I didn't know you were involved, but I did hear there were two women hospitalized with serious problems. As I remember, it was a result of a back alley abortion racket."

He angrily replied, "It was not a racket."

"But, they were your clients'?"

"Patients, patients, not clients. When they seek medical treatment they're patients."

"I heard one of them died." He was silent as I continued. "I don't know about the other one."

He lowered his voice and said. "Yeah, well, all surgery has it's risks. There aren't any guarantees."

I asked, "Were you arrested?"

His voice rose, as he replied, "Hell no. I was gone."

"There's probably a warrant out for you."

He angrily said. "It was a long time ago. No one cares now."

"There isn't any statute of limitations for murder. There is always someone who cares." I started to add, "I care," but he interrupted by shouting. "Fuck you," and a loud click told me the mike was dead.

# CHAPTER THIRTY FOUR

At least the warm wash down had knocked the chill off, but I was still cold. My head was throbbing simultaneously with each heart beat. While my eyes kept pace with my pulse and faded in and out of focus. Nausea was still a problem, but there was nothing left to regurgitate. Even bile, during violent retching, had vacated my system. It was hours ago and I'm still gagging.

The illuminating glare obliterated the definition of the overhead. It took great effort, coupled with staring into lightning brightness, before I could detect lights and faucet heads. They were inserted into a framework of beams about twenty feet high. Anything above that was concealed by the brightness. Damn, there was bound to be a camera concealed among those fixtures. It would elude all efforts of detection unless I could knock out some of the lights. A monumental task, considering they're several feet beyond my reach. Also, there is nothing to stand on, or to use as a prod. Then, being completely naked might not hinder, but it sure as Hell didn't help.

I moved slowly running my hands along the walls. The only sounds came from the rubbing noise of my flesh on metal. The near silence added to my feeling of stress created by solitude. Time exists, but cannot be calculated, I thought, as I considered my options. I laughed and realized my only option was wait and see.

I heard several clicking noises before a flat unemotional voice said. "Mr. Evans, this is Johanna. Doctor Cutter says, I'm with child."

I quickly asked. "Johanna, are you all right?"

The voice tone did not change as she said. "I am with child."

I said, "Johanna wait," as a click sounded. I continued, "Johanna, Johanna speak to me. Johanna please speak to me." My requests were met with silence.

I resumed my scrutiny of the ceiling. Now I knew, not only a camera, but a speaker as well, was concealed among the spigots and lights. Yeah, now I realized the door slamming I heard earlier came from a speaker. There isn't a door to this tank. I wondered, How in the Hell did they put me in here? I hated to admit it, but this chamber was created by an ingenious bastard.

Having given up on finding an exit, I tried to think of someway to pass the time. If I glanced at the walls, vertigo quickly returned. I hesitated to close my eyes since I was cooling down and feared freezing to death. They say people get sleepy before they die. I curled up trying to stay warm and concentrated on staying awake. It proved to be a losing battle and I slept.

I jerked awake as a loud voice boomed into the room. "Hey, Dutch are you alive?"

I answered. "Just barely. Where are my clothes? I'm freezing to death."

There was laughter followed by, "What are you going to do tomorrow?"

I hesitated then said. "How in the Hell would I know?"

He laughed, then said. "Well, Hell, it doesn't matter if you die today. What difference does it make, since you don't know anything about tomorrow?"

"Is that your plan. Freezing me to death?"

He quickly replied, "No that would be too easy. I have other plans for you. I will warm things up and give you another warm shower."

His words were followed by the water and this time it was uncomfortably hot. I yelled. "Damn it, You're scalding me. I don't want a shower, I want my clothes."

His voice lowered as he said. "Oh, too hot huh." Then there was laughter before he continued. "Okay, I'll turn it down a little."

I asked, "Why can't I have my clothes?"

The water went from hot to warm as he said. "If everything goes as planned, I'll buy you a nice dress."

There was a click before I could answer.

# CHAPTER THIRTY FIVE

The synchronize throbbing in my head told me my heart rate had escalated to over a hundred. I sat down, crossed my arms over my knees and tried to calm down. I cursed the bright lights, closed my eyes and rested my head on my arms. Searching for a positive thought, it came to me, in spite of the brightness, the lights did give off a little heat. I did fade in and out of what could be called cat naps.

Surprisingly, I wasn't hungry, even through, it had been hours, maybe days since I'd eaten. The periodic showers, coupled with a slow drain, provided drinking water. The only opening in my enclosure was the drain. I check it for any possibilities. Ah yes, a black hole, drilled deep through solid steel. It was so small, I couldn't even insert my little finger into it's depths. I quickly pulled out hair from the back of my head and jammed it into the drain. It was a long shot, but the only one I could think of. Now if there is enough showers the waters will flood this chamber. The only problem would be trying to keep from drowning until I floated to the top.

I moved back to the wall, squatted, and used my arms to pull my knees up to my chest. I was contemplating pulling out more hair for the drain when I heard a click. It was quickly followed by Abel's voice.

"Well Dutch, old boy How you doing?"

I thought about not answering, but if I hoped to gain any information I had to enter into a dialogue with my captors.

"Johanna called you Doctor. Did you finish school?"

He laughed and said, "Not in the real sense. I did more studying on my own and learned more than I ever would at school."

"What you're saying is you feel you're entitled, so you conferred the title on yourself."

"Yes, that's partially true. You see I had to go places and do things. The title of Doctor gets respect and opens doors."

I laughed and said. "I guess it would be handy for reservations at the big restaurants. Where else will it open doors?"

"You would be surprised. It's really amazing how medical supply houses, banks, and pharmacies just can't do enough for me."

"I heard you steal your medical supplies."

He laughed and said, "Only when the opportunity pops up."

"Yeah, like when Junior hijacks a truck."

His voice became serious as he said. "Yes, it does help when something good falls into your lap."

I asked. "Why did you kill him?"

There was a long silence before he answered. "It's really none of your business, but I guess you should know part of the problem. You see, Junior had a thing for Johanna. He somehow found out my plans for her. He threatened to kill me if I touched her. So he had to go. It's really as simple as that. No one threatens me or tells me what to do."

I said. "That was all. A threat he probably couldn't carry out?"

"Oh, he might of been capable of pulling it off. He did a lot of hunting and I know he was a crack shot. In fact, and you'll like this. He taught me how to shoot."

"If that's true, why didn't he shoot you."

He laughed then said. "He could of, but we never gave him the opportunity. He was so dumb, he thought I would keep him around until he had the chance."

I said, "Maybe you should have held off and used him to shoot Haystack. Your shooter missed."

He said, "Missed, not hardly. Haystack moved, but it was still a good shot." I asked, "How about me? You only killed my horse."

"Now that was a good shot. We thought you would come up looking for the shooter. Hollis came through the woods at the wrong time and we had to get out of there."

"What if I had gone up the ridge. What would have happened?"

"You would have enjoyed my hospitality a lot sooner."

I asked, "You mean, you wouldn't have killed me, like Hollis?"

"No way, I wanted to keep you alive at all costs. Hollis wasn't on our must do list. We let him live, until he got to snooping around."

I asked, "What about Bella?"

There was silence, except for the sound of him breathing. It seemed like an eternity before the quiet was interrupted by a deep sigh. A few more seconds passed before he said. "Ah, yes, Bella. She knows what she has to do."

"And what's that'" I asked.

The solemn tone in his voice faded and he replied in a serious voice. "She only has to become my partner." He hesitated, then laughed and continued. "I need women and she has women."

"Why do you need women?" I asked.

He ignored my question and said. "You know, she has a long list of whores wanting to go to work for her. There could be even more if she would only listen." He hesitated then continued. "She won't even hire young girls. I told her professional teams, like baseball, have farm teams. She could do the same. Yeah, young whores in training. I guess you could call them, apprentice sex machines." He laughed then said. "I don't give a damn what they're called, as long as they're available to me."

I started to speak, but stopped as a click ended the contact. What a sick son-of-a-bitch, I thought, as I resumed my position with my head on my arms.

# CHAPTER THIRTY SIX

I felt the cold metal against my cheek. It took extra effort to open my eyes. Everything was blurry, but slowly began to focus. I realized I was face down on the tank floor. What could have happened? The last thing I remembered was squatting with my back against the wall. Now, I was spread eagled in the center of the tank. I was woozy and unsteady. I pushed myself up to a crawling position and moved to the wall.

I felt an emptiness, yeah, a time lapse of nothing. My head was starting to throb again. It was strange I hadn't noticed it before. My throat was dry, but as dry as it was, it couldn't mask the horrible taste in my mouth.

I crossed my arms on my knees and cradled my head. The throbbing increased as I searched for answers. Did I black out? Is my head injury causing temporary amnesia? It didn't seem I was having any problem contemplating. The problem was there wasn't anything to contemplate. I needed a drink, but the floor was completely dry. I ran my hands along the wall, searching for moisture. Then greedily licked each drop of condensation from my fingers. I didn't hear the click and was startled when Abel spoke.

"Wake up, wake up, you lucky bastard."

"I'm awake."

"Good, did you have a good sleep?"

I hesitated then asked. "Was I asleep?"

He laughed, then asked. "Don't you remember?"

"No, but I know, I'm cold. I don't know how I could sleep when I'm so damn cold."

"Oh, about that, I'll warm it up for you. It's unnecessary for now."

I asked, "Why was it necessary?"

"Well, for one thing you know your metabolism slows down when you are real cold. Therefore, you have a better chance of surviving major surgery."

"What major surgery?" I asked.

He laughed and replied. "Brain surgery of course. You lucked out, and I will blow in some warm air. That's the good news. The bad news is you have a subdural hemorrhage of the frontal lobes of the brain. It's strange though, since Hans swears he hit you in the back of the head."

"He did, and what you're describing sounds like a contrecoup injury. In plain English, a blow to the back of the head causes the brain to oscillate in a forward thrust. The lacerations are caused by the edges on the inside of the skull. Was there a fracture?"

He hesitated, then said, "No fracture."

"That's good news. Sometimes, there is a fracture with this type of injury. What did he hit me with?"

"Just his fist and only once. He's very strong, but I warned him to be careful."

"I wish you had warned me to duck. You said I was asleep. Did I go into shock?"

"Naw, you'll appreciate this. You were asleep on your arms. I pumped Nitrous Oxide into the chamber. It's heavier than air and encompassed your position. You inhaled enough to get woozy. Then I enriched it with Enflurane and it was sleepy bye time for you. To make sure you stayed immobile while I did an examination, I hooked you up to an IV of Morphine and Scopolamine."

"How come you didn't go to sleep?"

"Easy, I wore a breathing apparatus when I entered. You know like fireman wear. Once I hooked you up with the IV, we pumped out the gas and ran in oxygen. Then we took x-rays and blood samples. The x-rays revealed the blood on your brain. So, no operation today."

I nodded as I said. "Too bad. I guess you were very disappointed. Now, please tell me, why I have this terrible taste in my mouth."

He laughed and said. "Oh that, well we cut down the anesthesia until you were semi conscious. Then we made you drink formula 27. One nice thing about Scopolamine and Morphine it lets you respond to pain, but you don't retain any memory. So you don't remember drinking, Huh, I'll be damned. I may have brought you back to far, since you raised a Hell of a fuss. It must taste really bad. I'm both pleased and surprised you don't remember."

I looked at my left arm and noticed the red puncture mark in the crick of my elbow. The muscles of both arms and my shoulders were sore. I said. "You must of had a hard time restraining me."

"We did, but muscle can overcome resistance. Most people quit struggling when increased pain becomes too intense. Unfortunately you don't. Lorraine was right when she told me you were tough. She also said you had a line shack mentality. The tough, I understood, the line shack, I never understood."

I ignored his comments and asked, "What's formula 27?"

He was silent, but I could hear his breathing. Finally I asked, "Are you still alive?"

He replied, "Yes, formula 27 is a coagulant. It will inhibit blood loss."

"I never heard of it. where is it used?"

'Well, it has quite a history. During World War Two it was one of the medical experiments in Germany. People would drink it and then be shot. The doctors proved it would work."

I yelled, "What, you have given me a coagulant. My blood may now clot. You son-of-a-bitch, you have set me up for a stroke or heart attack."

He replied, "Yeah, maybe. The research papers I read didn't go that far. In fact they claimed it to be a success."

I lowered my voice and said. "What success. They killed their victims."

"Yes, but their experiments didn't have the same set of circumstances like we have, It might work for you and you might live. In fact it may save your life."

"What, and where did you study? I'm getting a feeling of a strong Nazi influence. Hans hit me. Gas is pumped into what you call a chamber. A blood coagulant is created by killing people. In fact, I seem to remember your ancestry is German."

A loud click told me our conversation had ended.

# CHAPTER THIRTY SEVEN

I know now, what they mean by, "it hurts to think." I was huddled against the wall trying to remember what Lorraine said. It had something to do with Abel Cutter. Yeah, he told some female classmate and she was spreading it around. No doubt it was pure gossip, but worth remembering. My head throbbing seems to cancel out all thoughts of the past. In fact, it wipes out some of the present. Damn concussion, I hope someday to meet that iron fisted son-of-a-bitch on more equal terms. Yeah, someday, like I dare think there is a someday. I wish I had paid more attention to the gossip. I remember there was a lot, involving Abel. It wouldn't make much difference, if I can't remember.

I do remember on Sunday night we usually studied in the kitchen. It was late and I came in with a sack of takeout. Lorraine was seated at the table dressed only in a bra and panties. Damn, she was pretty. That, I clearly remember. Then later, whoa, I can't think about that now. I even have an legitimate excuse. I have a headache. Now back to other things. There was several books scattered on the table top. She smiled, pushed them aside, and said, "Lets eat, I'm starved." I nodded and told her I had hamburgers, fries and soft drinks. She made a comment about med students and unhealthy food. I agreed, but pointed out it fit our food budget. She took a bite of the burger, followed it with two fries and mumbled. "Someday." In those days we each believed there would be a someday.

I don't remember how Abel came into the conversation. I remember I never liked him. He was one of those people who, no matter what experience anyone had, he had one better. Oh yes, there was the time I saw his name on a class register as Adel Cutler. When I mentioned it to him, he said, It was just a missed communication. They couldn't read his handwriting. When he pointed out the mistake they told him, his handwriting was so bad he was going to make a great doctor. Maybe, I mentioned this while we ate.

I remember, Lorraine, finished her burger, wiped her mouth and dropped her paper napkin on the table. She was quiet for a moment then said, "I was having lunch with Maribel, when Abel joined us. After a few minutes of small talk he asked if we would give him copies of our class notes. I didn't answer, but Maribel had a crush on him and said she would. She handed him her notebook and said, he probably wouldn't be able to read her writing. He replied, it was no problem since he came from a family of doctors and he could decipher bad writing."

She fingered the straw in her drink, then continued. "Abel thumbed through a few pages without speaking. He looked at Maribel and said, Some of this looks like Hebrew. Are you a Jew? She said, Yes. He replied, Oh, and handed back her book. Then he abruptly left without any further words."

I remember commenting how crude I thought his conduct was.

Then Lorraine continued. "Maribel was hurt, then she got mad."

I nodded and said, "I don't blame her. I probably would have hit him with the table."

Lorraine laughed and continued. "Well, she didn't hit him, but she knows people. She checked with a Jewish Documentation Center and discovered his real name."

My mind wandered as Lorraine's lips encompassed the straws. She stopped when the sound of suction reverberated in the empty plastic container. She stood up, smiled and gathered up the remnants of the meal. The walk to the sink was tantalizing and culminated when she bent over the waste basket. I stood transfixed, without shame, and enjoyed the view. She retrieved her purse from the counter and returned to her seat. She pulled out a folded sheet of paper and said.

"Maribel's source send her this information. She gave me a copy." She started to hand it to me, but pulled it back and said, "He was telling the truth." I nodded and she began to read out loud. "His maternal grandfather was a Nazi Doctor, who conducted medical experiments on inmates. He was sentenced to death for war crimes. He committed suicide before the sentence was carried out. Abel's father was born in England to a German couple, who had achieved English citizenship. The family returned to Germany where the father was raised and educated. He married the oldest daughter of an associate of his Grandfather. After his marriage he became interested in medicine. He started in late 1944 assisting his father-in-law at Toirdealbhach Women's

TED KNUCKEY

Camp. In early 1945 he feared, it Germany fell, his English background would be a problem. He took his wife and fled to Argentina. He eventually entered medical school and did become a Doctor. Adel was an only child and was born when his mother was in her mid-thirties. He later changed his name from Adel to Able to conceal his German background. The name Cutler easily became Cutter as he distanced himself from the family."

Now it made sense. Abel is Hebrew, Adel is German. I must of had some recollection of this when I made the comment about his German ancestry. It does seem strange that he would take a Jewish name when he seems to be so prejudiced. Then again, maybe he believed it's the best way to hide his hatred. Yeah, it gives new meaning to the theory, the best place to hide is in plain sight.

I was glad he turned up the heat in here before I upset him. It's amazing what I could remember if I connected my memories with Lorraine. Damn, if I kept thinking about her I would be begging Abel for another cold shower.

# CHAPTER THIRTY EIGHT

Time moves, it doesn't stand still. How fast it moves is the question. Minutes become hours, hours become days, and on and on. When a light constantly shines with the same brightness there isn't a night or day. I wished I had a watch, then, I could at least calculate hours. I don't know how long I'd been here. Maybe long enough to go crazy. I thought, If I'm not crazy now, I will be, especially if I keep thinking like this. Crazy would be better than being in here. Yeah, crazy might be even a blessing.

This philosophical meandering wouldn't help. I had to concentrate on escape. Abel had the key. He always was an egotistical bastard. That included, cocky, conceited and self-centered. He was quick to put others down and acted superior on all occasions. The most annoying thing about him was his bragging. Yeah, his boasting, particularly to the females. He was easily insulted, but acted favorably to flattery. I needed a way to use his bull shit character against him.

It seemed like a long time since a contact. I wondered if he would speak, or was I in for a gas attack. Maybe, laughing gas, Yeah, another dose of Nitrous Oxide. I needed a good laugh, but not from a blast of anesthesia. My thoughts were interrupted by the familiar click. There was silence, except for the barely audible breathing. Finally I spoke.

"My head is killing me. How about a couple of aspirin?" There was a quick reply.

"No aspirin. Aspirin thins the blood. We want it to clot."

"You're all heart. What took you so long to speak after you turned on the mike?"

He hesitated then replied. "I was thinking. I'm going to x-ray you again. Since you know about it, I don't need to worry about the odor. I have more Ether than Nitrous Oxide. Maybe this time I will use Ether."

"I wouldn't, if I was you. Ether is highly combustible. Nitrous oxide and Enflurane is not. Hell, if you fill this tank full of Ether, any type of spark will make it blow. There won't be anything left of your little operation. This tank full of Ether would make one Hell of a large hole."

There was another short period of silence then he said. "I hate to admit it, but you're smart. I may have to reconsider on how to use your brain."

"Do you mind if I ask. Just what do you have in mind for my brain?"

He laughed and said. "I guess, I don't mind if you ask. After all it's your brain, but I will control it. All you need to know, is I have a body in need of a brain."

I asked. "Are you trying to create a Frankenstein's monster?"

He said, "No, not really. My creation will be smart."

I replied, "Don't you know a brain cannot live outside of the body? If you deprive it of blood and oxygen, it will die."

"Now, I have to go back to believing you are dumb." He hesitated, then continued. "The brain will live as long as it is supplied with Oxygen. There's a ton of evidence to prove the brain lives even after the body dies. In France they beheaded people with a guillotine. They noticed, the brain lived, even after being severed from the body. In many cases there was eye movement, in others, lips moved. In one case a handler was bitten when he picked up the head."

"Yeah, and I know a freshly killed rattlesnake will strike if picked up. Once a gun fighter was executed by hanging. When the rope snapped his neck, he went through the motions of drawing his pistol and firing six times. Those are conditioned reflexes. Maybe your examples are the same?"

"No, no." he said then in a softer tone continued. "Several brilliant doctors studied the aspects of life and death. Many concentrated on the brain. You know, there are hundreds of preserved brains in Germany. In Hamburg alone there are over 400. Their research confirmed my hypothesis."

"Hamburg Germany?" I asked.

"Yes, of course Germany. I've seen them. They're in formaldehyde jars."

I replied, "If they are in formaldehyde they wouldn't help you."

"No, that's right, but it is an small indication of the extent of brain research."

I asked, "Who are these great Doctors?"

"I didn't say great. I said brilliant, even though you might say some of them were great."

"I stand corrected." I said.

"Well, to start with there was, "The Angel Of Death," Josef Mengele. He was probably the most famous of them all. Then there were numerous others. Those, I am the most familiar with includes. Doctors, Percy Treite, L. Hardt, and Dr. Hintermayer."

I said, "Those sound like German doctors involved in the holocaust. Unless you're Dorian Gray, all but Mengels, died before you were born."

He laughed and said. "Right you are. That's a good one. I'm back to thinking you're smart. They were found to be war criminals. Hardt and Treite committed suicide, Hintermayer, I believe was executed. Mengele was a close friend of my father. He died a natural death in 1978, that is, if you call drowning a natural death."

"Was Mengeles death an accident?"

He replied, "I believe the jury is still out. It has been confirmed he died and death was by drowning. He certainly had enough enemies. A lot of them would have been glad to help him drown."

"If all these doctors are dead, how did they assist in your research?"

'Good question, I'm proud of you." He said, then laughed and continued. "Mengeles was a genius. In 1944 there was a landing of troops that changed everything. Do you know anything about that event?"

"Yes, it was June 6th. They landed at Normandy."

"Yeah, that was it. Well, Doctor Mengele and others felt the war was lost. They gathered all their research papers and smuggled the files to Argentina. Most of them were afraid of a war crimes tribunal. They sent their papers, but deleted all references to their names. Those papers were stored in a lab near the Argentina/Bolivia border. I was given access to them by my father and Doctor Mengeles."

"Very interesting." I said, then added, "I guess you learned from their experiments."

"You had better believe it. Hell, I learned more than I could in a hundred years of medical school."

"How did they get all the papers out of Germany?"

"I guess it wasn't easy. Doctor Mengeles had friends in high places. They weren't all doctors. He and my father talked a lot about SS officers. One they mentioned often was a Alphons Klein. He was a big help in organizing everything. He failed to get out and was sentenced to hang. Somehow he had it changed and he was shot. There is some belief of military officers that shooting is honorable."

I nodded and said. "I've heard they feel it's a disgrace to die by hanging."

"Well, they do say, live by the gun, die by the gun. He wasn't involved in shipping things to other countries. My father had contacts and being English he had a greater opportunity to travel. It wasn't just paper either. There was tons of money moved."

"Oh yes, money. Is that how you financed this luxurious accommodations?"

Suddenly there was the sounds of chairs violently being slammed around. Abel's voice seemed distant from the microphone as he yelled. "Stop that, You son-of-a-bitching freaks. Get the hell out of here." Then the sound of breaking furniture drowned out the words of several voices. All the commotion was interrupted by a gun shot, then silence, as the microphone went dead.

"God, I hope the scores, Freaks one, Cutter zero." I realized I had spoken out loud. Shaking my head I quietly resumed my squatting position against the wall and waited.

# CHAPTER THIRTY NINE

The silence was agonizing as I waited. My emotions were mixed and confusing. I didn't know if I wanted to hear Cutters voice or not. Maybe some other voice would be encouraging. The best scenario would be if a door opened and I could get out of here.

Abel's voice suddenly filled the tank, then became softer as he spoke. "Sorry, about the rude interruption. The cord pulled out and I needed to adjust the volume."

I asked, "What was all the noise?"

"Nothing important. Now where were we?"

I said. "Money, you said you have money."

He laughed and replied. "I don't believe I said that, but I do have adequate amounts. I've obtained the numbers of several large bank accounts. Many, who believed the war was lost, squirreled money out of Germany. They stash it in numbered accounts in several countries. The numbers were fortunately included with the research papers. Then as fate would have it, for one reason or another, the depositors couldn't recover their nest eggs."

"And you lucked out," I said.

"Big time and I'm not a bit sorry." He hesitated and continued. "My father was English and I have a British passport. As well as several others. It makes it easy to travel, So, you see the money being scattered around hasn't been a problem. Hell I've even gotten money out of German banks."

I said, "Since you are so damn rich, how about paying for my two calves you slaughtered."

He laughed and replied. "Lets see, beef is what, a quarter a pound. That would be butchered out, or maybe like you cowboys say, twenty dollars a head."

I said, "You have been watching too many old Westerns. Those were two young purebred Red Angus calves. One heifer and one bull. In other words, breeding stock, not beef."

"Oh, really. I'm a vegetarian so I don't know much about beef. They looked like any other cows to me."

I said, "Apparently you don't deny you butchered them. Please tell me why?"

I could hear him breathing as he hesitated before answering. "Well, for one thing, I wanted to entice you to come to me. I butchered the Haystack cows and felt you might respond if I butchered yours. I called in a tip to your Sheriff to call Dr. Healum, then called Healum to give him a lead. He did and you bit."

"It seems like there should be more to it, than that."

He replied, "There is, I wanted the body parts and especially the blood. Haystacks were handy and I needed to send a warning to Johanna. Yours were a message and an opportunity to get more organs and blood."

I said, "You mean, placing them nose to nose was a message?"

He laughed and said. "Yeah, clever huh, Two dead redheads, one female and one male, nose to nose. Like you and Lorraine."

"I see, I'm beginning to understand. One thing, I don't understand is how you placed them without tracks."

"Oh, that's easy. We butchered them and drained the blood in my lab. It's in the back of a semi trailer. Then I have a large air supported craft that is wind driven. It was built for me in Argentina, It's capable of easily carrying two tons in flight. We load up the dead cows and drop them wherever we want. It doesn't make much noise, in fact you can barely hear it. Animals are different and they hear the noise. Dogs and coyotes bark and howl like hell. Then for some reason, horses seem to go crazy."

"Okay, that explains a lot. I still don't understand, if you don't eat meat why do you want cow blood and entrails?"

He sighed and said, "Ah Dutch, you're so far behind the times, I can't believe it. Man, you know those three blonde whores of Bella's."

"Yes, what about them?"

"Well, I wanted their hair to begin with. Then there was a bonus. Their brains are still alive in my lab. I told you the brain will live as long as it gets oxygen. Well, we live in a wonderful age. We can make a blood substitute by chemically stabilizing cross-linked cow hemoglobin in a saline solution I have a continuous flow of this into the brains and it works."

I remarked, "Wow, that's amazing. Can you explain it to me?"

He said, "It's only the beginning. There are other substitutes, but they require human hemoglobin as a part of the formula."

I asked, "Whole blood has a shelf life, how does the cow substitutive blood compare?"

He answered, "Better, a lot better. three years, compared to less than two months."

"That's great, and you know how to develop it?"

He hesitated, then said, "Yes, but I'm limited as to supply. It's easier to buy what I need. It has been developed and approved for use in South Africa. We have a contact there who can furnish enough for now. Eventually I'll be able to develop my own. Until then, they ship it to my supplier in Argentina, who ships it to me. It comes by air freight, ready to use. Unlike human blood it doesn't need refrigeration."

I said. "In South Africa they would be using it for living breathing patients. The necessary oxygen would come from their lungs. How do you supply the oxygen to the brains?"

"Good question," he said, hesitated then continued. "As I understand the cells pick up the oxygen the same as red blood cells. I pipe in a steady eight liters of oxygen into the fluid as it enters the brain. It works and the brain lives."

I said, "That explains the shipment of oxygen."

"Just part of it. I used some to keep you alive."

"I guess, I appreciate that," I said, and then asked. "Cow blood types, as I recall are B, and J. Humans. of course have types A, B, AB and O. Is this a problem?

"No problem with the finalized solution. Did you know they now can convert donated type A, B, or AB, blood into O, the universal blood type. That means it can be given to anyone."

"Wow, you are dazzling me with your knowledge, Dr. Cutter. You have explained the blood, but why the body parts?"

He replied, "Oh about that. Well, if I'm going to create cow blood, I need my own cows. I mean I can't keep looking for cows to butcher. I can, with the organs, I have, clone my own. Then I would have an endless supply. I wouldn't even have to kill them. I would merely take the blood as I needed it. It would be like people donating blood." He hesitated then said. "I guess I should let you in on the next step. You'll be astonished."

He didn't continue until I impatiently asked. "How are you going to astound me?"

He hesitated for what seemed to be minutes then said. "Okay, I want to explain this so you can understand. I guess since you are a cowboy you know cows. Well, Angus cows have a gestation period of 281 days. Others differ a few days. Some more some less. By the way what is a Hereford?"

I answered, It's a different breed of beef cattle. They're red and white."

"No matter," he said, and then added, "Angus are better, I guess."

I said. "It's just a matter of preference."

"Yeah, well Hereford's gestation period is 285 days. Not much difference, but I'll stick with the Angus."

"Are you raising beef?"

He quickly answered. "Hell no. Damn it, you're not paying attention. Now listen, Women take 280 days. Get the picture?"

I answered, "The picture I'm getting is scary as Hell. Now, please explain exactly what you're talking about."

He said, "I can see I will have to give you the cloning course 101. First, in order to clone, you need eggs. Girls have eggs. Second, contrary to popular belief, clones do not climb out of test tubes. They have to be developed in the womb. Girls have wombs. I take the oocyte, or unfertilized eggs, from the female donor. Then her nucleus is sucked out of the egg and replaced with the subjects nucleus that is to be cloned. This simulates a fertilized egg, i.e. zygote. Then it is inserted into the womb of a chosen female for the normal pregnancy development." He hesitated, then deeply sighed, before continuing. "Well, the whores are good, but, there aren't enough of them. They can furnish eggs on a steady basis. Providing they aren't pregnant or surrogate mothers. If you remember the egg factory shuts down when pregnancy sets in. It comes down to whores have eggs, cows don't have usable eggs but they can be surrogates. Now, have you figured it out?"

I replied, "Yeah, it you are going to create huge numbers of clones you need a large supply of egg donors and surrogates. That's where Bella fits in, right'?"

"Right, but I need hundreds. Now that we can modify cows blood and make it compatible with humans, the rest is simple. We can modify the human clones to be compatible to cows. This area around here is covered with good Angus cows. I can use them to make numerous clones. This is why I came here to build my laboratory."

I said, "I thought they have lots of cattle in Argentina."

He replied, "They do and they also have gaucho's who hold court at the nearest tree. I would be dangling from a limb if they caught me messing with one of their cows.

"That might happen here. Especially it the right cowboy catches you. Anyway, I don't believe it will work and even if it did, no rancher will risk his herd for anything so ridiculous."

"That is the beauty of it." He laughingly replied then added, "Many of your herd are already impregnated. Haystack's entire herd is involved. See, I don't need their permission. I also have a small herd of my own. I use them to study and so far so good."

I started to speak when I heard a female voice. It was soft and I couldn't make out the words. I did hear Abel yell, "Shut up," before a click and then all was quiet.

# CHAPTER FORTY

I had no idea how long I'd slept. My arms were still crossed over my knees. They were both numb from cradling my head. I started to move, but stopped as there was a noise. I'd heard it before, but not so distinct. I wondered if I was hallucinating. I didn't know why I'd slept. I didn't feel like I had been drugged. I was still in my adopted squat against the wall. I studied the noise and recognized it as cats. Yeah, lots of cats. The microphone was on and the volume up. When he plugged it back in he hadn't adjusted it to the usual level. Now, I wasn't sure. Maybe the female voice had just been a cat.

Flattery seems to be working to some small degree. Cutter wouldn't leave the mike on for my benefit. No, and he certainly is not interested in my entertainment. I almost laughed, but my thoughts concluded as he yelled. "Who in the hell has been playing with this mike." Then there was the familiar click off.

I raised my head and wiped the slobber from my lips. I was amazed there was enough fluid in my system to slobber. I must have been in a deep sleep with my mouth open.

My activity wasn't unnoticed and the cold shower commenced. I cupped my hands to catch the water and eagerly drank. Once, I had my fill I stood allowing the flow to caress my body. I wondered if I had a fever since the cold water felt damn good. When it was apparent I was enjoying myself the shower ceased. I ran my hands through my hair as Cutter asked, "Feels good, huh?"

I hadn't heard the click of the mike and his voice startled me. I shook the water from my hands and asked, "So, what's with the cats?"

He asked, "What cats?"

I didn't answer and after a brief silence, He continued. "So, you heard my pet cat. What's the problem. I know you're not the type to object to a little pussy hanging around."

I said, "I'm not talking about pussy or a cat. What I heard was a lot of cats. Are you also cloning cats?"

He laughed and replied. "Come on Dutch, where's your sense of humor. The old Dutch, I knew, would have come back with something like, 'If you're cloning pussy, count me in. You disappoint me. In fact you're becoming a terrible drag."

I said, "If I'm such a drag, why not let me out of here?"

He said, "Now, that's funny, real funny." he hesitated then continued, "No, I'm not cloning cats. What I hear, there are too many cats in the world anyway. So why clone them?"

I asked, "If not cloning, what are you doing?"

He answered, "I didn't say I wasn't cloning. I just said I wasn't cloning cats."

I noisily exhaled and said. "You don't strike me as the type who has set out to save cats. I, also, don't believe you want to save the world and kill all cats. So, please tell me what is it with the cats?"

There was an uncomfortable minute of silence then he spoke.

"Okay, I'll give you a crash course in catology." He hesitated and I asked, "Catology, what the hell is catology?"

He laughed then said, "If you'll shut up, I'll tell you."

"Okay, okay, I'm listening." I said.

He sighed then continued. "Acromegaly, in cats is caused by a growth-hormone secreting tumor of the anterior-pituitary. It seems to be more prevalent in the males, but it exists in some females It causes the cat to have abnormal growth. Unfortunately it occurs in older cats and is slow to develop. I've developed a procedure to speed up the process. In addition, by combining the secretion of several cats, I can inject it directly into the pituitary. You recall that the pituitary can be accessed for injection up through the nostrils. This allows me to create one super cat. Have you ever seen a two hundred pound house cat?"

"No."

"Well, I have one, a female. You know I always accept a challenge and we had a female hanging around. So I used her. She's big, very strong and is no longer a pussy cat. In fact she's mean as hell."

I mumbled, "I hope she kills you."

He continued, "In answer to your unasked question, she hates everybody. You do believe me, that I have such a cat. Don't you?"

"I don't know," I replied, hesitated, then continued. "I believe you probably made up the word catology, I don't know about the cat."

"I might have made up the word, but the cat is real. If I didn't have other plans for you, I'd drop her in there. I might do it anyway. Damn, that would be great entertainment."

I wiped the water from my shoulders, then said. "It occurs to me, if you can make a super cat, someone can make a super mouse."

There was silence as I ran both hands several times through my hair. Then said, "Yeah, a super mouse that can kick your cats ass."

He said, "You know Dutch, you would have more hair if you would quit stuffing it down the drain." The resounding click ended my attempt to respond.

# CHAPTER FORTY ONE

I wondered it my head ache was subsiding or maybe I was just adjusting to it. Either way was fine since it was not as severe as before. That could be bad, since it might convince Cutter to operate.

The quiet gave me a chance to think. To start with, what do I know about cats? Not much, they're classified as being felines. There are two or three around the barn at the ranch. They keep the mouse and rat population in check. I suspect, Mary may slip them a saucer of milk, once in a while. Sport gives them a chase every so often. As far as I know he never caught one. I'm sure he wouldn't want to catch a two hundred pounder. For that matter, neither would I. I would be willing to give, such a cat, a gallon of milk. Yeah, if I had milk. Maybe Cutter's lying, but I did hear cats. I guess it's possible that he does have a cat with an overactive pituitary.

It's been a long time since I gave any thought to the pituitary gland. I remember it lies just below the brain, between the temporal lobes of the two cerebral hemispheres. As I recall it has two parts. The larger anterior lobe secretes hormones into the blood stream. One of the secreted hormones controls growth. I know humans have such a gland and I guess all mammals are the same. If I believe Cutter, cats have the pituitary and it reacts the same as in humans.

Cutter's voice broke my concentration as he said. "You seem to be in deep thought, Dutch."

I answered, "I am, I was wondering if you could create the same kind of growth in a person?"

He said, "I can, but some times, it just happens."

I shook my head and replied. "Really?"

He said, "Yeah, you probably knew the most famous of them all. André the Giant?"

"I've heard of him. I believe he's dead, isn't he?"

He replied, "Yes, he died in 1993. He was born in 1946, too late for Hitler's experiments. Well, anyway, he suffered from acromegaly. He grew to seven foot, four inches tall and weighed five hundred pounds. He was strong as a gorilla and very agile. In fact he was a professional wrestler for most of his adult life."

"I remember, he came from France and called himself, The Eighth Wonder of the World. He also went Hollywood and was in movies and TV."

He said, "That was him and he was a victim of the acromegaly or gigantism disease. They're caused by the same disorder. His just happened. I can make it happen."

I said, "And, you're making it happen in clones?"

He laughed and said. "Yes, in fact, you met one of my subjects at Haystacks. What did you think of him?"

"Big, damn big, very impressive."

He said, "Good observation. I have the potential of several more. Right now there are only sixty in various stages of development."

I said, "You mean different ages?"

"Of course," he replied, hesitated, then continued. "They are born the same way as any baby and then, they grow. My father started the program and the older ones are the result of his successful endeavors. The younger ones are mine."

"Do they all have acromegaly?"

He replied, "Yes, and I give them an extra boost. First you have to know, acromegaly is not hereditary. The exception is in clones, If you only clone from infested tissue and cells it will appear in the new clones. I have sophisticated the process and I can use tissue and cells from clones to make new clones. Then I inject the new clones with both growth hormones and muscle building steroids. I continue the treatments and the end result is supermen. It's like Hitler's plan, only he was doing it by breeding, I do it by cloning."

"Hitler's way sounds like more fun," I said.

"True, but his way required using too many people. My way is best."

I asked, "All males?"

He answered, "For right now, but soon, I may create females. You know I've observed that the ugliest female is still more attractive than the best looking male, If I make females, and they breed, no telling what will happen."

"Maybe, I will order a couple, if you clone the right females."

He said, "Wait until Bella hears this. You know, she's working hard at making a deal. The problem is, she wants your freedom in exchange for her girls."

"She's the one I want cloned." I hesitated then asked, "Are you going to clone her girls?"

"No damn it, I want their eggs. Some of them can be surrogates, but I need eggs. You're not paying attention. I want eggs."

I said, "If cows can be surrogates, use chickens for eggs. Yeah, get a bunch of chickens?"

"Don't try to be a smart ass. Just try to keep a scientific mind."

"Sorry, I guess you control the clone's sex, by only cloning males. You once said you were going to put me in a dress. What was that all about?"

"Yeah, well, don't worry about it. I once had the idea of trading your brain for Bella's and giving her yours. I wanted to see how you two would react to each other. Bella has made herself too valuable to experiment with, so that's off."

I sighed and said. "That's a relief, I don't have the legs for a dress. Bella wouldn't be happy in my body. I don't understand the connection between cloning and brains. What am I missing?"

"Bella's company for one thing." He said and then laughed."

I didn't respond and he continued. "Well, clones are born like people. They don't know anything about anything. Knowledge comes from exposure and they have to experience in order to learn. I intend to give them lots of experience when they are three. When a baby is born the skull bones are linked by unossified fibrous membrane called fontanels. These gradually disappear and the skull becomes solid. This process is complete in about eighteen months. Then due to my control of the accelerated growth the skull can accommodate an adult brain by age three. Then a strange thing happens. The inside of the skull remains the same in people with acromegaly. The outside increases and matches their growth. So even though the head seems large the brain cavity remains a normal size. This allows me to give a three year old a life time of knowledge to build on. I will not only have supermen, but they will be smart. I intend to start harvesting only males with the highest intelligence. My procedure still needs to be proved and that's where you come in."

I said, "For a couple of seconds there, I was flattered. You say the clones are born like people. Don't you believe they're human?"

He replied, "Human, hell no, they're freaks. I'm not like Frankenstein, I don't love my monsters. They do what I tell them to do. I created them and I can destroy them. That's all they need to know."

I said, "If you give them knowledge they will start to think for themselves."

He replied, "I've considered that, and I will only give brains to a select few. Only those who are totally dedicated to me will get the knowledge."

I asked, "How can you make that decision when they're only three years old?"

"I will keep them secluded and totally dependent on me. It has been shown many times if you deprived them of everything, then give just the necessities they will worship you."

"I just wonder how you can make it work. You call the women sex machines and incubators. The clones you refer to as freaks and monsters. I always believe you have to give respect to get respect. You don't seem to respect anybody, yet you expect everyone to respect you. I suppose you're going to say your cat loves you."

He said, "She does and catology is a real word, smart ass."

The now familiar click signaled the end of our conversation.

# CHAPTER FORTY TWO

Damn, well, so much for flattery. I stood quietly and contemplated my mistake. Suddenly the chamber went black. It was the first time I'd been without light since my confinement. I casually inched backwards while feeling for the wall. There was a brief flash of light and then a return to darkness. I felt the cold metal and pushed my back tightly against it's firmness. I sensed another presence and cursed the fact I might no longer be alone. I braced myself, waiting for the unexpected. I tried to control my breathing, but could hear my heart pounding. My instincts kicked in and I felt there was a danger. My breathing and heart beat could be detected by whatever was sharing the space with me.

The darkness and silence seemed endless as I waited for the unknown. Then simultaneously, the click of the microphone accompanied the return of the lights. I rubbed my eyes seeking focus as Cutter said. "Good morning, Dutch. Say hello to my pussy cat."

I blinked as the shape took form. Involuntarily I pushed harder against the wall. Standing just inches from me was a huge black and white cat. There was laughter and Cutter said, "Don't worry Dutch. The tank is round, so she can't corner you." This was followed by more laughter, punctuated by comments of "Sick um, Pussy, sick um."

Neither the cat or I moved as we stayed transfixed by the others presence.

Cutters voice continued as he said. "You'll notice it's a black cat with a white neck and chest. It's a long haired feline with four white paws. It looks like she's wearing a tuxedo, You know, with white tie and gloves. Neat, huh? I understand she's called a tuxedo cat. I hope she doesn't get blood on her white chest and paws." He hesitated, laughed, then continued. "I told you she was two hundred pounds. Well if you pull out enough of her long hair, she might weigh, maybe, one ninety. I'd say it's about even, and you would have a fair fight." There was more laughter, as he said. "I'm going to shut off the microphone. I can't stand screaming."

If I move, I'm prey, If I stand still, I'm dead. I wish I'd paid more attention to the ranch cats. Hell, better than that, I'd trade my ranch for a bucket of milk. Maybe even a can of sardines right now. They can smell fear, so don't show fear. A neat trick under the circumstances. Be calm, she's just an animal and you can handle animals. Yeah, but she is two hundred pounds of unpredictable muscle. Don't forget she's an attitude with teeth and claws. So far she hasn't moved. Is that good or bad? Maybe she's afraid of me. This is my space and she may feel insecure. Ah, yes, dream on and die confused. Wait, cats are hunters and they catch and kill prey. If she doesn't recognize me as prey maybe I'm safe. They're territorial and will fight for their space. This is my space, She has probably never been here before. Then there is the worst reason why animals attack. They feel trapped and threatened. In this case we're both trapped. I hope she doesn't believe it's my fault, or that I have the key.

Let's see what her reaction would be if I moved. First I extended the right hand slowly toward her. Was that a purr or a growl? It wasn't a hiss. I thought cats only hissed. Whatever it was, it was a defensive threat. She did rear backwards as to bolt. No, maybe she was just preparing to pounce. Wait, think before moving again. She's a two hundred pound cat. Cutter has loaded her with growth hormones and steroids. The hormones probably wouldn't alter her personality. Steroids, on the other hand, are probably synthetic derivatives of testosterone. That would make her more aggressive. I saw a lion tamer once and he had a whip and a chair. I only have brains and nerve. They both might fail me. Cutter didn't say he did anything to her brain. No transplant or anything. Maybe she was still mentally a ten pound cat. I slowly squatted down to where I didn't appear as a threat.

The purr was now real. There is nothing more relaxing than a cat stretched out with her eyes closed. This is probably as close as she will come. I'm willing to wait for friendship on her terms. The purr, however was getting louder, and I hoped she didn't meow. In this tank it would reverberate and break my eardrums. The purring seemed hypnotic and I felt my eyelids getting heavy. I crossed my arms over my knees, put down my head, and allowed my eyes to close.

# CHAPTER FORTY THREE

Cutter's voice at first seemed far away, It rapidly got louder and seemed closer. I snapped awake as he yelled. "Wake up, wake up, you son-of-a-bitch. What did you do to Pussy?" I looked around without speaking, while my eyes focused. The cat was gone. Cutter yelled again, "What did you do to my big Pussy?"

My mouth was dry as I replied. "I hope no one is listening to this conversation." He didn't respond and I asked. "Nitrous oxide again?"

"Yes, damn it, this is serious. Pussy won't wake up. What can I do?"

I asked, "Who are we talking about? If it's the cat, why do you keep calling her Pussy?"

He said, "Damn it, that's her name. The clones named her. I wanted Kitty, but they think all cats are Pussy. She won't wake up. What can I do?"

I replied, "You're the one with Doctor before your name, why ask me?"

He said, "Don't get smart. You're the one who knows animals."

I replied, "Yeah, well, I never put one to sleep with nitrous oxide. Besides why should I care one way or another?"

His voice became softer as he said. "Let me tell you, why you should care. I told them Pussy was fine, until she was in with you. If she dies they're going to blame you. Right now, I have a five hundred pound clone holding her and crying like a baby. Two others are blubbering and several more have tears running down their cheeks. I told them cats have nine lives. They want to know which one she has now. Dutch I'm scared. I don't know what they will do. Hans wants to come into your chamber and tear you apart. This is the first time I've seen them exhibit any emotion."

I said, "Okay, she has an overdose of an anesthetic. I only know what to try. First, put a mask on her and make her breathe pure oxygen. Keep it going at eight liters. Second, take a ten cc syringe. Fill it with adrenalin and slowly inject it intravenously. Stop the injection, if she starts to respond."

'Good, good," he said, then added. "I hope I have adrenalin."

I said, "You should have plenty. You're the one who has been hijacking trucks carrying medical supplies. Look for it as adrenalin, adrenaline or epinephrine."

He left the microphone open and I could hear excited voices. At least two were female. I couldn't make out any of the words. I wondered if they might be Bella and Johanna."

The microphone clicked off, then on, as Cutter said. "Pussy is awake. She staggers and falls when she walks, but she's alive."

I said, "That's good news. I'm always glad to hear when an animal beats the odds."

He sounded relieved as he said. "Yeah, I did have everything I needed. I guess those clones had me so upset I wasn't thinking right. For one thing, can you believe they cried? Hell, I didn't believe they had any emotions."

I said, "It seems you were trying to create robots. Now you know clones are people. They walk, they talk, and they feel pain. It seems they can think for themselves. They might even be wondering why there aren't any girls to play with."

Cutter was quiet for several seconds then said. "I've thought about that and I'm ready to start cloning females. This will help me speed up my plans. They will breed and I will have more clones to work with."

I replied, "One big problem. If they breed their children will not be clones. The male will have one set of DNA and the female another. Their children will share both of their genes. Just like people reproduce today. You'd be back to square one."

"Damn you Dutch. How did you figure that out."

"I raise stock and breeding animals is pretty much the same as humans. We're all mammals" I hesitated, then continued. "I thought I heard female voices."

He laughed and said, "You did, I had Bella and Johanna helping me. I thought their maternal instincts might save Pussy's life. I had to promise, if you helped, I would turn you loose. You won't be surprised to know, I lied. The clones had to lock both of them up, they were so mad."

I said, "You're right, I'm not surprised. I would be surprised if you ever kept your word."

He sharply said. "Don't push me, Dutch. You and Bella are back on track for a brain switch." He coughed and added, "And it will be soon."

The microphone clicked off.

# CHAPTER FORTY FOUR

I resumed to my position of suspended animation and wondered, what's next? Cutter seems to be losing touch with reality. Even if he creates female clones they need several years before being capable of child bearing. I seem to recall hearing something about clones, Some scientist predicted they would be like mules. Therefore not capable of reproduction. If that's true, maybe they wouldn't feel testicle pain. That's ridiculous, if they have balls they can feel pain. I wonder if a solid kick in the groin would work. They are too tall for a knee and a foot would have to be over the head like a football punt. That means it would take a fourth and twenty desperation kick to the groin to bring them down. I don't know much about clones. I do know about mules. If you're crazy enough to try to kick a mule in the balls, you would find your head in the next county. Hell, he'd kick you hard enough, the magpie's would feast on your brains in the three adjacent counties.

I sure would like to kick that Sunday punch bastard in the nuts. Yeah, Hans, I'd kick him hard enough to drive his balls up into his tonsils. He'd look like a squirrel with his jowls full of walnuts. Then maybe he'd be like a mule. A good solid kick could end all his breeding capabilities. It would be worth a try. It might be the only chance I'd have. It could equalize the situation. Since I never saw him, how would I know it we meet. Hell Cutter said he has sixty of them. They probably all look alike.. Damn, I wish I had my boots.

My thoughts were interrupted by a piercing screech of shearing sheet medal. I looked up and had to jump out of the way of falling lights. Darkness set in and then a large hole appeared in the ceiling. The only light came through a gaping hole.

I pushed my back against the wall as a huge hulk of a clone wiggled through the jagged edges. He grabbed a protruding steel bar, lowering himself as it bent with his weight. His legs were swaying erratically as he swung toward the floor. He dropped the final four feet and stood facing me. He smiled and said something in a language I didn't understand.

Hello Hans, I thought, and quickly kicked high and hard catching him between the legs. He moaned and sank to his knees. He started gasping, while clutching his crotch with both hands. I followed my advantage by using my right fist to punch him in the throat. I was about to use my fingers to poke his eyes when Bella yelled. "Dutch, stop it. Damn it, stop it. I sent him down there to see if he could lift you high enough to get out. Now I think you've killed him."

"I didn't kill him," I said, and watched as he folded to the floor. He was holding his crotch with one hand and his throat with the other. He started retching and then violently emptied his stomach. I looked up and said, "He tore the roof off like he was opening a christmas present."

Bella said, "Yes, it was a locked door. I asked him if he could break the lock?"

I said, "I don't believe he broke the lock. He just removed the ceiling. Throw me a rope or something."

Bella said, "We're looking for a ladder, but would a rope do?"

"Yes," I said, and looked toward the still suffering hulk on the floor. I quickly added, "Please hurry, before he regains his composure. I don't want to have to hurt him again."

She laughed and asked. "Is that the real reason? You don't want to hurt him again?"

I answered, "Yes, of course. We'll talk about it later. Please get me a rope or something. And hurry, like right now."

I heard two women laughing as a rope snaked it's way through the ceiling hole. I grabbed the end and pulled hard. It was a quarter inch soft twist rope secured to something outside of my sight. I was concerned it might not hold my weight. I heard moaning from my isolated companion and started the climb. It had to be hand over hand since the rope was too small to grasp with my legs. As I neared the opening electrical wires were sparking and partially blocking my path. My motion caused the rope to sway making the wires swing into each other. The instant result was arcing flashes. Each spark was accompanied by a sharp crackiong noise. It reminded me of the fly zapper in my barn. Yeah, a fly hits it and zap, a dead fly. I wanted freedom, not a quick death from electrocution. Still it might be less painful than a rematch with a mad injured clone. This thought was enough incentive to make carefully maneuvering through the wires worthwhile. I was near the opening, when I noticed the rope was sawing itself on the ragged edge of the torn metal. It was only a three strand rope and one strand was already separated. I moved upwards, just as the second strand severed with a snap. I grabbed a light support bar and used it to relieve part of my weight. This allowed me to inch my way toward the opening. My movement was cautiously slow when suddenly the rope below me snapped tight. I glanced down and saw the clone starting to climb. I swung over through a barrage of sparks and grabbed a second support bar. He was just below me when the rope gave way. He fell back to the floor, landing flush on his back. I heard a loud whoosh as the air left his lungs. The electrical sparks illuminated the opening and I managed to reach a non jagged edge. I pulled myself up and out, surprised to find the opening, level with a cement floor.

I was amazed how much strength I had lost during my confinement Hell, I didn't seem to have any endurance left. I was face down, trying to catch my breath. A pair of hands rubbed my neck and across my shoulders. I tried to push up as Bella asked, "Are you okay, Dutch?"

I rolled over and looked into the tear stained face of Bella. She was on her knees and without speaking, bent down and kissed me. I managed to control my shock at seeing her head had been shaved. That son-of-a-bitch had really prepared her for brain surgery. In spite of that, she looked damn good. Even her overalls, several sizes to big for her, failed to distract from her beauty. I noticed Johanna standing just behind her with tears running down her cheeks. I pulled myself up on one elbow and wrapped my other arm around Bella. I looked toward Johanna and asked, "What are you two crying about?" Then my eyes became moist.

# CHAPTER FORTY FIVE

Bella, glanced up and pushed back. I followed her eyes and observed we were now surrounded by clones. Their faces were expressionless and devoid of any emotion. They were inching forward, each stretching his neck to seek a closer look. Johanna said something in a loud voice. I didn't understand the words, but the clones stopped, then started backing away. Their expression was now one of surprise.

I asked, "What did she say?"

Bella replied, "I don't know. It was in Italian."

I asked, "Johanna speaks Italian?"

Bella said, "Yes, and I don't understand a word. I only speak English and German."

I stood, looked around, then asked, "Where's Cutter?"

Bella took my arm and pulled herself up. She tossed her head in a motion that would have arranged her hair. Then smiled as she realized the futilely of her action. She spoke in a low voice as she asked, "Don't it surprise you, that I speak German?"

I shook my head and replied, "Nothing surprises me right now." I hesitated and then continued. "How in the world did you swing these monsters over to your side against Cutter?"

She and Johanna both laughed and then Bella answered. "Well, we told them, Cutter hurt Pussy and you saved her. They liked that. Then, they never have been around women before. Now they think we're pretty cute."

Johanna chimed in and remarked, "They don't know why, they think we're cute, but they all agree."

Bella added, "Actually, they really changed when Cutter had my head shaved. He ordered one of the clones to do the job. The poor fellow tried to refuse and Cutter had one of his close henchman beat him with a whip. I tried to comfort him, but he cried as he cut each strand of my hair. The rest of the clones became restless and Cutter ordered his so called officers, to shoot any of them who complained."

Johanna said. "That might of helped, but I still say it was because we're cute."

I said, "I can't argue with that, Now, where in the hell is Cutter?"

Bella pointed to a staircase and said. "Over there, is his office, but you're too late. He's gone."

There was broken glass scattered down the stairs, A shattered door was teetering on the top rail. I glanced at Bella as Johanna said. "The door was locked."

Bella giggled and added, "We have friends who don't like locked doors."

I nodded and started toward the stairs as Bella grabbed my arm. She shook her head, "No," and whispered. "You II cut your feet on the glass."

"Yeah, thanks, but where did Cutter go?"

Bella looked at Johanna and Johanna said. "He and six of his officers took off about an hour ago. They were in one big hurry and they all were carrying bags."

Bella nodded and said, "Yeah, one Hell of a hurry. We heard yelling, to get on, Then it sounded like the wind was blowing. It didn't last long and then everything was quiet. I think it was a wind plane. Cutter told us he had one. Anyway they're gone."

I looked up at the cluttered stairwell and asked. "Who broke into the office and made that mess?"

They both giggled and Bella said. "We had a couple of our friends open it up. We wanted to see what was in there. We hoped to find a phone or something. We did find where a radio had been. Now it's gone, a couple of wires are all that's left. It was torn from the wall."

I said, "Maybe he got a message?"

Bella replied, "Maybe. For sure, something happened. I know they were listening to police calls. We did,"

She stopped speaking as doors on three sides of the building crashed inward. Each was accompanied by the blinding flash and explosion of Flash, Bang, grenades. Every entry was simultaneously filled with multiple well armed officers. They were dressed for combat, but the uniforms were significantly different. Several identifying different agencies.

Most of the clones started screaming and cowered together in a tight mass of humanity.

Johanna and Bella were shouting in different languages to stop. It appeared to me that the organized confusion was out of control. I moved toward the nearest officer, but stopped when a voice from behind me asked. "Dutch, are you all right?"

I turned to find the Sheriff approaching. I nodded, and added, "Yeah, can you calm this situation down?" Before he could answer, I noticed Captain Savage moving toward the crowd. I could tell how many days he had worn the same shirt from the sweat rings on his back. I thought this was a hell of a time to notice his lack of a clean shirt. Then, again maybe he had worked steady. Yeah, probably hadn't had time to change. He hadn't even shaved since I saw him at Maude's. Yeah, true dedication. Even now he's proving his worth. A man in charge and calm, in spite of all Hell breaking loose. A voice blared from a bull horn. It was loud and came from the far wall. The words seemed lost in the confusion, but all action slowed down. I turned to face the Sheriff and said. "Ben, I'm damn glad to see you."

He looked around, nodded, then said. "We found a note on the windshield of a squad car. No one knows where it came from. No one was seen in the area or leaving. It mentioned you, Bella and Johanna. So here we are. Now, What in the Hell are these monsters?"

I laughed, and replied. "They're giant clones,"

He shook his head and asked, "Are they human?"

I said, "Of course. The worst you could say of them, is like Shakespeare's Macduff. They were not from a woman born."

His face wrinkled up in a studious look as he said. "You mean, they came from a test tube?"

"Not quite, they were carried in a women's womb until birth."

He starred at the group for several seconds then said. "The women who carried them, wasn't their mothers, but only incubators."

I nodded as his look turned to understanding. Then I said. "I believe they would be called surrogate mothers."

He started to speak when Bella walked up and said. "Hi Ben, I'm glad you got my note. I sent one of my friends with it two days ago. I was beginning to wonder if maybe you had killed him."

He replied, "I might of, if I'd seen him. Your directions were pretty close. It just took us a while to figure them out." Then he looked at her as if he was seeing her for the first time. In a shocked quiet voice he said, "What happened, you're bald?"

She ignored his comment as if it didn't exist and said. "I had to guess at most of the directions. I only had a vague idea where we were."

Ben said, "I can't take the credit. Hollis's agency knows this country better than I. It was their knowledge that pin pointed your position. You know I haven't slept since Dutch disappeared. Damn you Dutch you never told me what you were going to do."

I glanced at the back of his shirt and noticed a total absence of sweat rings. I asked, "How did you find so much help. Hell, half of these officers are Feds."

"Hollis's bunch is responsible. They have connections in high places."

Johanna was talking to Captain Savage and they both were laughing as they joined us. Savage said. "Damn, this is a gold mine. I have to call the NFL. I can teach this bunch to play football and develop one Hell of a team."

I shook my head and said. "Forget it. None of them can pass the steroid test."

Savage said "You're going to have to explain that to me. I will warn you, it had better be good. If it isn't I will tell Haystack you really did run off with Johanna."

"What in the Hell are you talking about?" I asked.

Ben laughed and said, "Oh, by the way Jim Haystack is home. Johanna is missing, you're missing and he's convinced you ran off with her. To add to his suspicions, his leg wasn't broken. He says you only told him it was, so you could take off with her."

I asked, "His leg wasn't fractured?"

"No, the bullet only nicked the bone. A little surgery and he's home with a big bandage and a limp."

I said, "That's great, How about Bella, does he believe I ran off with them both?"

Ben said, "Well, I was about to believe it, until Jill confessed she was keeping a secret. Damn you Dutch you should have told me the whole story."

I started to agree when an officer ran up and said. "Sheriff, those Deputies you sent up to Haystack's have just called for Homicide. Central wanted you to know and asked if you could call in'?"

Ben looked at me and said. "On the way up here there was a call of a problem at Haystack's. I ordered two of my Deputies to turn around and check it out I haven't heard from them. I'd better fine out what happened?"

I nodded as he started to walk away, but he stopped, turned back toward me, and said. "Dutch, do me a favor. Put on some clothes. Damn you're disgusting."

# CHAPTER FORTY SIX

Johanna was sobbing and muttering, "I want to go home, but I can't. I can't, I can't, damn it I can't." Bella held her and kept repeating, "It will be okay. You'll see, we'll fix everything." They both looked at me for reassurance. I bit my lip and silently cursed my Sir Galihad syndrome. I wanted to hold both of them in my arms. I nodded and only said, "We'll take care of it." Words that for the moment meant nothing. I had no idea what the problem was, I was about to ask when Savage, followed closely by a Clone, arrived with my clothes. He looked at the women, then at me with an expression of confusion. The Clone looked only at the two women and started to weep. I started dressing and said, "Thanks, where did you find them?"

Savage didn't answer and his gaze returned to the two women. He asked, "What the Hell is the matter? You're safe now, what's the problem? Come on talk to me."

I caught the look from Johanna, then Bella and realized they were concerned about Johanna being with a clone child.

Bella started to say, "She is," and then stopped as I shook my head and mouthed, "No."

Bella took a deep breath and continued. "She's upset because her husband thinks she ran oft with Dutch."

I continued to dress and again asked. "Captain, where did you find my clothes?"

Savage, now appeared to be satisfied with Bella's answer. He turned toward me and said. "Oh, yeah. This Clone took me to a hidden trap door that led to a lower floor. There is an entire lab down there. You know test tubes, gas burners and everything. Those were in the main room. There are several smaller rooms and some are refrigerated. They have shelves with containers filled with animal entrails In one area there's what look like brains in glass containers. They are hooked up to tubes and floating in some kind of solution."

Bella blurted out. "My girls and their body guard."

Savage looked surprised and said. "You mean they're real. You know, like from people?"

I nodded, as Bella held Johanna to her breast and joined her in uncontrolled sobbing. Savage shook his head and said. "The solution around them seems to be bubbling. It's weird, I swear I saw one move. Do you think they're alive?"

I said, "They very well may be."

Savage shook his head and said. "Wow, I almost pulled the plug on the machines. It was weird enough, that I wanted it to stop. What do you think would happen if I did unplug them?"

I said, "They would die and you would have committed murder."

Savage looked startled and said. "Murder! How in the Hell could it be murder? They're not people, They're just brains.'

I said, "They're human brains. The medical and legal fields have set the standards, A human is not dead until they're brain dead. I'm sure you have heard that expression. You know when that's determined, people are dead."

Savage said, "Yeah, and when brain dead, they can harvest their organs for transplants. I don't see where that could apply, if there isn't any heart, lungs or body. It doesn't make any sense. I think you are just playing with my brain. Hell it couldn't be murder, could it?"

I said, "I don't know. I'm neither a doctor or a lawyer, and if I was, I still might not know the answer. I do know I wouldn't want to be the one to pull the plug."

Savage was silent as he surveyed the room. He seemed confused then shook his head and said. "No, I wouldn't want any brain deaths on my conscience. Damn it, I wish Ben would get back."

I said, "Yeah, he left here, code three. I could hear the siren screaming and gravel flying as he took off. What was his hurry?"

Savage said, "I don't know. Something big up at Haystack's"

I nodded and said, "It must of been real important. Look, do you know where my truck might be? I would like to get out of here."

He replied, "I'll tell you, if you promise to wait at Maude's. One other thing, take those two weeping females with you. Between them and those crying clones, I've had it. You would think as big and ugly as they are they wouldn't be so emotional."

I replied, "Yeah, that's where Cutter made a big mistake. He forgot they are human and they have human emotions."

Savage said. "Cutter, is that the name of the stupid son-of-a-bitch responsible for this set up?"

I said, "Yeah, Abel Cutter. The jury is still out on whether he's stupid or maybe a genius. I guess only time will tell." Then I mumbled to myself, "Hell yes, an evil genius and win lose or draw, still a son-of-a-bitch."

# CHAPTER FORTY SEVEN

Maude was alone at the cafe counter. She was on the middle stool with her back to the door. We walked in and without looking up she slurred the words, "The joint is closed."

Bella said, "Maude, it's me. Bella."

Maude swung around, half falling from her stool. She tried to squint her eyes into focus. Her elbow bumped a newly emptied wine bottle causing it to fall from the counter, It noisily crashed to the floor, rolled and came to rest under the first booth. She watched until it stopped, then tried to rise.

I moved forward as she fell against me and looked up into my face. She said, "Dutch, oh Dutch am I glad to see you. It's been Hell around here. Bella is missing and there are cops all over the place. You would think that would be good, but it's not. Hell they won't even eat here. They have their own damn kitchen in the parking lot."

I said, "It's okay, Maude. Bella's with me."

She looked at Bella, then Johanna and allowed her eyes to linger on them both. Then she said, "They don't buy a damn thing. They just come in and park in the booths. Oh, then they feel tree to use the rest rooms. I point at the sign saying the rest rooms are for customers only. The bastards only laugh and use them anyway."

She started to sag in my arms and I half pushed and lifted her back onto the stool. She grabbed the front of my shirt with both hands and tried to pull herself up as she said. "You'll find Bella, you can do it. I know you will find her."

I said, "I found her. she's with me."

Maude didn't loosen her grip while pulling me forward. We were face to face as she said, "You find her and tell those cops to get their chuck wagon or what ever it is, off of my parking lot.

I took her wrists and pulled her hands free from my shirt. Bella moved forward, took one arm as Johanna took the other. Bella said, "Come on Maude. We're going to the kitchen. It's coffee time."

They half carried her through the door as Bella kept assuring Maude that she was Bella. Maude insisted she wasn't and kept saying Bella had long hair.

I eagerly checked out the parking lot for the chuck wagon and found it was long gone. It probably moved with the raiding party. Even now it probably was serving officers and hungry clones. Damn, I was hoping for a free meal since my billfold was not with my clothes. I returned to the cafe, poured myself a cup of coffee and grabbed a couple of bags of chips from the rack. I'd confess to my theft before Maude counts the bags and rounds up the usual suspect.

# CHAPTER FORTY EIGHT

I was engrossed in thought as I munched the chips and didn't hear a vehicle drive up. I did hear the door open and looked up as Sheriff Ben walked in. He said," I have been looking for you." I took a swig of coffee, wiped my mouth with a paper napkin and said. "You work fast. I didn't think Maude was sober enough to call." I held out my hands and continued, "I'm guilty, take me away."

He parked his rear end on the stool next to me and said. "What in the Hell are you talking about?"

I laughed and said, "These chips and coffee. I don't have any money. I will have to ask Maude for credit. I did hope it would wait until she sobers up."

Ben nodded and said. "She's still soused, huh. She has been on the bottle for days now. I don't know when she will sober up. She isn't the problem though. What was the bastards name, who ran the lab?"

I said, "Cutter, Abel Cutter."

He said, "Yeah, Cutter. What did he look like?"

"I don't know. All the time he held me I never saw him. He use to have long blond hair, blue eyes and was about my size."

He said, "Well he changed some. Now he's a red head. A recent dye job, but red like yours."

"You saw him. Did you catch him. Where is he?"

Ben smiled and said. "Jim Haystack got him." He hesitated, then took out a wallet from his back pocket and dropped it on the counter.

I reached for it and said. "That' my wallet."

Ben smiled and said. "That's the only identification Cutter had on him. The drivers license says his name was Dutch Evans. I guess it's yours and there is twenty five one hundred dollar bills inside. Then, a couple of ones, a few tens and some twenties. Now you can pay for your own damn chips."

I thumbed through the money and said. "Wow, The son-of-a-bitch was going to be me."

Ben took a couple of chips, nodded as he chewed and said. "Yep, he was on the run and was going to use your identification. He even scratched up the picture on your drivers license. Tried to cover up your nose so he could pass for you. He couldn't do it. Nothing could change that nose. Anyway Haystack stopped him?"

"Wait a minute. Did Haystack think he was stopping me? You said he thought I ran off with Johanna."

He laughed and said, "Naw, he thought he was a space man. By the way, are you sure those clones are human?"

"Yes, they're human. Come on give. What's the story?"

Ben stepped from the stool and walked to the chip rack. He grabbed two bags, threw one to me and opened the other. He resumed his seat and said, "Reach into your fat wallet and drop a ten by the register. Otherwise, I may have to ask how much you had when the clone hit you in the head."

I took out a ten dollar bill and placed it next to the cash register. Ben smiled and continued. "The way I figure it, you got amnesia when the clone hit you, so it wouldn't do me any good to ask."

Ben was enjoying his position of power and was playing it for all it was worth. I said, "You're right, total amnesia. I hope it's not catching and you will remember the story. Damn it, What happened?"

He filled his mouth with chips, chewed, swallowed and brushed the crumbs from his lips Once finished he said. "Well, Haystack was a little upset when he thought you had run off with Johanna. No, that's not quite true. He was mad as Hell. He told me, he didn't know why she left with you. Hell you're uglier then he is. Well, anyway there is one thing he hates more than a wife stealer and that's a coyote. He has an old buckskin horse he calls Buck. Believe me you couldn't spook that horse, with a cannon blast. Anyway just before first light this morning he rode up to the pasture by the cemetery. He intended to take out his life frustrations on a few coyotes. When he started to step down old buck went nuts. Haystack grabbed his rifle from the scabbard and hit the ground. The horse took off and smashed into the cemetery fence. Jim was standing there cursing the day old Buck was born, when a big flying machine came over the ridge. Well, Haystack thought it was a flying saucer from outer space. It came right at him and he fired hitting the pilot. Then the craft just barely missed him as it continued on into the trees. It was still in sight when it crashed and six monsters jumped off the wreckage. They all started running right at Haystack. He emptied his carbine, hitting them all. They were dead when the Deputies I sent up there arrived.

"Was Cutter the pilot?'"

"Yes, Jim got him dead center chest. If Cutter lived, it was just for long enough for him to know he was dying."

I nodded and said. "I shouldn't be happy about that, but I am. What about the Clones?"

"Two head shots, three chest and one stomach. The stomach briefly lived, but died before they could get aid. The Medical Examiner is guessing he bled to death from a ruptured aorta. The others were all dead within seconds."

I said, "It sounds like good shooting and with a good self defense excuse."

Ben took another mouth full of chips, slowly chewed and swallowed, Then said, "Damn good shooting. He was using his lever action 30-30 carbine. I know he's fast and a good shot. We've been hunting together for years and he always prefers that rifle. My self, I want something bigger. When I have to shoot I want to feel the power. Jim told me you prefer the 30-30, something about it being light and easy to handle."

I nodded and said, "That's true and I always believe it's small enough for varmints and large enough for bear."

He said, "He sure proved it was big enough to stop a space invasion."

I said, "Well, six giants, with mayhem on their mind, coming at you. There's no time to make a mistake. I guess Jim, is probably pretty shook up."

"Yeah, but he is settling down with a pint of one hundred proof. I gave it to him. Then told him to drink up and quit shaking. It's hard to believe a man that big and strong could be so shook up. He did make one mistake, I wish he hadn't, since it did create a problem."

I asked, "What problem?"

"Well, Jim really believed he was under attack by aliens from outer space. He got on his phone and called the Air Force. They flew in and tried to take over. I finally convinced some of them to fly up to the lab and join the other feds. I even sent one of my Deputies to show them the way. They were still arguing jurisdiction as they flew off. Hell, to make matters worse, they left four armed Air Policemen behind. They are standing guard. and said they have orders not to let anyone near the Space Ship. I told them I'm the Sheriff and I wanted to check it out. They replied their orders meant especially me. I guess they'll probably take the air craft I don't give a damn if they do or don't.

Hell what would I do with it. We were fortunate to get Cutter out before they arrived. I hope by now they realize we are not dealing with spacemen and the dead bodies are mine."

I said, "So Cutter is dead. Damn, it I don't feel cheated. Oh well, I wonder if there is something to eat in the kitchen, I'm still hungry.?"

Ben said, "Have another bag of chips. You don't want to dig into your bankroll for another ten. I figure we still have a bag apiece coming."

I walked over and grabbed two more bags, threw one to Ben, and said, "You're all heart. Bon appetit."

He open the bag and said. "Thanks, I need to reward your generosity. Cutter had hand guns in the seat beside him. My crew managed to stash them before the Air Force arrived. I believe three of the pistols are yours and one is Bella's. I have them in my truck and you should grab them before the feds ask questions."

I nodded and headed for the door.

# CHAPTER FORTY NINE

Johanna came from the kitchen carrying a tray with two cheeseburgers. In addition to a generous meat patty they had all the trimmings. She placed them in front of us and said. "We gave Maude a shower and put her to bed. Bella thought you might be hungry."

Ben grabbed one and said. "I wish I had known I would have told you to hold the onions."

Johanna shook her head and said, "Shut up and eat. We already had one and they're good. Now we have to clean up the kitchen. It's a mess and not all of it is ours. Why don't you grab a couple of bags of chips from the rack. Burgers go better with chips."

We watch her disappear into the kitchen before Ben said. "I believe she's right. We need chips. I'll grab a couple while you try to find something other than coffee to drink. I mean coffee is okay, but this coffee must of been made last month."

I said, "I think you're right. The pot was cold and close to full. I just put the fire under it."

Ben had the chips and the burgers when he moved toward the booths. He said, "Bring those sodas over here. We'll take a booth and act like we're customers."

I had two sodas and started toward the booth when the door opened. I stopped and smiled as Gus walked by. He was carrying a six pack of beer in each hand.

Ben said, "Gus, where in the Hell, have you been. Put those sodas back Dutch. Gus bring that beer over here."

Gus didn't answer as he walked to the booth, put the beer down, took a seat and scooted over next to the wall. I took the seat next to him and across from Ben. Gus handed each of us a bottle. I twisted the cap off and remarked it was very cold.

Gus said, Yeah, I had them on ice in a cooler. I was going to take them to one of the cabins and stash them in a refrigerator. Then I saw you two and thought you might like a beer."

Ben took a drink and said, "Damn right, and they really go well with a burger and chips."

Gus nodded and said, "I think a cold beer on a warm day is like a woman."

Ben and I both stopped and looked at him as he took another large drink. He ignored our stares and said. "Yep, just like a woman. When hot and dry the first drink of a cold beer is great. In fact it's so pleasurable, it defies description. The second drink is still good, but not even close to the first. Then, from then on each gulp is not as good as the last, but it doesn't stop us from wanting another one."

Ben seemed to contemplate Gus's theory. as he chewed.

I said, "Interesting concept, but a beer won't replace a woman in my book."

Gus said, "Not to replace, only to compare too. I don't want to do without either of them."

Ben said, "Me either. Hand me another bottle."

I said, "I guess I don't entirely understand. I mean, tomorrow you can start with a new bottle of bear. Is it your theory you need a new woman each time?"

Gus said, "I think that's a great idea. You have to remember I'm married to Maude"

I said, "I'll ask Bella and get her opinion."

Ben said, "Hell, Bella would certainly vote for it. She runs a whore house and would make money like you wouldn't believe."

I said, "I don't know if that's true or not. I will say, I certainly never had a reason to notice any decrease in pleasure in my experience."

Gus said, "Wow, another reason I should never have married Maude. Where is she anyway? I figured she would be in here raising Hell about my being gone for a few days."

I said, "Bella and Johanna put her to bed."

Gus said, "Still drunk. Damn it, Ben, some of this is your fault."

Ben said, "My fault. How did you figure it's my fault. I didn't marry her."

Gus said. "Well, not entirely your fault, but some of it is. She started hitting the bottle after Junior's funeral. Then you moved all your troops in. They ate everything in sight. We had a freezer full of Angus beef, They cleaned it out. We're still waiting for the county check you promised. Bella disappeared, then Dutch is gone. You move in your own mobile food wagon. Maude becomes just the keeper of the rest rooms. It was too much. I hid or poured out all the booze. Then she drank the cough syrup and my after shave lotion. She raised Hell and your Deputies felt sorry for her. You know the ones going to and from town for supplies. They brought her at least one case of wine and a couple of bottles of whiskey. That's when I took off for a few days."

Ben said, "Yeah, and when you left Maude ran short on supplies. Then with Junior gone she couldn't keep up. She said she was even out of horse cock. They told me they brought her ground beef and other food essentials. She was told she was welcome to eat at the chuck wagon. You should be grateful instead of bitching about a little wine. If it wasn't for my Deputies, she could have starved. As a matter of fact, these burgers probably were brought by my Deputies. Damn you're one hell of an ingrate." He hesitated, took a large swig of beer, belched, and continued. "While we're at it, we couldn't even buy gas since you took the pump keys with you. You could have made some money if you hung around. Where in the Hell did you go anyway?"

Gus said, "I did take the keys. Maude would have tried to run the pumps and in her condition she might have blown the whole place up. Hell, she might have even burned herself up and in spite of everything. I'd miss her."

Ben opened another beer and said. "Okay, but where did you go?"

Gus said, "I went up to Haystack's. I was there when all Hell broke loose this morning. Now it's so damn crowded, I left."

Ben nodded and asked, "Were you with Jim when he shot?"

"No, I was still asleep in the house. I didn't even know he was gone. The first I knew about anything was about eleven. I had slept in, got up, washed last nights dishes and cleaned up a little. I was getting pissed since I was planning on fixing breakfast and Jim wasn't around. I finally went out on the porch and saw him walking in from the upper pasture. His leg is still bothering him, but it seemed he was limping more than usual. I figured his horse had bucked him off and he was going to be real mad. He had his gun and I wondered it maybe he had bucked off, got mad and shot the horse. In that case I sure wasn't going to raze him. I went back into the house and started breakfast."

The thought of breakfast engulfed me. It was a luxury, I'd missed most, while in Cutters tank. I asked. "What did you fix for breakfast?"

Ben gave me a dirty look as Gus said. "Biscuits, gravy and ham."

"Coffee?" I asked.

He nodded, "Black and strong."

I said, "Haystacks ham has to be the best in the West."

Ben said, "Damn it, what did he say when he walked in?"

Gus said, Well, he didn't come right in. I had breakfast on the table and went out to see where he was. He was sitting in his truck, talking on his cell phone. He was out there for a long time. When he did come in, he didn't eat. All he said was he killed some space men."

Ben repeated, "All he said, was he killed some space men?"

Gus nodded and said. "Yep, and I didn't ask any questions."

Ben asked, "What happened then, was he shook up?"

Gus said, "Yeah, He didn't seem to want to talk. I thought maybe he had gone crazy. What, with Johanna missing and maybe his horse bucking him off. Then maybe he shot somebody. I didn't say anything and pretty soon your Deputies arrived. They were heading up toward the pasture when a helicopter landed. Then Detectives and you came later. I grabbed my cooler of beer and headed out. I drove into some trees above the ranch and saw the Medical Examiner drive in. Then the helicopter left."

Ben asked, "Did you go back to the ranch?"

Gus said, "Yeah, quite a while after you drove off. I went to see if maybe they had arrested Jim. He was alone in the kitchen drinking some 100 proof stuff. He said you gave it to him. Damn, I don't know how he could drink it straight. I can't even handle it in a mix. Anyway I gave him a couple of beers to use as chasers. I think he already had too much to drink, I asked what he was doing and he said, he was developing amnesia."

My mind flashed back to Bella and Johanna saying, "They were carrying black bags." I looked at Ben as he said. "Yeah, Jim had a terrifying experience and his mind could shut out the events."

Johanna came from the kitchen and walked over to the booth. She said, "Gus, I want to stay here tonight. I want to rest and clean up, before going home. If it's all right with you?

Gus said, "Of course it's all right. You can use cabin four. We have a new stronger door on it now."

She smiled and said. "I'll take cabin three, I have that key and four is taken."

Gus said, "Well, okay, suit yourself. Who's in four?"

Bella came in swinging cabin four's key and said. "I am."

Gus said, "Bella, for, what, what happened to your head. Where's your hair?"

She said, "I went to a new hair salon. I believe the hairdresser may have gone a little too far. Then maybe this is the latest style."

Gus said, "I sure hope not."

She smiled and said, "Coming Dutch?"

I said, "On my way," while slipping from the booth, She smiled, handed me the key, and we walked out without looking back.

# CHAPTER FIFTY

It was quiet, except for the sound of pots and pans being bumped around in the kitchen. The chili was hot as ever. The ice tea offered some medicinal relief after each spoon full. Bella's smile was infectious. The bandana covering her head with a small knot under the chin added to the intrigue of her beauty. The cute use of her right hand as a fan being waved in front of the full, luscious lips increased my desires to carry her back to cabin four. I tried to concentrate on the chili, but with each burning swallow, I felt I needed the heat to cool myself down.

Shortly after noon, Ben arrived and walked directly to our booth. I moved toward the wall as he took a seat next to me. He smiled at Bella, just as Maude arrived with a bowl of chili and a glass of ice. She raised her chin toward the half full pitcher of ice tea. Ben looked up into her face as she said. "Pour your own and hurry up. I will bring a refill, but I have to get back to the kitchen."

Ben said, "Thanks, believe me it's nice to see you and hope things are getting back to normal."

She said, "You mean it's good to see me sober and not the sloppy, slobbering, bitching, drunken, Inn keeper."

Ben refilled our glasses, then poured his own before handing her the now empty pitcher. He smiled and said. "I never said sloppy or slobbering."

She said. "You don't deny the bitching drunk though."

He said, "No matter what I say, you'll never believe me or let me win."

She laughed and said. "You never had a chance."

We silently watched as she returned to the kitchen. Once out of sight we returned to the serious task of dining. Ben commented on something like liquid fire, then cleared his throat and said. "I was surprise to hear you two are leaving. Gus told me he thought after two weeks you were homesteading cabin four."

I said, "Well, cabin four is nice, but it's not home. Besides there's a party today and they threw us out. Said cabin four has always been a favorite, It seems some of the regulars are superstitious and demand the same cabin. It's okay, since I have to get back to my ranch."

Bella said, "I'm going to his ranch and stay until my hair grows out."

Ben looked at me as I said, "I have a good pair of horse clippers and she is a sound sleeper."

Ben said, "Electric clippers make so much noise."

Bella giggled and said, "I can do a good job of pretending to sleep."

Ben said, "Yeah, that would work. Those hand clippers catch and pull. I had a barber once, who I swear, used them."

Maude returned with a full pitcher of ice tea. She set it in front of Ben and said, "Drink up. It's going to be a long night."

Ben nodded and said, "Yep. I thought I saw a couple of cars pull in a few minutes ago."

Maude said, "They did. They saw the Sheriff car and kept going. They are parked about a half a mile down the road. They'll be back when the others start arriving."

Ben said, "I'm sure they will be back. Bella since you're leaving, whose running the show.?"

Bella said, "Jill. She has been doing a great job since I've been away. I have a lot of confidence in her and this way, I keep her away from Dutch."

I said, "Eat your chili. Maybe it's hot enough to erase those erroneous evil thoughts."

Bella said, "Baloney."

I said, "No, chili, now eat."

Ben said, "You know Jill recommended a Health Spa to Johanna. Told her she needed to take a break after her ordeal."

I asked, "Is Haystack, okay with her leaving?"

Ben wiped his mouth, exhaled a huge breath of air and said. "Strange as it may seem, he's all for it. He said, down deep he knew you didn't run off with her. He said, You're ugly, but that don't make you evil. Then he said, "Ugly does not equate to evil." I was surprised, it's pretty impressive talk for Jim."

I nodded and said, "I didn't think he knew that many words."

Ben said, "True, he don't like to waste many words. He likes to get right to the point. He is a happy man right now. He's bringing in a shipment of a hundred head of Angus cattle this week. He said to tell you, half of them are red."

I said, "Wow, that will really build up his herd." I didn't mention the cash outlay he needed. Sometimes amnesia really pays off,

Bella said, "I hope some of them are bulls."

I said, "I'm sure, a couple of them will be. They're needed to keep the herd going"

Ben said, "That reminds me. You know Cutter had a fair sized herd of his own. Well the Feds are using them to feed the Clones. They are butchering two a day they tell me."

I said, "That surprises me. I figured, since Cutter was a vegetarian he wouldn't feed the Clones meat. They probably wouldn't have a taste for beef."

Ben laughed and said, "You're right. Not only beef, but any kind of meat. It changed when some on them got ahold of Haystacks hams. Now they devour everything in sight."

I said, "At two a day. The herd won't last long, what will they do then?"

Ben said, "I don't know, but it's the Feds problem. Immigration is handling the whole shebang. I hear they might even deport them back to Argentina. It seems that's where they were created. None of them have any connections here."

I said, "Born not created. They're human, remember."

Ben said, "You keep telling me they are, but I have my own opinion."

Bella said, "They're human. I'm glad Immigration is involved and you're not."

Ben said, "Ouch. I usually don't like the Feds coming in and interfering. This time I'm grateful. D.E.A. found cases of Coumarin, Somatropin and Somatrem in one room. In another there was Andogen, Durabolin and Methyltesosterone. There were a lot of others that I can't even pronounce."

I said, "Yeah, Those are growth hormones and muscle building steroids. Cutter really had an elaborate set up."

Ben said, "He sure did. Oh, yeah Dutch they found where the Nitrous Oxide and Oxygen tanks were piped into your cell."

I nodded, and motioned for another beer, as Ben continued.

"Captain Savage is up there and he told me, those brains were being preserved by a constant flow of Oxygen mixed with Coumarin and cow's blood. They told him the Coumarin is an anticoagulant. Damn, who would have thought of anything like that?" He hesitated, seemed thoughtful for a minute, then said. "Haystack and neither Maude or Gus knows this and I don't think they should. They found the rifle that shot Haystack They ran finger prints and DNA. There's no doubt it was Junior's, Hell, he's dead. I don't see any reason to spread it around."

I said, "The fact it was his riffle doesn't make him the shooter. In fact, Junior was dead when Haystack was shot. Not only dead, but dead for two or three days."

Ben nodded and said. "You're right. I think maybe the big Clone, who killed Junior was the shooter."

I started to agree when Ben said. "They tried to get DNA's on the Clones. They all have the same DNA's. Ain't that weird?"

I asked, "Where did they find the rifle?

Ben said, "Savage said they found it in the store room with all the oxygen tanks. You know, I believe Junior had it in the truck the night he was killed. His finger prints were all over it, but the Feds wanted to double check and ran the DNA."

I said, "Tell the Feds to check for Cutter's prints and DNA on the rifle. He has to be considered a possible suspect."

The sound of tires crunching on the gravel parking lot announced the arrival of several cars. I said, "We ought to get started, I want to leave before the party starts."

Bella smiled and said. "Yes, I want you well on the way West, before Jill gets here."

I said, "Maybe another bowl of chili wouldn't hurt."

Ben said, "Yeah, The traffic will be bad. Then, the Highway Patrol always patrols these roads on party days."

Bella said, "Dutch, remember the sooner we get to your ranch, the quicker we can start working on a Clone of our own. You know, one with both our DNA's."

Ben stood, as I quickly slid from the booth and said. "Yes, Horace Greeley once said, "Go West, young man," and I will add with a woman. We're out of here."

Bella said, "I believe, John Soule, may have said it first. Greeley maybe just borrowed it. Dutch is the first to add, with a woman and I like it that way. Let's go."

Ben said, "Who in the Hell is John Soule?" He hesitated and added, "Besides I think you're both wrong. Will Rogers said it."

Bella said. "I'll explain it to you someday, but right now I'm in a hurry."

Ben laughed and said "I know you're in a hurry, but be careful. Remember Dutch, if you do get stopped, I don't want to hear you tried to badge your way out with my badge. You know, the badge, you claim you can't find."

I said, "I told you some Clone is probably wearing it. If the Feds find him, you'll have to explain why you deputized a Clone."

We heard him laugh and yell, "Good luck and have fun. Let me know if there are any surprises."

I whispered to Bella as we entered the truck. "We may all be in for a surprise come spring calving time."